INCUBUS

CHARLOTTE DOBSON

Hard Shell Word Factory

For Michael, who still lies beside me when the lights go out.

ISBN: 978-0-7599-0131-5
Trade Paperback
Published September 2002
© 2000 Charlotte Dobson

Ebook ISBN: 1-58200-556-7
Published May 2000

Hard Shell Word Factory
PO Box 161
Amherst Jct. WI 54407
books@hardshell.com
http://www.hardshell.com
Cover art © 2000 Dirk A. Wolf
All electronic rights reserved.

Chapter 1

"DAMN IT. How could I run out of coffee?"

I slammed the cupboard door and turned to stare at the paper-strewn kitchen table I used as a desk. I needed a heavy dose of caffeine to keep me awake through Kendrick's dry, unimaginative article on burial customs of the ancient Aztec. And get through it I must, if I wanted to reestablish my name in the academic community.

I glanced at the clock. Cabot's would still be open but I knew I'd have to hurry. I pulled on a heavy parka, paused just long enough to apply coral lip gloss and check my hair, and raced out the back door.

My face and hands started to sting from the cold. Fishing around in my pockets, I found a pair of lined leather gloves and slipped them on. Then, to counteract the cold, I took off at a brisk jog, carefully avoiding patches of snow and ice.

The old-fashioned Pennsylvania town I now called home looked like a Currier and Ives sketch. The houses perched on the side of a mountain, their rooftops coated with blankets of snow that glowed under the moonless sky. The spire of the church stood tall and serene against its backdrop of twinkling stars. Gigantic yew trees, their laden branches bending under the weight of icicles two feet long, flanked the church on either side. Chimney smoke scented the town with the pungent aromas of maple and pine.

Memories of another time struggled for recognition. Although I was only nine when my mother walked out of my life, I still recalled pleasant Christmases spent with her here, in this very town. She had grown up here, in the house I now occupied. Being there should have brought me closer to her, but it didn't. Every empty room reminded me this was the last place I wanted to be. It was also one of the last places that would have me since my exile from the scientific community four months before.

And what had I done, really? I published an innocent theory explaining Mayan religious rituals based on the physical evidence uncovered over the past hundred years. The book, intended for limited distribution among my fellow specialists in ancient South American cultures, caught the public imagination.

The resulting publicity spawned renewed interest in the long-forgotten civilizations of our neighbors to the south, and made my name a household word. Unfortunately, that also proved to be my downfall. Could I help it if the theory excited a small, somewhat eccentric segment of the population? The fact that I didn't endorse the many heart-eating cults and snake-worshipping sects that sprang into existence didn't help me at all. Weirdos of every description followed me mercilessly, invading my privacy and that of my neighbors.

Within two months of the book's publication, I was a scientific and a social outcast. The university withdrew my funding, claiming I had slanted the data to make a sensational point. They tarnished my name so thoroughly I couldn't get a job anywhere else. Worse, my neighbors banded together to request my immediate departure. Publicity made it impossible to find an apartment, hence my banishment to the backward town where my mother had been born.

I had to prove to everyone my theory wasn't wrong. But how in the world was I going to do that? I couldn't even call the university for information on the latest discoveries without some pit-bull of a receptionist recognizing my voice. By now, I expected to hear the click of a severed connection the minute I opened my mouth.

I pushed the depressing thoughts away.

I looked toward the center of town, hoping to find something to hold my attention. At that late hour, I had the street to myself. The 436 residents of Cabottown rested behind dark, plastic-sealed windows.

One block ahead, the business district came into view. Two tired streetlights – the only two the town boasted – stood like defeated soldiers at opposite ends of the tiny street. Smack in the center of the block, the welcoming lights from the drugstore spilled out onto the sidewalk, illuminating the facade like a beacon. I increased my pace, drawn to the warmth and light.

Whispered voices emanated from the dark, narrow alley beside the drugstore. I slowed, shocked to discover someone else outside.

Someone giggled. I paused for a minute and glanced at the mouth of the alley. Something compelled me to draw closer. My feet obeyed, taking the first steps inside. Then I caught a glimpse of shifting shadowy figures standing just within the streetlight's minimal influence. Two people, locked in intimate embrace. One male and one female.

I averted my gaze and retraced my steps, thankful the couple had not caught me watching. Back on the street, I smiled and hurried past the alley. There must be at least a dozen places more suited to an illicit rendezvous, I thought.

Inside the drugstore, I removed the gloves and opened the parka to let warmth surround my skin. I threw back my hood and looked around the store.

The place smelled of an odd combination of perfume testers and stale coffee. Paperback books, newspapers, and the latest editions of popular tabloids occupied the space to the left of the door. The lunch counter, bearing scratches and stains, monopolized half of the store. The space between held shelves containing a small mix of just about everything anyone could want.

Alan Wilson, the county Sheriff, sat at the lunch counter, sipping what appeared to be the dregs of the coffeepot. Blue eyes crinkled with amusement, he returned my nod of greeting and held up the newspaper he read. It was the latest edition of *Trust Me*, one of the more tenacious of the tabloids. I saw my picture on the cover and rolled my eyes.

The Sheriff winked and went back to his reading. He used to be a Philadelphia police lieutenant. I was certain his cozy, good-old-boy facade hid a keen, analytical mind.

"Evenin', Doc," Jason called from behind the counter. He flashed me a lopsided grin and continued to wipe the space in front of him.

Jason was the sixteen-year-old son of Irene Cabot, owner of the town's combination lunch counter, post office and drugstore. I had the feeling he worked there because his mother, Cabottown's leading citizen, told him he had to. He didn't seem interested in anything but video games and computers.

"Whatidya forget this time?"

He was used to my irregular shopping habits and expected me to visit the store at least three times every day.

"I'm out of coffee, and please, call me Martine, or Marty. Even Miss Murdoch would be better than Doc. It makes me sound like one of the fossils I studied in college."

"What ever ya say, Doc."

Gnashing my teeth, I made my way through the store until I found the coffee. Irene didn't stock my favorite brand, so I selected a gaudy red can and headed back to the counter.

"Anythin' else? It's almost closin' time."

"Not that I can think of." I handed him five dollars and waited for my change. "Oh, yes. I forgot to pick up my mail this afternoon. Is there anything for me?"

"I think so. Let me look."

He turned to the slatted wall behind the stamp machine and ran a hand over the polished wood.

"Yep. Looks like you got a letter from the University of Virginia. Another rejection?"

I flashed him a quelling look and held out my hand. "Anything else?"

"Bills. Telephone, electric. What's this? Telegram. Wow. Someone die?"

"A telegram? Let me see."

Jason held it up to the light, trying to peer through the flimsy envelope.

"Just hand it over."

I accepted the envelope with a nod of thanks.

"Ain't ya gonna open it? Might be important."

Of course I wanted to read the telegram, but Jason's love of gossip stopped me. I didn't want its contents spread all over town before I got home. I slipped it into my pocket and smiled.

"That's all right. I can wait."

He looked deflated when I turned away, purchase in hand.

A jolt of anticipation quickened my step when I walked out the door. I paused under the dim streetlight beside the alley to open my mail, too excited to feel the biting cold.

The letter from the university started out in a positive way, but quickly turned sour. They didn't have a position for me. I sighed. It was what I expected. I stuffed it into my pocket with the bills and tore into the telegram. It was from my father's old friend, Emil Larson. The message was brief and vague.

"I need you. Have arranged flight at 1:00 afternoon of Feb. 17. Philadelphia airport. Have arranged an escort. Bring book."

He wanted me to drop everything and meet him in Mexico. Like I had anything to drop in the first place. I read the telegram again, then shrugged and slipped it into my pocket. I stared at the sidewalk for several seconds, debating.

Why would Emil take the chance of tarnishing his sterling reputation by sending for me, the leper of the scientific community? I shrugged and re-zipped my parka.

After months of solitude it would be stimulating to speak with a fellow scientist, even if he was old enough to be my father. The last time I had seen Emil was three years before, at my father's funeral. Right after the ceremony he had hopped on a plane and gone back to his dig.

What could be happening down there? Shelley Peterson, the one friend I had left at the university, might be able to answer my questions. I'd give it a shot when I got home.

A muffled noise escaped from the alley behind me. I listened, trying to identify the sound. Before I had a chance to think about it, I heard it again. Scratching, and a subdued hiss of alarm.

I sighed and entered the alley, guessing that a cat or small dog was in distress. I swore under my breath, realizing the people I glimpsed on my way to the store must have been some of the local kids, out for a bit of fun with Mr. Manning's timid kitty. It would only take me a second to be sure.

I paused after a few paces to let my eyes grow accustomed to the deeper darkness between the rough stone buildings. The distinctive odor of day-old garbage hit me. I wrinkled my nose in distaste.

The street-lamp didn't penetrate this far. The meager light that did find a way through only served to highlight the shadows. Outside, a lone truck rumbled through the street, its headlights distorting the litter and debris. For an instant, the shadows seemed to lunge and close in.

I had the feeling that something moved closer. I took a quick glance over my shoulder, but the darkness was complete. I strained my ears, listening. Nothing moved across the frozen crust of snow.

Claws scratched metal. I remembered my errand and quickened my pace.

"I'm coming, I'm coming. Hold on for a second."

I placed the bag containing my coffee in the snow piled beside the dumpster, then pulled my gloves on. The last time I had tried to touch a frightened cat the resulting scratches had left my hands sore for more than a week. Lifting the lid, I bent to look inside. The smell of rotting food made me gag. I turned my face away, drew a deep breath of cleaner air, and tried again.

Green eyes, reflecting some hidden source of light, stared back at me from the darkness inside. I heard what sounded like a slithering rustle, followed by a deep hiss. I was about to reach in when my brain screamed a frantic warning.

Those luminous objects couldn't possibly belong to something as ordinary as a cat. I sprang away.

A long, thick, shadowy shape emerged from the dumpster before I could slam the lid. I took another step back. The step brought me up against something massive and hard.

Something clenched my right hand in a grip I couldn't break. I glanced behind me, too numb with shock to do more than whimper. The thing was large and warm and appeared to have the general shape of a bull. Although the creature could have chewed my hand off my arm, it seemed to wish only to restrain.

I choked back a sob of fear and turned toward the mouth of the alley. At that moment, I thought of nothing but the need to get away.

Something twined around my feet, preventing my escape. It was too big and thick to be a rope. Through the fabric of my jeans I felt muscles flex and relax. The thing wound its body tighter. The hissing noise increased, then subtly changed into a shattered whispering of my last name. The frigid air around me pulsated with the sound.

"Murdoch."

Fear gripped me. My heart pounded within my chest. My free hand, greasy and cold from sweat, beat ineffectually at the hard shape at my back. It refused to release me. My breath, coming out in ragged gasps, solidified as soon as it left my mouth, creating a cloud of vapor that clung to the moisture-laden air. Thick, green, iridescent fog rose up to surround my attackers and me.

The slithering shape at my ankles tightened and inched its way up my legs. It paralyzed me.

The coiling reached my knees and exerted pressure to force me to the ground. I sobbed. The sound bounced around inside the cloud of hazy vapor, then died away.

The thing around my legs contracted, forcing me down into the snow. I knelt. Through the fog, I saw blazing green eyes.

The glowing eyes staring up at me had a fringe of long brown lashes encircling lids that appeared almost human. A thick shock of dark brown hair grew from the crown of its head.

It was a snake, but unlike any snake I had ever seen.

I looked upon the plumed serpent of Mayan myth come to life and felt my heart constrict painfully.

I shook my head and screamed in fear.

Glistening scales contorted, squeezing, cutting off circulation. My legs tingled from lack of blood.

The massive head reared back and opened its jaws. Slavering teeth dripped venomous juices down the legs of my jeans. Terrified, I turned my face toward the street and screamed again.

"Who's there?"

To my right, near the open end of the alley, the street-lamp's golden glow outlined the shape of a human silhouette. The hard, muscled shape at my back vanished, freeing my hand. The serpent released me before the echoes of my last scream died away. Robbed of support, I fell face down in the snow and tried to catch my breath.

My unwitting rescuer moved an arm and turned on a flashlight.

The powerful beam found me, then moved on to rake the alley. With the aid of its light, I turned to take a wary look around. There was nothing behind me but a few wildly shifting shadows. The rustling sounds died away, leaving me to wonder if the whole bizarre event had taken place at all.

And then I saw it, a shiny oblong lying on top of a churned pile of week-old snow. In the uncertain light, it looked like a sliver of polished glass. It was huge—almost as large as the pad of my thumb.

It made me shudder to look at it. There was no time for closer scrutiny. The man drew nearer. I put out a gloved hand to take it, then froze.

My right hand still ached from the bull's grating teeth, but there wasn't a mark on the smooth leather glove covering it. I clenched my hand, searching for scratches, punctures – anything. The glove looked as smooth and untouched as the day I bought it. Within seconds the soreness dissolved. Both my hand and my leg felt whole and uninjured.

Footsteps approached through the crusted snow. I grasped the object with a shaky hand and slipped it into my pocket.

A mobile transmitter hissed into life, scaring me. I jumped and covered my head with both hands. In the same instant, I heard the soft crackle of a leather bomber jacket and discerned the tall, muscular shape of the newcomer. Sheriff Wilson grabbed the instrument from his belt and asked the dispatcher to send two cars around. Then he replaced the transmitter and continued his approach.

"Doc Murdoch? That you?"

The Sheriff, closer now, called again. "Doc? You all right?"

"Yes. It's me."

All around me, the drifted peaks of snow appeared uniform in their coating of grime. Besides my own, there wasn't a single fresh footprint—or paw-print or snake print—to prove I had not been alone.

I bent over to retrieve my package, then stood to greet the Sheriff. I noticed then that he had his gun out of its holster. He pointed it straight at me.

"What the hell you doin' here?"

"On the way to the store, I thought I heard a noise in here. I saw two people, kissing. On the way back, I heard the noise again, but the people had gone. So I came in to investigate. Something attacked me."

"I heard you scream from inside the drugstore."

He moved around the alley, shining his light over every square inch of the place. Two doors lead to adjacent shops, but both were padlocked from the outside. Nothing could escape that way. The

Sheriff stopped beside the dumpster, letting the light wash over its rusted exterior.

"Find anything?"

Before I could answer, he turned the flashlight inside. I gave an involuntary start of nerves and backed away a pace.

The Sheriff, after one careful look at the contents of the dumpster, holstered his weapon and turned to me.

"Tell me everything that happened, young lady," he said. "The people you said you saw. One was male, right?"

"Yes. I'm sure of that."

"Can you describe him?"

"No. I didn't get a very good look at him. Why?"

"I'm askin' the questions. Tell me the rest."

I told a censored tale, omitting any mention of the serpent's plume of hair or glowing eyes. When I finished the Sheriff turned his flash again, shining its glaring light on my face. I winced in sudden pain.

"Hey, have a little mercy with that thing, Sheriff. You're hurting my eyes."

"Did you see anyone the second time?"

"N-no."

"I think you should tell me the truth."

"I am telling you the truth. I didn't see anyone. I thought a few of the shadows moved, but it must have been my imagination."

"It wasn't your imagination."

The Sheriff pulled me over to look inside the dumpster. Nestled atop a pile of trash at the bottom of the container lay the twisted, tortured remains of a young woman. The body was fresh. Steam rose from the torn flesh of her stilled and lifeless chest.

In spite of a lifetime of studying such things, my stomach tightened reflexively. This was no ancient burial. The chances were good the body belonged to someone I knew. After the first nauseating glance, I found I could study it without emotion.

"Her chest has been ripped open," I said in awe. "By the look on her face, I would say it happened while she was still alive. Notice the flesh has been peeled from the long bones, yet there is no evidence of blood."

The inside of the dumpster should have been coated with the stuff. Instead, there wasn't a drop that I could see. I reached out a gloved hand, only to have it batted away.

"Don't touch her. Look at these marks on her ribs. You ever seen anything like that before?"

I swallowed hard. "I think I have. They look like . . . teeth marks."

His steely eyes met mine. "Just like in that book of yours. Yes, Doc. Some of us do read, you know."

"You can't think I had anything to do with this."

He didn't answer. Instead, he looked the body over with a practiced eye. "She was around five-foot-five, chunky build, long wavy brown hair, brown eyes."

"How can you tell that?"

"I recognize her. She's one of Evans' girls. Sarah, I think."

My hands dropped to my sides. I shivered, suddenly cold. "You realize you just described me."

"Yeah. Makes you think, don't it?"

"I swear, I had nothing to do with this."

"Relax. I saw you leave Cabot's and stand under the light to read your mail. You weren't out of my sight for more than about thirty seconds, not long enough to commit this murder. I know you didn't do it on the way in, neither. She hasn't been here that long. In this temperature, the body would cool down fast. You're clean."

"Of course I am. I study burials, not make them. If you hadn't come along when you did I'd be the next victim."

"I think that's mor'n likely true."

"But why?"

He shrugged. "Publicity Some kid out to make a name for hisself by killin' Doc Murdoch usin' her own ancient MO."

"You can't be serious."

"I'm deadly serious. In a way, I been expectin' this since the day you moved into town."

I shivered again and looked away.

The Sheriff closed the dumpster and, taking my arm, led me to the mouth of the alley. Two white cars, each bearing the emblem of his department, were parked at the curb in answer to his summons. He led me to the first one and opened the passenger door.

"Get in. Drucker'll drive you down to the station and take your statement. Then he'll take you home. I don't want to hear about you spreading this all over town, neither. I want you to stay inside that house of your'n and keep your mouth shut. If you even think about talking to a reporter, I'll haul you to jail."

"The last thing I want is more publicity." Before stepping into the car, I spared one more horrified look for the gloomy alley. "What are you going to do about her?"

"None of your business," he said, his eyes flashing with anger. "This isn't one of your archaeological sites, damn it. This is murder."

"If I can be of any assistance in your investigation—"

"If you want to help me, get the hell out of my county," he said in a tight voice. "These copy-cat psychos will follow you and leave the rest of us alone."

"Are you telling me I'm free to go?"

His eyes narrowed in suspicion. "You plannin' to?"

I explained about the telegram.

"Let me see it."

The Sheriff studied it for some minutes before making up his mind. "I want to do some checkin' on this. Don't get on that plane unless you hear from me. You got that?"

"Are you ordering me to stay?"

"Call it a polite request."

There was nothing more I could say. I got into the car and let Drucker drive me home. No doubt the Sheriff was right. Add another black mark to the growing list of catastrophes the book and its publicity had caused. My presence in the town attracted every loony in the Northeast. The longer I stayed, the worse it would get.

Now, finally, I had a place to go. Emil's telegram couldn't have come at a better time.

Chapter 2

DRUCKER PRECEDED me into the house and checked every room. I must admit his solid presence reassured me. After the episode in the alley, my nerves were shot to hell.

When he finished his tour of the house, I offered him a cup of coffee. He saw through that tactic and declined, saying he had to return to his duties. I sipped coffee and watched his car until it rounded the corner at the end of the street. I glanced at my watch and counted the seconds. Before I reached one hundred he returned, found a space across from the house, and parked. I waved and let the curtain fall back into place.

I felt better knowing he watched the house. If some psycho was on the loose in town, I was in great danger, especially if he thought I could identify him. I wandered around, locking the doors and windows in a fit of nervous activity.

The caffeine restored my equilibrium. By the time I had downed the first cup I dismissed the animals in the alley as a product of my over-worked imagination. The strain of my solitary lifestyle was beginning to get to me. I shrugged it off and turned to the phone.

Lifting the receiver from its cradle, I punched seven digits and sat back in my chair. I didn't try to reach Shelley Peterson at her house because she never stopped working until midnight. The switchboard operator didn't recognize my voice. She put me through to the anthropology department right away.

Shelley answered the phone on the first ring.

"Yeah."

I smiled, picturing her at her desk. By this time of night, her well-worn jeans usually resembled shapeless sacks and her favorite Loony Tunes sweat-shirts were covered with ink spots and toner from the temperamental copy machine. Her brown hair would have long since escaped its pony tail to straggle around her lined face like Medusa's snakes, and her green eyes would be red-rimmed and swollen from squinting at the computer screen. It wasn't that she was too vain to wear glasses - she just refused to take time from her research to visit the eye doctor.

"Yeah yourself. Is that any way to answer the phone?"

"Is that you, Marty?"

I hushed her. "The whole building is going to hear and know who you're talking to."

"There's no one else around. And what if there were? Most of them know I still talk to you, and they don't really give a damn."

"Even Doctor Mathews?"

Norman Mathews was the primary reason I had to resign my position at the university. He took greatest offense when my study of burial customs topped the best-seller list. He convened the board to denounce me, claiming I fabricated the data and slanted the evidence to make a sensational point. Because of him, I was relegated to the lunatic fringe of archaeologists.

His conduct would have been unforgivable even without the little detail of our engagement to complicate the issue.

"Screw Mathews," Shelly said, moderating her voice nonetheless. "He'll get his one day, and I just pray I'm there to see it."

I couldn't help laughing. "Are you kidding? I'll sell the tickets."

"Speaking of tickets, why aren't you on a plane to Mexico? I hear you're joining the team."

"You heard that? How?"

"I hear most of what goes on in the exciting world of bones. Are you going?"

"That's still up in the air. The Sheriff hasn't decided if I'm his prime suspect or the next most likely victim. Until he decides, I'm confined to house arrest."

"Suspect in what? What are you talking about?"

I filled her in, adding, "Sounds like I should leave before they run me out on a rail."

"I'll say. Wow. The killer is using the methods you wrote about in your book? He ripped the victim's heart from her chest?"

"Yes. And gnawed her bones for good measure."

"Jee-sus. That's disgusting."

"Tell me about it. I'm sick to death of publicity."

"Then you should think twice before you go to Mexico with Larson. If half what I hear is true, you're going to have more publicity than you can handle."

I sagged into a chair and tightened my grip on the receiver. This is what I wanted to hear. "Why? What's going on down there?"

"I don't know anything definite. Emil called Mathews yesterday afternoon, and there was a whole lot of shouting in his office. I caught your name, along with a lot of disparaging remarks about your theories and methods. Then he was quiet for so long I thought he'd hung up on Emil."

"What did he say exactly?"

"You know how he gets. I'm sure it's nothing you haven't already heard from him."

"I get the picture. Go on."

"After the long pause, there was more shouting, and he finished by telling Emil he'd better be right. If he wasn't, Mathews threatened to deal with Emil the same way he dealt with you."

"He actually said that?"

"Yes, he did."

"Too bad you didn't record it. But what could be going on down there? Why would Emil need me?"

"All I have are rumors. You know how there are always rumors associated with digs."

"So give me the rumors."

Shelley hesitated. I knew her so well I could almost see the shrug when she relented. "Okay. You know Emil found a city in the jungles of Mexico."

"That's no secret. He's been working there for four years. It's reported to be of relatively recent date, though, and he hasn't uncovered anything new. Just your basic Toltec civilization."

"That's the published data. What if I were to tell you that Emil stopped issuing his monthly reports, all non-essential personnel were dismissed, and the jungle surrounding the site is patrolled by armed guards twenty-four hours a day, all at the expense of the university?"

I uncrossed my legs and sat up straight. "Are you sure?"

"Of the guards I am. I've seen the expense accounts. But that's not the half of it. Just before the area went into quarantine, a couple of the ethnography fellows came back to the campus to finish their dissertations. They told me under the foundations of one of the pyramids, Larson's team had found the remains of an older structure. Much older. Olmec."

My pulse started racing. "Olmec? Are you certain?"

"There doesn't seem to be any doubt about it. Larson himself dated the structure to around four thousand BC."

"He found Tamoanchan," I said. Unable to sit still, I stood and paced in nervous excitement.

"I've heard that name before."

"I hope to hell you have."

"You're the specialist on American civilizations, not me. Refresh my memory."

I complied. "The Olmec civilization existed from about eight thousand to twenty-five hundred BC. They're thought to be a primitive hunter-gatherer society. The only artifacts from their culture are a series of huge stone heads that litter the terrain and are thought to represent the boundaries of their hunting lands."

"Hunter-gatherer societies don't build cities," Shelly said.

"That's just it. We always thought the Olmecs were primitive. I guess Emil found the proof he needs to refute that hypothesis. There are legends about a ceremonial center of the Olmecs called Tamoanchan, but it was assumed the stories were only legends because we couldn't locate the site. Its supposed location differs with whoever you talk to. If Emil has indeed found structures that ancient, it could revolutionize American anthropological theory."

"Instead of the Mediterranean being the cradle of civilization, the American continent's cultures either pre-dated or co-existed with the other civilizations," Shelly said. "This is exciting."

"I still don't see how this has anything to do with me, or why Emil would call Mathews and insist I come down there."

"If you'd shut up for one minute I might be able to finish the gossip."

"You mean there's more?"

"Not much, but I think it'll answer your questions. I've heard whispers that they've uncovered a huge cemetery, one that was dug into the ground."

"The Olmecs, Toltecs and Maya frequently used mass graves, especially for sacrificial victims," I said, unimpressed. "Honduras and Guatemala are littered with such sites dedicated to the god Gucumatz."

"I swear, the next time you interrupt me I'm out of here and you can wait until you get to Mexico to discover the rest on your own."

Chastised, I resumed my seat. "I'm sorry. Please continue."

"The reason this particular cemetery is of so much interest, and the reason I think Emil needs you down there, is you're the only one who can provide information about the strange condition of the remains. The skeletons on the bottom of the heap correspond to the date of the structure that surrounds them. About six thousand years old.

"The skeletal material on the top of the pile is much more recent. If the reports are true, it would indicate the cemetery is still in use. Rumor has it the bones on top are less than ten years old." Shelly's voice shook slightly when she finished.

"I thought you told me this underground cemetery was sealed

under the foundations of a more recent building," I said, drawing out the sentence to cover some rapid thinking.

"I did. And, so far, they haven't come across another way into the place."

"This is exciting."

"The thing that really has them in a tizzy is the condition of the remains. I've heard every bone is split open, from the bottom of the pile to the top. Each bone large enough to contain marrow in significant quantity has been split lengthwise."

For a moment I couldn't speak. Shelley gave the ghost of a laugh.

"It looks as though you might have the final, irrefutable proof your theories are correct," she said. "Someone split open all of those bones and took the marrow out. But that's not all."

"The rib bones on the left side are broken in half."

"Yes. It looks as though that book of yours was correct. Someone tore open the ribs of all those people to get at their hearts, then broke open the long bones to extract the marrow."

I was sick with excitement. I saw the opportunity to exonerate myself and prove to the world I wasn't a crackpot. Then another thought struck me. My eyes grew wide with the horror of it all. I groaned aloud.

"I wondered when you'd get to that point," Shelley said in a grim voice. "Now all you have to do is find him."

"Find him?" I couldn't believe the implications. Maybe I misunderstood. Her next words, however, dispelled that comfortable thought.

"If these rumors are true, it proves that your heart-eating cult existed in pre-historic times, just as you said it did," Shelley said. "But it also proves that there's still someone out there today—"

"Who eats human hearts," I said.

"Exactly."

I HAD BARELY replaced the receiver when the doorbell rang. I jumped a mile. Crossing to the living room, I peered through the peephole and flipped on the porch light. When I saw who it was I unfastened the deadbolt and opened the door.

"Sheriff Wilson?"

"Evenin', Doc. This is Sergeant Zimmerman with the State crime lab. Mind if we come in?"

Zimmerman nodded in response to the introduction. Of medium height and lean build, he looked more like a scientist than an officer of the law. His three-piece suit bore the stains of chemicals and the knot of his colorful tie rested under his right ear. His thin, graying hair stood up in frozen tufts. Next to the tall, commanding presence of the Sheriff, he looked frail and insignificant. I bit back a grin and opened the door as far as it would go.

"No. Of course not. Would you like a cup of coffee?"

"Not just yet. Zimmerman here would like to get your fingerprints and measure your jaw. You got a problem with that?"

"No. Not at all."

The Sheriff's rigid stance relaxed a bit. He nodded to Zimmerman, then took a tour around the room. "Mind if I look around?"

So that was the reason for his visit. I wondered when he'd get around to searching my house. I considered asking for a warrant, then thought better of the idea. I had nothing to hide.

"Help yourself, Sheriff."

"Is there a place where I can set up my equipment, Doctor Murdoch?" Zimmerman asked.

"Certainly. Is the kitchen table all right?"

"Fine."

I cleared the table of articles and notes and tried to remain calm. Despite what the Sheriff said in the alley, I must be a suspect for him to return so soon, bringing another officer with him. He moved around the rooms on the ground floor, then proceeded up the stairs. Later, I heard the creaky attic door open with a crash.

Zimmerman placed a large black case on the table, then shrugged out of his coat. A strong wave of formaldehyde accompanied the gesture, leaving no doubt of the origin of the stains. After tossing the coat over a chair, he opened the case, set out inkpads and fingerprint sheets, then pulled out another chair.

"Sit here, please." His voice didn't fit the rest of his body. It was deep and strong.

He took two sets of prints. When he finished, he turned again to the black case and extracted several pairs of precision calipers.

"Now I want to measure your teeth and jaw."

I nodded. He went through the same procedures I used to measure remains in the field, jotting the findings on a chart of the human skull. He measured every tooth in my head three times. I had the feeling he was deliberately stalling to give the Sheriff time to complete his search. Finally, Zimmerman replaced his instruments and closed the case.

"Thank you for your cooperation, Doctor Murdoch. Goodnight.

No, don't get up. I can see myself out."

I settled back in my chair, guessing he wanted to have a private word with the Sheriff. Even though I knew I was innocent, I couldn't help feeling nervous. My stomach churned.

"This the door to the basement?" the Sheriff asked, startling me. I hadn't heard him approach.

I looked and nodded. "Yes."

"Mind if I have a look?"

"Want me to go with you?"

"No. You stay here. I won't be long."

I poured myself another cup of coffee and resumed my place at the table. I heard occasional noises from the room below, indicating the Sheriff was thorough in his search. The noises died away and silence returned.

"You packed yet?"

I jumped again. "I'm going to get you a cowbell to hang around your neck. No. You didn't find anything?"

The Sheriff leaned against the doorframe, looking relaxed and friendly. "Nope."

"You mean I can catch my plane?"

He nodded. "Your teeth don't match the marks on the bones. I checked out that telegram, too. It did come from Mexico."

"I told you they wouldn't match. I had nothing to do with the murder."

"Zimmerman agrees we can't hold you, but I want to give you a little piece of advice," he said, his blue eyes flashing. "You go down to that dig and you stay there. I wanna know how to find you, just in case."

"In case of what?"

"In case. Night, Doc."

"Goodnight."

After I let him out and made sure the doors were locked, I managed to get down to the task of packing. While rooting through closets and file cabinets for the material I wanted to take, I remembered the incident in the alley and recovered my parka. Sliding my hand into the pocket, I extracted the piece of glass.

Without the awkward gloves, I knew the minute I touched the object that it wasn't glass. Despite its smooth appearance, pits and veins roughened the surface on both sides. I took it to the light and trained a magnifying glass on it.

It was not glass - not unless they were making it with tiny veins running through it. It was slick and oily and rough, just like the skin of a reptile. I closed my eyes and let my fingers move over it.

When I thought I had the answer, I opened my eyes and stared at the thing, remembering the long tubular shape that slithered from the opened dumpster. I was certain the object was a snake's scale, but unlike any I had ever seen.

But so what? The sheriff said the marks found on the bones of the victims were made by human teeth. No doubt the scale represented the passage of someone's exotic pet, escaped from its cage to wander the night in search of food. It might have crawled into the dumpster, attracted by the warmth of the girl's mutilated body.

I sighed, then laughed out loud. Of course. When the poor animal saw me, it naturally sought the comfort my living body heat could provide. It was as simple as that.

I got out of my chair and went into the kitchen. I opened the trashcan and stood for a minute, poised to drop the scale inside. Something stopped me.

I remembered fringed eyes, staring up at me with human expression.

The creature that held me in the alley was not human. I conceded it was not the plumed serpent of my earlier imaginings, either. But what did that leave?

I grinned at my foolishness, but couldn't bring myself to dispose of this small piece of evidence. For one crazy second, I considered calling the Sheriff to tell him of the discovery. Then I thought better of the idea. No good would come of producing the scale at this late hour. He might even revert to his earlier suspicions and make good his threat of locking me away. That I couldn't allow. Not when I was so close to clearing my name.

Holding the object carefully, I retraced my steps to the living room, found my backpack, and slid the scale into a pocket of my wallet.

I felt better the minute it was out of sight. I turned away to resume preparations for the trip, and soon forgot all about the scale.

I couldn't wait to leave Cabottown, and its psychotic visitors, behind me.

Chapter 3

THE AIRPORT WAS crowded, as if everyone in Philadelphia decided to fly on the same day. And who could blame them? The cold-snap was in its second freezing week, with no let-up in sight. The line for curb-side check-in reached almost to the next terminal. My cab driver pulled up at the rear of the line and opened the trunk to remove my bags.

While we were unloading duffel bags, I noticed a small crowd just inside the terminal. The lights and cameras present told me the press was out in full force, probably awaiting the arrival of some celebrity. I turned away, relieved that they couldn't be waiting for me.

When the last of my bags stood in line for baggage check, someone gripped my arm. I glanced up, ready to scream. When I saw who it was, I almost screamed anyway.

"What the hell are you doing here?" I asked in a surly growl.

"It's good to see you," Dr. Norman Mathews said in a loud voice for the benefit of the security guards close by.

Following his gaze, I noticed several guards eyeing us with interest. One, a young man no doubt anxious to make his first arrest, placed a hand on the holster at his side. Perhaps he thought a mugging might be about to take place. He wasn't wrong. The urge to strike the condescending smirk off Mathews' face was strong.

"It isn't good to see you," I said, pulling away. "Leave me alone."

"Lower your voice. I don't want the press to know you're here yet. I need to speak to you privately. My car's parked over there."

Following his pointing finger, I saw his long, sleek Towncar sitting at the curb. "You've got to be joking. I'm not going anywhere with you."

The cabby, waiting to be paid, stood close enough to hear my angry comments.

"Hold on, buddy," the cabby said, taking Dr. Mathews' arm. "The lady looks like she doesn't want to go with you."

"I'm not trying to abduct her," Norman said haughtily. "Nothing could be further from my mind. I just want to speak to her in private for a moment. Tell him it's all right."

"I'm not sure it is. What do you want?"

Norman looked from me to the cabby and sighed. "Somehow

word leaked out that you're going to Mexico to join Larson's dig. Those reporters are waiting for you."

"I didn't leak it, if that's what you're insinuating."

"I don't recall accusing you. All I want to do is brief you on what to expect so you don't tell them anything important until we know exactly what we have."

I thought for a minute, then decided it was better to talk to him than to the reporters. "Okay. But you can say what you want to say right here. Pay the cabby for me, won't you? That's a good boy."

He dug deep into his pockets, then counted out the fare plus a generous tip. I nearly bit my lip to keep from laughing when he asked for a receipt.

I took the opportunity to study him at close range. His thinning hair fell in well-trained lines to just above his ears, then tapered to rest along the collar of his starched white shirt. His face, unlined and carefully schooled, never revealed what he thought. The same went for his hard, flint-colored eyes. Even though we were engaged to be married just six months ago, I didn't know him at all. The realization depressed me.

When the cabby left satisfied, Norman turned back to me and took a deep breath. "I imagine you've heard some rumors regarding the dig in Mexico," he said in hushed tones.

"I've heard some pretty wild stuff, but nothing that could be considered believable."

"Believe them. I also imagine you know I'm opposed to your involvement in this project."

I had to give him points for honesty. "I'm aware of that."

"Good. I don't want there to be any illusions regarding your role. Larson seems to think you can help, but the others in the department have serious doubts. Including me. However, Larson insisted. We're sending you as an observer and to help with the cataloguing of finds, not as a physical anthropologist. I want that clear from the beginning."

He paused for so long I thought the discussion was at an end. I moved forward in line, relieved to see that there were only eight people between me and the counter.

"Just a minute, Doctor Murdoch. I'm not finished."

His tone angered me. I was through taking orders from Norman. "I thought you'd never acknowledge my title again. Let's have no hypocrisy just because you think I might say something detrimental to the press."

"I might have been a little hasty. You earned the degree. The preposterous sensationalism you managed to attract since then should have nothing to do with your previous academic record."

"I didn't expect the book to become popular, nor did I want the publicity I received as a result. It's a theory, nothing more."

"Perhaps I misconstrued your motives."

I knew it was the closest thing to an apology I'd ever get from him, and I bowed my head in polite acceptance.

But Norman wasn't finished. "The fact is, Larson uncovered some questionable artifacts and I feel it my duty to inform you that, in my opinion, the evidence has been planted."

"Wait just a minute. Are you accusing me of going down to Mexico, digging a hole, and throwing thousands of bones in it just to prove my theories?"

"The thought did cross my mind."

"You self-centered ass," I said, no longer caring who heard me. "You just can't stand to be wrong, can you? If you weren't such a pompous shit you'd have looked at my data before you denounced me. The thing that bothers you the most is I might have independent corroboration of my work and, if I do, you're going to be exposed for the narrow-minded jackass you are."

He gripped my arm and made me face him. "Shut up. You're attracting attention."

I glared at him and twisted my shoulder until I wrenched free. Pulling the bags behind me, I moved closer to the counter. "What if I am? You care so much about public relations you've forgotten the importance of good field work. If Larson has found Tamoanchan, and the site proves my theories to be true, I'll broadcast it from the rooftops. I'll make sure everyone knows you were the shit-for-brains who tried to squelch the news."

Norman turned red with anger. For a minute I thought he wanted to strike me. Luckily, the ticket agent approached. Norman hurried away, losing himself in the crowd.

Within minutes I had my boarding pass in hand. I felt much calmer. Reporters approached the minute I stepped on the pad to open the automatic doors. I made myself pause and take several deep breaths before turning to face them.

"I'll be happy to answer your questions, but I haven't been to the site yet. I doubt I have anything to add to the information you've already heard. Doctor Larson and his team uncovered an ancient city in Mexico. The ruins haven't been conclusively dated, but I hope to be able to help in that area."

"Is it true Doctor Larson found proof your heart-eating cult still exists?"

I recognized the reporter from Channel 2 and flashed him a smile. I froze for a moment when I caught a glimpse of Norman standing behind him.

"You know better than to ask me a question like that. I haven't even been there yet. Ask me when I get back."

"Are you going down there to take over the dig from Emil Larson?" another reporter asked.

"Heavens, no. Doctor Larson is an eminent archaeologist. There couldn't be a better man in charge."

"Then what is your role?"

"I'm an anthropologist. It's my job to examine and catalogue the physical finds, and to offer theories about the culture of the civilization—their religious beliefs and normal, daily activities."

The crowd of reporters parted for just an instant, and my eyes locked with a pair of unreadable blue ones. It was a man, standing at the back of the crowd. I'd never seen him before, of that I was certain. He watched me intently and flashed a brilliant smile. My lips twitched in response. Then the camera crews shifted again, erasing the lounging figure from view.

"Is it true the university black-balled you because your book was such a success?" a reporter asked.

I saw Norman stiffen and move away from the wall.

"Where do you guys come up with this stuff?" I forced myself to laugh. "If they'd done that, why would they send me to Mexico?"

I glanced at my watch and flashed an apologetic smile at the reporters. "I'm afraid that's all the time I have. I'm certain I'll have more information for you when I get back."

The reporters made way for me to pass. I almost reached the metal detectors before my arm was gripped for the second time. I turned, ready to lash out. Then saw it wasn't Norman. It was the man with the blue eyes I'd glimpsed at the back of the crowd.

"Do I know you?" I asked, trying to place him.

He smiled. "We've never met, but I've studied you. I know your name is Martine, but you prefer Marty. Your mother disappeared when you were eight, and you were raised by your father until his untimely death three years ago."

"Congratulations. You can read a book jacket."

I looked away, feigning indifference. His rich, deep laugh made the hair on my neck stand on end.

"My knowledge is more extensive than that. Perhaps we should go someplace more secluded to discuss it?"

I shook my head. "I have a plane to catch."

"It doesn't board for another thirty minutes. There's time."

"How do you know when I board? You don't seem the type to listen at keyholes. Or were you going to tell me you have ESP?"

"Nothing so crude, I assure you."

His eyes met mine. They were blue like a summer sky. He smiled. Tiny crow's feet around eyes and mouth added character to his face. Otherwise, it was almost too perfect. Although he looked no older than 25, for one brief second I had the impression I was looking into the eyes of recorded history.

I shivered and pulled my gaze from his.

At about five foot nine, he was slightly shorter than I would've liked. Otherwise, he was perfect. He had sandy blond hair curling just below his collar, and blond hair peeked from the opened neck of his shirt. His face, neck, and hands appeared evenly tanned, like he'd just stepped off some exotic beach.

He didn't look like the usual autograph hound. I had a hard time picturing him as the studious type, too. Which left me to wonder why he'd take the trouble to follow me. I looked away. Handsome men were usually already in love with themselves, and wouldn't give a second glance to a plain woman like me.

I glanced down at the bronzed hand gripping my arm. A shiny band encircled the ring finger of his left hand. So that was it. He wanted an exciting flirtation with the tabloids' favorite daughter. I should've known.

He followed my gaze and raised his hand up for a better look. "Unusual, isn't it?"

His voice held the merest trace of a foreign accent, but I couldn't place its origin. The tone was heavy with concealed amusement.

I took his hand and pretended to study the ring. "Yes, it is. I've never seen a wedding ring with a bull or a snake on it, let alone both. Is it a family heirloom?"

"You jump to conclusions. It isn't a wedding ring." His smile was unmistakable. "But you could say it's an heirloom, considering it's been in my family for thousands of years."

"Thousands," I said skeptically, drawing his hand back for a closer look.

"Yes. The artist who carved the figures was a true genius. Note the lifelike quality of the figures. My grandfather said if you look hard enough, you can see movement from the snake."

"Movement," I said, shaking my head in disbelief. I felt the first twinges of uneasiness. "What's it going to do, crawl up my hand?"

"A scientist is supposed to keep an open mind. Take a look for yourself. I'm certain you'll find it interesting." He curved his fingers over mine, turning the ring toward the light.

I made my gaze drop to his hand to study the ring. It looked and felt heavy, like white gold or platinum. There wasn't a trace of wear, which disproved his assertions about its age. It looked as if he'd just bought the ring.

The design intrigued me. Instead of the usual representation of a bull showing only the horns or head, the animal appeared in its entirety, with the dewlap and genital organs plain to see. The snake was even more carefully wrought. Each scale was well defined, and the eyes appeared so lifelike I thought they stared up at me. For a moment I thought I saw the thing slithering across the shiny surface of the band.

I stiffened and bent even closer. A plume of wispy hair sat on top of the serpent's head. The hair lifted and swayed as if blown by imaginary wind. I closed my eyes and backed away a bit. When I opened them again, I tried to ignore the snake and pay attention to the curious design.

At first glance, the serpent seemed to entwine itself around the hind legs of the bull. The optical illusion was frighteningly realistic.

I closed my eyes for a few more seconds.

When I chanced another look, the snake was again inanimate, caught in the act of strangling the bull. I leaned closer, hoping to find that there were two snakes and I'd initially missed one. I saw only one. I drew my face away from the man's hand, but I couldn't seem to pull my hand out of his.

I felt my whole body stiffen when my eyes met and locked with his. His amusement died. Under my fingers, his hand turned cold and damp, but I couldn't let go. I had the sensation he was testing me in some strange way. Then I remembered the dream-like scene in the alley the previous night. Fear contracted my throat.

"Who are you?" I whispered.

His eyes narrowed and he laughed. "Don't you know?"

I shook my head, breathing through parted lips. His gaze held mine. For a moment, I almost read his thoughts.

The push of the crowd broke my trance. I dropped my hand and turned away, telling myself I was being foolish. The scene in the alley could have nothing to do with this man. Although the light in the alley was poor, the male figure I saw there was several inches taller.

"You must come with me," he said, taking my arm again. "We must speak."

"Why? If it's an autograph you want, I'll be happy to oblige. Otherwise, I really must leave."

"What I have to say won't take long. I think you'll find it interesting from a scientific point of view."

"All right." I gave in with unconcealed irritation. "But I can only spare you a few minutes."

"It'll be enough."

I let him lead me into a vacant private lounge and took the seat he offered. By then I'd recovered from the shock of the moving ring.

"Do you mind telling me what you want?"

"We have to speak before you get on that plane. I thought this would be an appropriate setting."

His weak smile and soft voice bothered me. "I don't even know your name."

He looked at me searchingly for several minutes. "Then you don't know. I'm surprised. I assumed from your book that you knew all about me."

It was my turn to stare at him. "That has to be the most original pick-up line I've ever heard."

He laughed with such genuine amusement that I felt my cheeks flame with embarrassment. I stood up to leave.

"No, please, don't go. I'm sorry for laughing, but I'm afraid you misunderstood my meaning."

I stopped walking, but I didn't sit down. "Just what is your meaning?"

He indicated the vacant chair. "Please."

I found myself sitting once again across from him at the small table, then waiting while he flagged down a waitress and ordered drinks. I leaned forward slightly to get a glimpse of his left hand. The ring seemed still and lifeless, but somehow I couldn't bring myself to take a closer look.

The waitress placed a glass of white wine in front of me, then lingered beside my companion. His generous shot of whiskey came with a dazzling smile and a free brush of the waitress' ample chest. He ignored her and she moved away.

I took a sip of the wine. "Thank you. Perhaps now you'll tell me why you followed me here?"

"Followed?" The tone of his voice suggested I was wrong again.

"I suppose it does look that way to you, but I assure you I came here today only to protect your interests."

"And just what are my interests, Mr.—?"

"Call me Quentin. And I'll call you Marty."

I took another sip. I surveyed him and noted with a resigned sigh that he was physically attractive. Then I thought about the ring. I found myself attracted and repelled at the same time. I took a longer drink from my glass.

"As for your interests, the primary one is always survival, is it not? Speaking anthropologically, of course."

"Are you trying to scare me?"

"I'm trying to warn you. When I first heard of your book, I was convinced you knew everything. My people believed the same thing, of course, and they didn't like that. As a result, I allowed them the freedom to act as they thought best. It wasn't until this afternoon that I changed my mind, you see."

"Changed your mind about what?"

"About letting you live. That's why I'm here. If I let you get on that plane without some sort of protection, you'll be dead within a day."

I emitted a nervous bark of laughter. "Really? How? Is the plane going to crash?"

"Nothing like that. But I assure you it's true." The calm timbre of his voice made me uncomfortable.

"Then what do I do to prevent that? Take a different flight?"

"I'm afraid that wouldn't help. The danger has nothing to do with the mode of transportation, or even this particular trip. It has to do with you. Last night was a warning. They're all out to kill you because of what you know. Because of what they think you know."

I felt the first shivers of full-blown panic. I was alone in a lounge with some sort of homicidal weirdo. I glanced around at the surrounding tables, hoping to find something to use as a weapon. Nothing.

"Are you some kind of lunatic?"

His hand, warm and smooth, covered mine on the table, and my pulse leapt. It was strange. The instant he touched me, my fear of him faded.

"You know better. I came here because, after what happened a few minutes ago, I can't allow you to be hurt."

"You mean because of what I saw in your ring?"

His eyes flashed briefly. "That's part of it." His hand tightened in a gentle squeeze. "And so is this."

He reached into the pocket of his jacket and took out a seashell on a long chain that he placed on the table in front of me.

"Wear this medallion every minute you are away from me. It's imperative. Don't take it off, even for a moment. They will recognize and respect this sign, as they have since the dawn of time."

"Dawn of time? What kind of game are you playing?"

"I can't explain now, but I am concerned with your welfare." His smile almost dazzled me. "You might say it's my destiny."

The odd intensity of his expression brought on a fresh wave of fear.

His head tilted to one side. "You have to go now."

"Just a minute. You haven't told me who 'they' are."

He looked startled, then his face resumed its irritating grin. "You really don't know. I'll make the necessary arrangements. I think it might be time."

His skin seemed to take on a smooth, glassy texture. I knew if I touched him he'd feel cold and clammy.

His hand came up to caress mine. "Sstay away from dark alleysss, my dear."

The fear turned to terror. His voice hissed and his eyes glowed.

I jumped to my feet, knocking over the chair in my haste to get away from him. I bent to retrieve it, thinking I could use it to fend him off if he came any closer.

When I straightened up, he had disappeared. The only signs he'd been there at all were his untouched glass of whiskey and the shell medallion.

I shook my head and put the chair on the floor, laughing at my own foolishness. If I saw sinister intent in a friendly gift, I needed to get away worse than I thought.

The waitress hurried over to retrieve the glasses. I felt her gaze on me for several seconds before she spoke.

"Have a fight with your boyfriend, honey?"

"He's not my boyfriend. I never saw him before today."

"He sure knows you. Look at the pretty necklace he gave you."

"I hate to shatter your hopes, but he's married. He said it wasn't a wedding ring, but I guess that makes him a liar, too."

Her eyes narrowed and the glance she threw me held suspicion. "What're you talking about?"

"The wedding ring on his left hand. I saw you look at it when you brought the drinks." I shivered. "Did you see the snake on it?"

"Come off it, honey. I ain't blind. If you want me to stay away, say so. Don't make up stories. I looked, sure. But he wasn't wearin' no ring. You think I'd flirt with a married man?"

She gave the table a final wipe and stalked away. I watched her go, my mouth hanging open, more convinced than ever I was losing my mind. One hallucination could be put down to stress. But two? I closed my eyes and tried to get a grip on my rampaging emotions.

I shook my head and turned back to the table.

In order to calm down, I bent over to take a closer look at the shell, at first afraid to touch it. I'd seen thousands of those shells in my life. They were part of the burial rituals of almost every Paleolithic civilization, and they were still in use as ornaments all over the world.

I forced myself to pick it up and turn it over. A tiny star, skillfully carved into the pink interior, reflected the overhead lights whenever the shell moved. Under the glittering star, the etched outlines of snake and bull reclined. Though I stared hard, I could discern no movement from either figure.

I glanced around the lounge, then laughed at my inexplicable reactions to an attractive, enigmatic fan. He'd gone to a lot of trouble to find someone to engrave it using information from my book.

I picked it up and placed it around my neck. It had been a long time since someone gave me something as beautiful as that shell. The least I could do was wear it to show my appreciation. I gathered my papers and belongings, and headed for the exit.

When I got a glimpse of my hand reaching for the doorknob, I froze. The fear returned in suffocating waves. The scene in the alley came rushing back. I gasped for breath, recalling the smooth, clammy feel of his hand on mine.

There, in the center of my palm, was the glossy smooth scale of a very large snake.

Chapter 4

AFTER I STEPPED off the plane and started to make my way across the asphalt, I remembered how hot and sticky the coast of Mexico could be, even in February. By the time I reached the terminal the sweater I was foolish enough to wear was plastered to my sweaty skin.

The inside of the airport wasn't much better. Sweaty, excited tourists jammed the aisles. I paused inside the door to survey the bustling scene, wondering how I was going to find my promised escort.

I heard my name called in a deep, booming voice. I caught a glimpse of a man in a bright flowered shirt elbowing his way through the throng.

The closer he came, the more I had to tilt my head back to see his face. He was tall, well over six feet, and his clothes made him resemble a walking rose arbor. His sleek black hair was parted in the middle, then left to flop over his ears in a casual style that billowed with the breeze of his rapid progress through the terminal. He seemed unable to stop smiling, regardless of the people who stepped on his feet or jostled his body. His high cheekbones, flattened nose and full lips proclaimed his Mayan heritage, which made his height even more incongruous. His eyes were a warm shade of brown that matched his coffee-colored skin to perfection.

As he drew nearer, his dark gaze fell to the shell around my neck, then raised back up to meet mine. His full lips parted, revealing dazzlingly white teeth. He laughed heartily.

I searched my mind for the Spanish words to ask what was so amusing.

"There isn't a moment to waste," he said, taking my carry-on in one hand and my arm in the other. "We must hurry if we're to make the next connection."

He turned and retraced his steps, dragging me through the press of tourists. He shouldered his way toward the baggage claim.

"You speak English."

"My father's an American," he said.

There was no time for further conversation. I had to pour on the speed to keep up.

My luggage was waiting when we arrived at the conveyor belt.

My companion followed me around, scooping up the bags I indicated. Then he led the way at a breathless pace to a small door set in a deep recess of the terminal.

By the time we crossed the asphalt to a small charter plane I was panting. He threw my bags into the cramped cargo hold, tossed me into the nearest available seat, and buckled his angular frame into the one beside me. Before I knew what was happening, we were airborne once again.

"So much for the stereotype about Mexicans being slow and lethargic," I said darkly. "The least you could do is grunt and point when you want me to follow."

"Sorry," he said. His face pinkened, but whether with embarrassment or exertion I couldn't tell. "If we missed this flight there wouldn't be another for three days."

"My turn to say I'm sorry," I said. "Where're we going, anyway?"

"Villahermosa. It's the closest airport to the dig. From there, we go by jeep into the jungle. There are no roads, so the trip will take all of tomorrow, and we should arrive in time for the evening meal."

"I see. Who are you? And how'd you recognize me in that crowded airport?"

Under his swarthy skin the blush deepened. "I'm Ricardo Cerves. Doctor Emil gave me your picture to study so I could find you. But it wasn't necessary. I've read your book."

"From the sound of your voice, I take it you don't agree with my hypothesis."

He shrugged and crossed his long legs. "I think you've managed a fair evaluation of some of the more ridiculous legends of my people," he said.

"And you don't approve."

"No, I don't. The Maya are still a superstitious people. Although the Spanish succeeded in forcing us to accept their Christian God, they could never stop us from believing the legends. Lending credence to these myths by printing them in a scholarly treatise won't help my people progress into the twentieth century."

"That's fair," I said in a conciliatory tone. "Provided the stories are myth or superstition. But what if somewhere there can be found evidence that proves a certain portion of the legend once had a basis in fact? Wouldn't that help your people even more? For example, the god Kukulkan."

Ricardo nodded in approval.

"We know he was a man, driven out of his own region because he advocated human sacrifice," I said. "He arrived in the Mayan regions where the people were already practicing blood sacrifice on a small scale. Because his name meant 'plumed serpent,' as did the name of an existing god, Quetzalcoatl, the two were forever linked in the minds of the people. The fact that Quetzalcoatl was a benevolent god who didn't advocate sacrifice was forgotten, and over the centuries the two became one. Explaining the practice of human sacrifice was introduced by a mere mortal, not a god, would help the Maya understand their past."

"I can see your point, even if I don't agree with your methods," Ricardo admitted. "It'd be better to let the old beliefs die of their own accord."

"But they aren't," I said. "It's been almost five hundred years since Bishop Landa, and blood sacrifice is still practiced. Not in the open, but in secret, among small, secret sects. The only way to stop it is to make the truth known, and the only way to do that is to educate the masses in their own history. Expose the gods as human beings, with human beliefs and human failings, and they cease to be gods."

Ricardo looked at me with respect. "It could work."

"Thank you, Ricardo."

He laughed and relaxed into the cushions of the seat. "Call me Rich."

"And you can call me Marty. Do you live in Mexico or the U.S.?"

"I moved back to the village after I finished college," he replied. "One of the few to do so. I make my living by serving as guide and translator to scientists."

"Translator? Then you can help me with my Spanish. It's a little rusty."

"I don't speak Spanish. But I'm proficient in eighteen of the twenty-three Mayan dialects, along with English, French, and German."

"But no Spanish? How's that?"

"Quite easy, really. My mother was the daughter of a Mayan elder and wouldn't allow Spanish to be spoken in her presence, as is the way with most of the households in our village. My father insisted on teaching me English despite her protests. The other languages I learned in school."

"I take it you didn't attend the village schools."

"Right again. Dad insisted I go to school in the States, so I lived with my aunt in Chicago. But I spent every summer in the village, and I knew I'd return when I finished my education."

"Your father's from Chicago?" I asked, incredulous. "How on earth did he end up in an isolated Mayan village?"

Again he laughed. The sound soothed my frazzled nerves. "He came as a laborer with one of the American archaeological teams, hoping to find hidden treasure and retire. What he found was my mother. He said the moment he saw her it was love. Since she refused to leave the home of her ancestors, he stayed with her. He developed quite a reputation as a reliable guide, and I decided to follow in his footsteps."

There was a long, comfortable pause, during which I could feel his gaze upon me. "What about you? What made you decide to go into anthropology?"

"That was predestined," I said, laughing. "My father was a gifted man, and I spent my life accompanying him from dig to dig. It was inevitable that I go into the same field, I suppose, although I'm not half the scholar he was."

"I suppose you spent a lot of time in Mexico, then."

"How'd you know that?" I said, startled. "Oh, of course. The book."

"Yes, but also from this." He pointed to the shell hanging around my neck. "It's of excellent workmanship. I don't recall seeing another like it."

I held it up for his inspection. "I agree. I've seen these pendants in graves all over the world, but this is the first example engraved with such skill."

He knit his brows in a puzzled frown. "All over the world? I thought it was strictly a Mayan superstition."

"They've been found in Mexico, but they're common all over the world, from Nelson Bay Cave in Africa to the Indian settlements of Mesa Verde. It's assumed they were used as ornaments, but I have my doubts."

"They're more than an ornament for the Maya," he said, letting the pendant swing back into place. "The elders of my tribe believe such shells can chase away nightmares. The old legends speak of nightmares as actual entities, capable of stealing your heart from your body. Wearing one of these shells to bed is the only way to insure you wake up the next morning."

"That's interesting. Where did that belief get it's start, I wonder?"

"Who knows how superstitions get started," he said. "The practice is still alive and well. No self-respecting Mayan would dream of wearing their *tzem* in public, but neither would they consider going to sleep without it."

"*Tzem?* I thought that was the Mayan word for chest," I said.

"It's also the word for these pendants, I suppose because it's believed they protect the chest during sleep. When the individual dies and is buried, the *tzem* goes along with them as protection against evil spirits who would try to steal the heart, the repository of the soul. Without a heart, the body would be denied admission to the afterlife."

"That's fascinating," I said. "I should do some research into the beliefs associated with these shells. It'd make a great book."

We spent the rest of the short flight discussing the impending journey through the jungle. I was happy Emil had sent me a competent, knowledgeable escort, especially one so well versed in the customs of the Mayan people. I planned to take full advantage of our time together.

The pilot announced we were beginning our final approach to the Villahermosa airport, and I turned to the window. Although we were flying low, I could see nothing that resembled a runway. I did see dense vegetation that seemed to skim the bottom of our aircraft. Banyan trees, giant ferns, and rubber trees grew thick and dense in all directions. At the last possible minute, the jungle gave way to expose the paved runway beneath our landing gear.

I let out the breath I didn't know I was holding and the plane rattled to a smooth stop near the terminal. There was some delay while the flight attendant wrestled with the main hatchway. The usual mix of tourists, backpackers, and business travelers poured into the aisle. I realized the plane was crowded and took my place in line.

While awaiting my turn to shuffle out, I got a strange feeling that someone was watching me. I looked around, careful to disguise my glance, until I caught the eye of a figure in the back of the plane.

The person remained in his seat even though the line was moving. Though I watched intently, I could detect no movement from his body, not even the rise and fall of his chest to indicate breathing. I knew he was alive from the intensity of his unwavering stare. His eyes seemed to glow.

Humid air filled the cabin, indicating the steward won his battle with the hatch. Despite that, I shivered. I saw cold fury in the yellow eyes that held my gaze.

Beware the prophecy. There are those who are not yet ready for the time of fulfillment.

As I stood there, the strange thought ricocheted through my mind.

I stiffened, troubled, when I realized the man with the glowing eyes was speaking in my mind. His thoughts became increasingly menacing, striving for mastery over me.

He wanted me to follow him, to join with him.

In the back of my numbed brain panic began to build. I knew it was a contest of wills, just as I knew I couldn't afford to lose. My eyes ached with the strain of keeping them open.

Incredibly, he grinned, as if he knew my terror. I felt sweat break out on my forehead and under my arms. I fought to block my mind from his. In response, he doubled the assault. I gripped the seat in front of me and exerted every ounce of willpower I had to keep him from gaining entry.

After several minutes of silent struggle, I sensed his confusion. He seemed surprised I could resist, and he weakened the mental onslaught. Finally, the man's eyes dropped from mine. I almost sobbed in relief. Still, I kept my gaze locked on the assailant, fearful I wouldn't be able to resist another attack.

In the back of the plane, his eyes changed color. Benign yellow darkened and grew colder. I felt him brace for another attempt. When his eyes razed my trembling body I saw they'd shifted to a sickly, fetid green that matched his cancerous thoughts to perfection.

All my instincts screamed the need to get away from him, but my muscles refused to obey my will. His gaze rose, raking my body in its unhurried progress toward my face. I sensed renewed strength and self-assurance, as if he drew confidence from another source. I knew I couldn't hold him off.

The glowing eyes focused on my waist. I felt my skin tingle with alien warmth. His gaze shifted higher and I felt my ribs grow hot from the burning intensity of his eyes. Immersed in fear and hysteria, it was some time before I realized the burning sensation had ceased. His flickering green eyes locked on my chest, but they were wary, almost frightened. The odd glow faded until it was no brighter than a candle.

I stared at him, unable to fathom the reason for the change from malice to apprehension. His eyes widened in disbelief. I followed the direction of his wary stare. It was the pendant that frightened him. The light from his eyes caught the tiny carving of the star, causing it to emit an answering glow.

He looked at my face and I saw speculation in his glowing eyes. After several heart-pounding moments, he blinked, then closed his eyes, extinguishing the light. I sank back against the seat behind me, drained.

"Are you all right?" Rich said.

I became aware that he was shaking me.

"Wake up," he said.

"I'm okay," I said, croaking. My throat felt closed and dry.

Rich looked from me to the back of the plane, then shook his head. "Do you get sleeping sickness or something? I was talking to you for the longest time, and you just stared at the wall."

I dredged up a shaky laugh. "No."

I looked around toward the front exit and noted that the other passengers had already left. The flight attendant looked at us expectantly.

"Are you really okay?"

"Yes. Let's get the hell out of here."

"Sounds good to me. Give me that bag."

I surrendered the bag and stepped into the aisle. I was just about to make my way to the door when something made me turn my head and look toward the rear. He was no longer there.

"What's the matter?" Rich said, his voice heavy with concern.

"Nothing," I said. "I just don't see how he could've passed me without my seeing him, that's all."

Rich turned. "What're you talking about? See who?"

"The man who was sitting back there," I said. "The one who stared at me."

There was an odd mixture of compassion and doubt in Rich's gaze. He licked his lips. "Where was he sitting?"

I stalked to the back seat. "Right there. Don't even try to tell me you didn't see him. He practically glowed."

He licked his lips again and, meeting my angry gaze, shrugged.

"He sat right there," I said. "In that seat. And he stared at me."

Rich flashed me a wary, uneasy glance.

"I'm not seeing things," I said. "Is this a conspiracy? First the waitress denies seeing that gaudy ring, now you tell me you didn't see the person sitting there a few minutes ago."

Rich examined the chair. After a time he turned to face me, a curious expression on his face.

"What is it?"

"Are you sure you saw a man? Was it something else?"

"What do you mean? What did you find?"

He gestured toward the chair. I threw him a questioning look, then scooted into the cramped aisle until I stood beside him.

The cushions, worn and shabby like the rest of the plane, bore indentations made by hundreds of previous occupants. Lying in the precise center of the seat was a small, shiny object.

"Another scale," I said, unable to pull my gaze from the thing. "A snake's scale."

Rich's eyes narrowed. "Another scale?"

"I have two just like it," I said. "They seem to be following me."

Rich cleared his throat. "You think snakes are following you?"

I shrugged, aware how this must sound to him.

He met my gaze, then lifted the sample and dropped it into his shirt pocket. "Where are the others?"

"In my carry-on, I think. Why?"

"I know a guy who's an expert on snakes," Rich said. "He might be able to identify them. It's worth a try, isn't it?"

I smiled at him in relief and appreciation. "Thank you."

"Don't mention it." He gripped my arm and steered me toward the front of the plane. "I find this fascinating. I'm pretty well acquainted with just about every kind of reptile you're likely to run into in this part of Mexico. But this scale is like nothing I've ever seen. Either someone made it with the intention of frightening you, or..."

"Or what?"

"Or there really was a snake in that chair. Either way, you've a right to be scared. If it's a person, they're dangerous." He took a deep breath. "If it's a snake, it's from a species I've never seen before. And it has to be really big. Judging from the scale, that snake would have to be at least twice as big as I am. I don't know about you, but I don't like the idea of anything bigger than me following us into the jungle."

I craned my neck to look up at his face, six-and-a-half-feet off the ground. "I'll second that," I said, stepping into the glaring Mexican sunshine.

Chapter 5

LOCATED ON THE Gulf coast in the Mexican State of Tabasco, Villahermosa had grown beyond recognition since my last visit. The area experienced a boon from the discovery of oil in the vicinity, and the sleepy town I remembered had grown into a thriving metropolis of more than half a million people.

The Mexican government, overwhelmed by the growth, couldn't afford the funds necessary to conserve the antiquities within its borders. To carry out the important work of excavation and conservation, it encouraged universities abroad to set up field laboratories throughout the country. The coast was home to sophisticated research projects, ranging from archaeology to zoology, that studied the impact of massive drilling operations on their areas of interest.

Rich explained it all as we made our way through customs and claimed the Jeep reserved by Emil. The vehicle was heavy-duty, with an upgraded suspension system, wide tires, and a winch.

We stowed my cumbersome bags in the back and left the airport. I enjoyed the slow, cautious trip through the city, marveling at the odd mixture of modern architecture and old-fashioned adobe homes. As we turned off the main thoroughfare, I caught a glimpse of the long white robe and shoulder length black hair of a Lacandon, the people who still follow the Mayan ways, openly worshipping the ancient gods. I strained my neck to follow his progress along the busy street. It was rare that they would leave their jungle homes to journey into the city. I had never seen a Lacandon in a metropolitan area and I wondered what he was doing here.

Rich noticed my interest. "There is a settlement a few kilometers away, through the jungle," he explained. "Their privacy was invaded when the city expanded, and the village elders are here to negotiate with the government for a tract of more secluded land. Tourists who don't understand their need for isolation bother the tribe."

"Why doesn't that surprise me?" I said. The Maya still believed cameras were things of evil, robbing the individual of dominion over his spirit. "I hope the government will cooperate."

"I think they will. They're finally beginning to realize that the heritage of the Maya is a natural treasure which must be protected. It's the Christians that disagree with the new policy. They're tenacious in their attempts to convert these people to their way of life."

"What a shame it would be if they succeeded."

We drove the rest of the way to the hotel in silence. After check-in, I found that my assigned room was across the hall from Rich's. Leaving him in the hall, I entered my room and took a quick look around. Its design was bright and airy, with a coverlet and curtains woven from a re-discovered Mayan ceremonial pattern. Thick mats made of braided sisal covered the floor, lending an earthy scent to the air. A small refrigerator, containing the usual assortment of snacks and drinks, hummed from the corner by the balcony window. The bathroom facilities were clean and modern and there was hot water, so I availed myself of a shower and a change of clothes.

Since I promised Rich I would dig out the other scales, I turned to my luggage while I waited for my hair to dry. I had to open every one of my bags to find the small pouch containing my credit cards and other personal effects. I swore I had packed the pouch in the bag I carried on the plane, but it wasn't there.

While rooting through the last of the big bags, I felt something sharp brush my finger. My hand recoiled before my brain could register the cold, oily feel. I knew what it was and I sat back for a minute, too stunned to move.

My heart raced and my palms grew sweaty, but I forced my hand back into the bag. I took out the scale. It was a good deal larger than the others I had seen, and the room started to spin when I tried to imagine how it had come to be inside my bag. My mind conjured up pictures of glowing eyes and glassy skin. I backed away from the bag.

There was a loud knock at the door.

My first impulse was to scream for Rich, but I managed to run for the door. With my hand pressed to the panel, I whispered, "Who's there?"

"Who do you think?" Rich said, his deep voice indignant.

I flung open the door and hugged him. He gave me a gentle push to hold me at arm's length and glanced around my room.

"What's wrong?"

"I found another one," I said. "This time it was in one of my bags."

He stared at my pointing finger. "You're bleeding."

"The scale must have scraped it. It isn't serious."

He retreated until he stood in the hallway. Under his tan, his face appeared pale.

"What is the matter with you?" I said, brandishing the injured finger. "It's just a little blood."

"Cover it," he said in a weak voice.

I put my hands on my hips, ready to laugh. His ashen pallor stopped me. "I have heard of big men afraid of a little blood, but I never thought I'd see it."

I searched through another bag until I found some adhesive bandages, then went back to the bathroom to cover the scratch. When I returned, Rich looked almost normal again.

He grinned when he saw me. "Sorry about that."

"Don't mention it. What are we going to do about the scale?"

Rich picked it up and put it with the one from the plane. "Where are the others?"

I got the last bag and, taking a deep breath, plunged my hand inside it. I found the pouch on the bottom of the heap, extracted the scales from a side pocket, and handed them to Rich.

"I talked to my friend the zoologist," he said. "He wants us to join him at the lab as soon as we can get there. He also invited us to be his guests for dinner. You should be flattered. He doesn't often part with his hard-earned cash."

"Sounds great to me." The mention of food and Rich's comforting presence restored my flagging spirits. I was starving. "Let's go."

The research station was at the end of a rough dirt road in the jungle. The ferns and palm trees grew thick in spots, and I almost expected to see yellow eyes peer out of the gloom. As I got out of the Jeep I noticed two or three iguanas scuttle into the underbrush. A few more basked in the sunlight, unperturbed by our presence.

Constructed of thin sheets of steel with a thatched roof, the laboratory building stood near the edge of the woods, surrounded by trees. Inside, the makeshift lab held all the latest in scientific gadgetry. Sophisticated computers and a high-powered microscope stood at the center of the room. Cages of specimens lined one entire wall, and the opposite wall contained cartons of supplies. A wall of reference books separated the animals from the work area.

At first the structure seemed deserted. The only sign of life I could detect was the aroma of freshly brewed coffee. It reminded me I hadn't eaten since breakfast.

At the sound of our entry, a mass of black, kinky hair rose from the clutter of test tubes. All I could see was the thick patch of hair, some brown skin, and the twisting body of a large boa. The sight reminded me of a carved stone stelae at Chichen Itza.

"Hello, Mike," Rich said. "You're looking fine. Now, if you could only dump that useless beast, you might get someplace in the world."

"Ha, ha," a voice from behind the reptile said. "He would never dump me. Hey, Rich. How've you been?"

"Getting by," Rich replied. "I want you to meet a friend of mine. Doctor Murdoch, say hello to Doctor Hargrove."

"Martine Murdoch?" The voice beneath the snake said in awe. "I read your book. Fascinating." Dr. Hargrove pointed at the tattered copy on the shelf.

"I wish I'd never written it," I said before I could stop myself.

"That's an odd attitude," Dr. Hargrove said.

I shrugged. "Unfortunately, it changed my life, but not for the better. It seemed like a good idea at the time. It was my way of attempting to explain some of the stranger discoveries of the last hundred years."

"Until I read the material, I never realized so much has been uncovered all over the world," Dr. Hargrove said. "The artifacts are startlingly similar. It's as though every civilization has a common link."

"Exactly," I said. "And that common link has to deal with religion and the way primitive man looked at himself and his environment. Is it so difficult to imagine all races did the same thing at one point in their social development?"

"I think so, too," Dr. Hargrove said. "You really made a name for yourself."

"Yeah, and the name is unprintable," I said. I took the book from the shelf and frowned at the cover.

"What do you mean?" Rich said.

I shrugged. "My fellow anthropologists don't agree with my hypothesis. They accused me of slanting the data. When the book became a best-seller, they wanted me to announce the material was falsified. When I refused, they convened a board of inquiry. I didn't fit their image anymore, so I had to go."

"You've been black-balled?" Dr. Hargrove looked stunned.

"Right into the corner pocket." I put the book back on the shelf. "Call me Marty. And I'll call you Mike, shall I?"

Both the men laughed, and Dr. Hargrove unwound the serpent from around his body. The first thing I noticed was his mustache.

Large and thick, it dominated a face that was as thin and lean as the rest of his body. He looked comfortable in the field scientist's uniform of ratty jeans and t-shirt. "You could call me Mike, but I'm afraid that name is already taken by the snake. Mine's R.J."

I held out my hand. He took it in a firm grip and smiled. I returned the smile. "Well, do you mind if I call you R.J., then?"

"Not at all." He moved over to the lab's small kitchen and offered me a cup of coffee. I accepted and took a long refreshing sip. "Rich tells me you're joining the Larson dig."

I nodded. "Do you know Emil?"

"I did some work for him a few weeks ago, before they cordoned off the area."

"Why did Emil need a zoologist?"

R.J. shrugged and handed a filled mug to Rich. I noticed his arms, though thin, were knotted with corded muscles. "It's really not all that uncommon to call us in. Most digs turn up fossil remains in one form or another and, when you have such a high concentration of scientists close by, it only makes sense to take advantage of them. Which reminds me, I'm dying to see what you've got."

The abrupt change of subject caught me off guard, but I motioned for Rich to hand over the scales. R.J.'s reluctance to discuss the dig and his involvement in the project puzzled me. In this age of teleconferencing and laptop computers, it wasn't common practice for a research team to call in experts not associated with the venture.

A movement over by the cages drew my attention. I joined Rich in his study of the various specimens on display, leaving R.J. to his work. Most of the animals suffered from injuries or sickness. Farther down the line the reptile cages ended and the last remaining spaces were occupied by birds, also in various stages of convalescence.

While I studied a beautiful toucan, R.J. left his microscope and went to stand in front of the wall of books. After several seconds he grabbed a large tome, flipped through its pages, then replaced it on the shelf. He repeated the process until he carried a volume back to the lab's long worktable.

"Look," Rich said.

I followed his pointing finger. "It's a snake," I said. "There's another one over there."

"Look in the back of the cage."

"It's a snake's skin. I've seen hundreds of them."

"I have seen hundreds of them, too," Rich said thoughtfully. "Take a good look."

I bent over. Except for the hide surrounding the animal's head, the entire skin had come off in one long, perfect piece. "After all the whole snake skins we've seen, you'd think one of us would've remembered they don't shed individual scales," I said in disgust. "Well, since they can't be the scales of a snake we've found all over the place, what could they be? Fish?"

"They are awfully big to have come from a fish," Rich said.

"They are awfully big to have come from a snake, too, but that never stopped us from thinking that's what they were. Especially when we knew snakes don't have scales. At least not individual ones."

"You're wrong," R.J. said from across the room. "Come here a minute."

"You mean they really came from a snake?" Rich said, surprised.

R.J. nodded. "Yes. Or they did, to be precise."

"But what kind of serpent has scales, let alone ones that big?" I asked.

"Just because they don't have them now is no reason to believe they never did." R.J. smiled and gestured toward the microscope. "Reptiles have been around for millions of years. During those millions of years they've evolved, become more suited to their environment, just as we have."

"I think I see what you're driving at," I said.

R.J. grinned and nodded. "Two years ago, a team working in South Africa did another exploration of the Nelson Bay cave site. Evidence from the cave proves that primates have hunted, fished, and lived together in groups in that area for more than fifty thousand years."

I stood over the microscope and adjusted the focus. Beneath the lens, the veining pattern of a scale came into view. "From there we also have the earliest known ornaments – shells used as jewelry, like this one."

"According to your book, after this first evidence things were quiet there for about thirty thousand years," R.J. said. "Then humans began to occupy the caves again, and did so almost continually for the next twenty thousand years."

"Correct again," I replied. "The coastline, which retreated during the last Ice Age, returned to its normal location after the thaw."

"The deposit layers had been studied by anthropologists for almost thirty years for indicators that would tell us how these early men lived. But it wasn't until about five years ago that the finds from the various layers were studied by the rest of the scientific community.

Two years ago, sieving the sand from the second era of occupation netted us a group of scales. Eighteen of them, in fact."

"So they found scales. What kind of scales?" Rich said.

R.J. pointed to the open book beside the microscope. "That kind."

Rich and I crowded around, studying the color pictures.

"They look the same as our scales," Rich said, his voice filled with awe.

"That's because they are," R.J. said. "I've compared the known attributes of the scales found at Nelson Bay cave with the three you just brought me, and I have no doubt they're from the same species."

"And what species is that?" I asked, comparing the book with the scale under magnification.

"One that's extinct now," R.J. said. "We believe it was an ancestor of the rattlesnake."

"You mean it's poisonous?" Rich asked, his eyes widening.

"Without a preserved specimen to study, there is no way to be certain. But we think it was."

"Are there any other known representatives?" I asked.

"A fossil was unearthed in the deserts of China in nineteen thirty-three which proved to be the remains of a scaled serpent." He flipped through the book until he found the page he wanted and pointed to the picture. "The remains were in pretty poor condition. The bones of small reptiles like snakes are pretty flimsy things, and don't leave good impressions under the best of conditions. This specimen measured almost fifteen feet in length and was nearly a foot in diameter. The really interesting thing about the find is the scales left in the soft mud of the riverbed.

"It was the first time something like that had come to light, and it excited the zoological community of the time. Each scale was examined thoroughly. They all bore the same veining pattern, much like fingerprints. The veining pattern of each of the scales found in Nelson Bay Cave was identical to each of the others, but different from the ones found in China. Most scientists believe we have two different species."

"But you don't believe that," I said.

"No. It's my opinion we have the remains of two individuals of the same species," R.J. said.

"But what about the scales I brought?" I asked, indicating the pile. "This could allow you to prove your theory, couldn't it?"

R.J. looked at me out of the corner of his eye. For the first time I saw doubt. "Why don't you tell me how you came to be in possession of them."

I told the story about the alley, and how I met Quentin. I was careful to include my own perceptions of the two events, trying to impress upon my listeners the fierce repulsion I felt during the first encounter, and the uncertainty of the second. Then I supplied details about the plane and the scale found in my luggage.

"Interesting," Rich said. I knew he was trying to be polite.

R.J. stood across the table, looking at me with narrowed eyes. I felt like one of the animals in the cages. "Do you remember which of these scales came from the man at the airport?" he said with deliberate calm.

I looked at the four objects and pointed to one in the middle. "That one."

"Are you certain?"

"I'm positive," I said. "It's bigger than the one left on the plane, but smaller than the others. Why?"

He paced the room. "It's not possible. If anyone else came to me with this crazy story, I'd call the police in a second. There are two things stopping me from doing it anyway. Do you know what those two things are?"

"No," I said. The mention of police was enough to make anyone nervous. Especially me.

"The brilliance of your work, and that the scales from the Chinese find have been locked away at Oxford University. It's possible someone could have stolen one of them, but they're so famous they're guarded almost as well as the Queen. If one of them came up missing, every expert on the face of the earth would be notified. You'd be a fool to bring them here."

"What does a moldy Chinese snake have to do with these scales?" Rich asked, his brow furrowed.

"You can't be serious," I said softly.

R.J. didn't look at me. He didn't smile, either. Nevertheless, I knew he was agitated by the way his mustache quivered. "I'd like to phone a friend I know at Oxford and eliminate the obvious possibility."

"Wait a minute," Rich said, balling his fist. "Are you trying to say she stole the scales?"

I placed a hand on his arm to keep him where he was. "It's all right. He has to be sure. In his place, I'd do the same thing."

I nodded at R.J. and he dialed the phone. Since it was two o'clock in the morning in England, the person at the other end took a long time to answer and the conversation was brief and impassioned.

"They are all there, or they were when the museum closed," R.J. said, wiping the sweat from his brow.

"Are you certain of the identification?" I said. "Could you be wrong?"

"I wish I could." RJ. brought the book closer to the microscope and invited me to compare them. It was impossible to tell the two samples apart.

"So this scale, the one from Quentin, the man at the airport, is a match to the scales found in the fossilized remains in China," I said.

Rich's eyes widened. "Is that true?"

"Is it possible the man who calls himself Quentin is a zoologist who has access to these scales?" I said. "Could he have slipped me one to scare me?"

R.J. shook his head. "Not possible."

"Then what about the other scales?" I said.

"They're different," R.J. said. "They didn't come from either of the two known specimens. And they're very well preserved. They still contain some of the oils found in the bodies of snakes. If it weren't impossible, I'd say they were recently shed."

"How recent?"

"This one," he said, indicating the smallest, "is hours old. The other, a few days at the most."

"Are you trying to tell us there are at least two of these things still around?" Rich said. "Sorry, but I don't buy it."

"I already told you, the species is extinct," R.J. said in a patient voice.

"Then how do you account for the appearance of these scales?" I asked.

"I am hoping you'll be able to tell me," he said, leaning forward.

"Me? I have no idea."

"That's interesting." Reaching past me, R.J. opened a drawer and extracted a wrapped bundle. "We have a bevy of recent scales, and each is associated with you in some way."

"I'd hardly call four scales a bevy," I said dryly.

"Neither would I," R.J. said, brandishing the packet. "Emil Larson called me about three weeks ago, frantic. He begged me to come out to the site as fast as I could. It was so unlike Emil to be upset that I dropped everything and went out there."

"I know. He did the same thing to me." I nodded.

"When I got there, he led me to the remains of an ancient temple," R.J. said. "At the base of the ruin they discovered a shaft that went down under the structure. At the bottom of a thirty-foot drop there was a tunnel that went about fifty feet into the mountain. At the end of this tunnel was another shaft still awaiting excavation. Emil stopped digging out the temple when he found these."

R.J. opened the parcel, and he indicated the three scales that sat in the center of the wrap. I lifted one and trained a magnifying glass over its polished surface.

"They were found together, almost on the top of the pile of debris filling the shaft," R.J. said. "Emil knew I'd studied both sets of known scales. We can place these under the microscope, but I already know what we'll find."

"They're different from any of the others."

His eyes met mine. "Right." He re-wrapped the bundle and returned it to its drawer.

"What do these have to do with me?" I said.

"After I recovered these, I decided to hang around, just in case more turned up when they resumed the excavation," R.J. said. "It was a slow process. They'd been digging for almost two weeks when, about ten feet from the top of the shaft, they hit a dead spot. That's when Emil got excited. He took the light and ordered his men to lower him down. He was very quiet. I thought something had gone wrong. After about an hour, Emil told us to bring him up and, when we did, I almost cried out. He was pale as paper, and sweating. He ordered everyone out of the area, and the next day he made everyone go home except for essential personnel. I packed up, came back here and resumed my work. About four days ago, he came to the lab and asked me if I knew you."

"Why?" I said.

"I'm coming to that," he said, shifting his weight from foot to foot. His mustache quivered so much I thought it would bounce from his lip. "When I told him we'd never met, but I was familiar with your writing, he didn't seem to know what to do. He left the lab but came back even more agitated. I made him call Doctor Mathews and insist you get down here."

There was a pause, broken only by the rustling of the animals in their cages. I found I was leaning forward, hanging on R.J.'s every word.

"What was down there?" Rich asked.

"Bones. Some were contemporary with the original structure. Others aren't so old. But they found far more disturbing evidence that the shaft was still in use. There was graffiti on the walls, some of it written in the last six months."

"How can Emil know the time frame?" I said. "That has to be conjecture."

R.J. reached into another drawer and pulled out a sealed envelope. "I thought so, too, until he showed me these. Your book didn't even get published until six months ago, so the writing can't be older than that. Emil didn't want me to tell you, but I think you have the right to know, so you can decide if you want to risk joining him at the site."

"What risk? What writing?" Rich said. "What's in the envelope? If you don't get to the point I'll have to strangle you."

R.J. hesitated, his smile grim. After several seconds, he handed the envelope over.

Inside were photographs of what I took to be the inside of the shaft. The first two prints showed writing in ancient Mayan text. Few of the Mayan glyphs were understood, and I didn't recognize any of the symbols.

The next series was odd indeed. Seeing Egyptian hieroglyphs on the wall perplexed me so much that, at first, I couldn't read them. When I settled down enough to translate, I almost wished I hadn't.

"Murdoch must be destroyed," it read.

My hands shook so badly I had to put the stack of pictures down.

Rich looked in confusion from me to R.J. "Aren't these Egyptian? What do they say?"

R.J. looked concerned. "I don't think this is a good time—"

"Someone's idea of a joke," I said. "One of the scientists must have a sense of humor after all. It could've been Emil himself."

Rich worked down to the bottom of the stack. I caught a glimpse of another section of the wall, the message written in English:

"Tell Murdoch that the Prophecy will be denied. Know ye that, wherever she is, the Nightmare will hunt her down."

"Why would Emil want to do this to you? You know better," R.J. said in a reasonable voice.

"Why would anyone do it?" Rich said. He pushed the pictures away and wiped his hands on the thigh of his jeans. "It's sick. It has to be someone's idea of a joke."

R.J. braced his hands on the table and leaned forward. "What if it's not? What if there really is someone down there, waiting for you?"

"You expect me to believe there's someone, besides one of the scientists associated with the dig, in the jungles of Mexico who knows how to write in ancient Egyptian, Mayan, Chinese, Arabic, Latin, and English? A literate fiend?" My laugh of scorn came out sounding pretty convincing. "I stopped believing in the bogeyman a long time ago. One member of the team hates me, and that's all there is to it. At least I'm forewarned." I picked up my bag and headed for the door. "I am going to get something to eat, with or without the two of you."

I stalked to the door and wrenched it open. The darkness surprised me and I backed away. The men, after a wary glance in my direction, followed. We piled into the Jeep and drove in search of nourishment. My temper cooled with every mile that brought us closer to civilization.

I made a mental note to have a serious talk with Emil when I reached his camp. Maybe he could tell me who it was that hated me so much they would write they wanted to kill me on the walls of an ancient burial shaft.

Chapter 6

THE INLAND JUNGLES of Mexico hadn't changed in the fifteen years since I last visited my father at his secluded camp among the ruins. Every summer vacation and school holiday was spent here. As soon as we left the roadways of coastal Mexico, delightful memories came flooding back.

Rich informed me we would follow the Rio Grijalva for most of our trip. I felt a pleasant thrill at the prospect. He told me the site of the dig contained ample fresh water because of the numerous *cenotes*—small inland lakes formed by the flooding of underground caves—that dotted the landscape along the river's path.

The builders of the ancient cities always chose to establish their urban centers around *cenotes*. In ancient times, the largest of the flooded caves was sometimes designated as a holy place. Sacrificial victims were thrown there after removing the heart as an offering to the god Quetzalcoatl.

I tried to picture the land the way it might have looked before the landing of the conquistadors. Crude roadways built by the Maya linked ceremonial centers throughout their vast empire, making the journey through the jungle easier for devout pilgrims and priests. A low stone wall, rivaling even the most ambitious Egyptian architecture, encircled their entire domain.

I shuddered despite the sun, wondering how an organized civilization could vanish so completely. Pondering this mystery, I was not in the mood for idle conversation. Rich left me alone for much of the journey. It wasn't until late afternoon that he stopped the truck to give us a rest before we entered Emil's forgotten city.

Grateful for the opportunity to move around a bit, I stretched. It took several minutes to get the blood circulating before I could move off the beaten track in search of a convenient bush.

I moved away from the truck, careful to look for easy landmarks. The jungle was not a place where I wanted to become lost. The trees overhead echoed with rustling and the call of macaws and cockatoos. Monkeys swung from branch to branch, chattering loudly. Here and there, dappled sunlight penetrated to the jungle floor.

I finally located a suitable place, protected from the birds overhead by the wide leaves of a sick-looking banana plant. I emerged a little later and started back along the path I had marked and found my way to the clearing.

Once at the truck, there was no sign of Rich. I opened his cooler and extracted the water jug and some fruit and settled in the seat to eat a light meal.

Soon after, several spider monkeys appeared overhead. At first they stayed in the tops of the trees. However, two juveniles grew bolder and scrambled down to play in the lower branches just above my head. The larger of the two was very agile, easily eluding the other. I watched them for some time, amused by their antics.

When they retreated, I noted how far the sun had dropped toward the horizon. Rich hadn't returned. I hesitated, debating between going off in search of him or remaining where I was. Since he was the more experienced member of the party, I couldn't imagine he could get lost. But the jungle was home to many creatures, not all of them as benign as my dueling monkeys. As the minutes ticked by I imagined all sorts of mishaps.

I opened my mouth and let out a shout. The loud, unexpected noise startled the birds and monkeys, causing them to take flight before the echoes had died. The resulting silence was worse than the noise. I glanced at the sky and was shocked to realize it would soon grow dark. I decided to hazard a brief look around, keeping the clearing in sight. In case I didn't find him, I wanted to spend the night close to my only mode of transportation.

Armed with a branch and a flashlight I fished from the truck's glovebox, I went to the place where I had last seen Rich. I started to look around. Soon I found a path of broken and twisted leaves leading west. I headed down it, keeping the Jeep in sight.

My stomach grew queasy when I made my way into the jungle. There was no movement at all. A quick, nervous glance around failed to locate a sign of life other than the trees and vines that seemed to press in closer. I had an overwhelming desire to run back to the roadway. The vegetation took on a sinister personality. I stumbled on for a few more paces, then stopped.

"Just let me find Rich and I'll leave," I said. The realization that I was speaking to the trees didn't embarrass me.

I had the feeling I was not alone. The menace I experienced on the plane grew stronger with every step I took. I knew the entity was close by, watching. I knew it could hear me.

I went on for another ten yards, then the jungle parted and I walked into a small clearing. The darkness was almost complete. Even though the ground itself was free of tangled growth, the branches of the trees were dense and twisted. I could make out a large, bumpy shape in the center of the cleared ground. I prayed it was not a predator and turned the flashlight toward the unidentified lump.

Part of the shape was definitely my missing guide. It was evident from the scratches on his face and his muddy clothing that someone had dragged him into the area, presumably the person who still crouched beside him.

The person looked up when the light flashed onto his face. The glow that came from his eyes wasn't a reflection of the light.

It was the thing from the airplane. My brain screamed a warning to run, then shut down in terror when the creature started for me. My legs couldn't move. The only thing that worked was my bladder, which was about to lose control. The idea of wetting myself like a frightened schoolgirl in front of this creature was the final humiliation. I'd rather die first.

Brandishing my stick in what I hoped was a menacing gesture, I found my voice. "Who are you? What do you want? Stay away from him. He has nothing to do with you."

"You're right," the creature said. "But you do."

It continued to move forward one cautious step at a time, the yellow glow from its eyes growing stronger. Even though I saw the thing drawing closer, I could detect no movement from its lower appendages. The illusion that it was slithering along was powerful, though I couldn't bring myself to shine the flashlight at its legs to find out.

"What do you want with me?" I moved away from it.

"You are the Murdoch," it said. I could swear I heard it laugh. "The Murdoch must die."

I didn't try to respond. I panicked and turned to flee, crashing through the dense tangle of vines. I stumbled and scratched the palm of my hand on a nearby tree-trunk. The creature behind me lifted its nose in the air and sniffed. Its eyes widened and the light grew stronger. It hissed.

I sobbed and turned my back on it. I ran as fast as I could for more open terrain and the waiting truck. I didn't make it far before I came face-to-face with another of the creatures, yellow eyes glowing and hands outstretched. I screamed and tried to hit it with my stick. The fresh branch snapped in two but the creature didn't even flinch. I tossed the useless stump aside.

I shifted direction and poured on the speed. The creature moved to intercept me. Before I knew he was there I ran straight into his arms, sobbing when I realized it was over. I was going to die.

The first of the creatures, the one from the airplane, came up and turned me to face him. The other held my arms in a bruising grip.

"Where did you get this," the first one said, pointing to the shell pendant.

The second creature stiffened and looked at his companion. "You didn't tell me she bears the mark," he said in an uneasy hiss.

"Silence, fool. It's obvious she stole it. Didn't you?"

Anger brought me to my senses. Some of the fear died, allowing me to find my voice. "I didn't steal it. It was given to me by a friend."

That admission seemed to disturb the second creature even more. He spoke to his compatriot in a language I'd never heard before. The debate was impassioned, though brief.

"Name him," the creature from the plane said. "The friend who gave you this. Name him."

"Wait just a minute," I said, indignant. "What business is it of yours where I got it? I didn't steal it, and that's all you need to know."

"Yes, I quite agree," a calm, cultured voice that seemed to emanate from the trees said.

Although they didn't release me, the grip on my arms eased a little. Both creatures addressed the newcomer in the unknown language. The only word I was able to distinguish was *macadro*, a Sumerian word meaning "ancient one." It was odd. I knew the rest of the conversation was not in Sumerian.

The newcomer, who moved closer so I could see him, looked normal enough. He had no trace of a yellow tint to his eyes. They were as warm and brown as any I had seen. He appeared to be about forty, but his lean body didn't betray his age. His gaze focused on my face, except for a brief instant when it dropped to the shell at my breast. He stepped forward to get a closer look. When he finally spoke, it was in English. Though he looked into my eyes, I knew it was the others he addressed.

"In that case, I think it wise to wait and see," the newcomer said. "If it is his, we will know soon enough. If not, we will deal with that when the time comes."

"But Tolquen, she's the Murdoch," the first creature said, whining.

"All the more reason to wait," he said. He turned to face the others, his voice taking on a hardened edge. "I would not wish to be the one to disregard the warning of the Macadro."

"The Macadro," the first creature said with contempt. "Do you really believe there is such a one?"

"Yes, I do," Tolquen said. "And if I were you, I would not express my doubts so forcefully, Mycerro. If this is his mark, do you think he would leave it unprotected and unwatched?"

Mycerro licked his lips and stole a last glance at my pendant. "I didn't mean to show disrespect," he said in a loud voice. "But I don't understand. The word is out. The prophecy—"

"Careful, lest you betray too much," Tolquen said. "Now go, and do not act again without my signal. And make certain you tell the others."

I wondered how many creatures there were.

Mycerro looked at Tolquen, then nodded and turned away. The two with the glowing eyes seemed to meld into the trees. I relaxed, feeling the menace evaporate.

The movement from Tolquen when he glided over to Rich broke the spell of fear. My legs returned to normal and I found I could move again. I followed him to the center of the clearing. Tolquen hefted Rich onto his shoulders with little effort and carried him through the trees.

When we emerged from the thick tangle my nerves quieted. I made out the shape of the truck though the sun had already set. Tolquen went to the far side of the vehicle and laid Rich on the passenger seat. The sight of his floppy limbs frightened me.

"Will he be all right?" I asked, taking Rich's limp wrist between my fingers.

His forehead felt warm and there was a strong pulse beating in his neck. Drying blood caked his face and arms. His flowered shirt was in tatters.

"He's been shot," I said, indicating the hole in the shirt just over his heart and the ooze of blood. "Do something."

"He is not hurt," Tolquen said, amusement audible in his voice. "You came at the right moment. I think, if you would use the flashlight, you will find his wounds are not deep."

Dazed, I looked at my free hand. In my panic I had all but forgotten the light. I turned it on. Tolquen's prediction proved true. The wounds weren't very deep, despite the fact that they still trickled blood. I reached into the back of the truck, extracted the first aid kit, and went to work. I did the best I could and managed to stop the bleeding. When I finished, I took a careful look at Rich's face, noting that his color was still good. What I had assumed to be scratches were merely dried lines of mud.

Satisfied that Rich wasn't seriously injured, I turned to face my rescuer. Tolquen lounged on the hood of the truck, leaning his back against the windshield. I joined him there.

"I guess I should start by thanking you for your help," I said. "Then I should ask who you are."

His nod was barely perceptible in the darkness, but I knew somehow he would prefer I didn't use the flashlight.

"You may call me Tolquen."

"Is that your first name, or is it Mister Tolquen?"

"It is only Tolquen," he said.

"Great. I seem to be meeting a lot of men who give only one name."

"I am not surprised."

"I see you're the strong, silent type, too. Tell me, are you any relation to Quentin?" I asked, my tone sarcastic.

He froze and turned his gaze on me. His eyes held a mixture of surprised delight and wariness.

"Then you did meet him." He sighed heavily. "Where did you meet him?"

"In Pennsylvania," I said.

"When?"

"Does it matter? I take it you know who he is, and you already assumed I'd met him because of this." I held out the shell pendant.

"Yes."

"I guess there's no way you're going to tell me who he is, is there?"

"Not yet. Not without a more definite sign." He hopped to the ground in one fluid motion and, placing his hands under my arms, lifted me off the hood of the truck.

"You know how to operate this vehicle, I assume," he said. He pointed in the direction the truck was facing. "Keep going straight south. You will reach the patrols in about half an hour, and they will direct you from there."

He turned to walk away.

"Wait a minute. Will I see you again?"

He laughed for the first time, a delightful sound that lifted my spirits. "I think you can count on that."

"When?"

"That depends. But soon, I think."

"Can't you be a little more definite?"

Again he laughed. "Be patient, young one."

He was about to disappear into the jungle when he turned. "Do not take it off. Not even for a minute. Next time I might not be close enough to stop them."

"Who are they? What are they?"

The glare from the headlights showed me his face. For a moment he looked stunned, then he broke out in great gales of laughter.

"What the hell's so funny?" I said.

"I apologize. It is just that we thought you were the one. Tell me something."

"Why should I? You won't tell me anything." I was about to slam the truck into gear when he jumped onto the running board.

"What did you see when you looked at him?" he asked.

The urgency of the question brought my gaze up to meet his. All traces of amusement vanished.

"The ring."

His eyes widened. "Then it is even more imperative you do as I say. Do not take the pendant off, nor allow it to be taken. I will try to stay close in case you need me."

I closed my eyes and leaned my forehead on the steering wheel. "Then there was a ring. I'm not going crazy."

"There is a ring, although most do not have the eyes to see it."

"Can't you tell me what the hell is going on? It's frustrating to be in the center of something and not know what it's all about."

"If I could, I would. But I cannot, not without a sign. Be patient. And be careful."

"Wait a minute. You obviously have some sort of control over the two who attacked me tonight. Couldn't you stay with me, as protection?"

"Doctor Murdoch, that shell is all you need. If it cannot protect you, nothing can. But I have a feeling the help you seek is closer than you think. I must go. We will talk again soon. At that time I may be able to answer your questions."

He disappeared so quickly I almost wondered if he'd ever been there. I found myself staring into the trees, resisting the urge to run after him. Beside me, Rich groaned. I put the truck into gear, heading in the direction Tolquen had indicated.

In half an hour I came across the armed guards, showed them the identification they requested, and received directions to the camp. Thankfully, there was a well-marked road.

At the crest of the small mountain the truck's headlights picked out two huge stone heads marking the only navigable entrance to the long-abandoned city. I braked to a stop and sat for a few minutes, studying them.

The heads were unmistakably Olmec in origin, and seemed to be older than the twenty-three known examples found to date. They were also larger, standing eight to ten meters high. I estimated their weight at fifteen tons or more. I couldn't wait for better light so I could inspect them.

Rich, who had moaned almost continuously since we entered the guarded perimeter, came to and made an effort to sit up. I leaned over to help him, but my touch made him flinch.

"I'm sorry," I said. "Does it hurt that much?"

At the sound of my voice he stopped fighting and ran a shaking hand over his face. I saw glistening perspiration on his brow and cursed myself for wasting time.

"We're almost at the camp." I put the truck into gear and was ready to go when Rich's trembling hand stopped me.

"What happened?" he said. "That man."

"I don't know for sure. When I went to look for you, I found you in a clearing with the creature from the plane bending over you."

"The last I remember, I was in the jungle, about twenty feet from the truck. I don't recall a clearing."

"It looked as if he'd dragged you there."

"You said he was the one from the plane? With the glowing eyes?" He shuddered. "I didn't see him until it was too late. I tried to run, but he was so quick and strong. He had me on the ground before I even saw him coming. I couldn't move."

"I know what you mean," I said, relating my own experiences with the creatures. "Who knows what might've happened if Tolquen hadn't come along."

"Tolquen?"

I explained. "He speaks their language, but I don't think he's one of them. I know it sounds stupid, but I don't get the same feeling when I look at him. He doesn't scare me at all."

Rich shuddered and looked at the floorboard. "It wanted my heart," he said, his voice hoarse.

I hadn't realized he was delirious. He looked up and caught me staring at him. "You saw the wounds on my chest," he said. "Five little punctures, five fingers on his hand. He said he was going to rip my heart out. And he damned near did."

I sat there, fighting the urge to be sick. I should've been elated. I should've been excited that we'd somehow stumbled upon one of the members of the heart-eating cult. But I wasn't.

I felt Rich's bewildered gaze on me and turned to meet it, flashing a reassuring smile while I shifted into neutral.

"What're you going to do?" he asked.

"I'm going to try to get some answers," I said with renewed determination. "It seems to be me they want, although I haven't been able to figure out why. The key to the puzzle seems to be Tolquen. At least, he seems the best place to start." I took a deep breath. "This is getting dangerous. You've done your job, and now you can get out of here."

"I'm staying," he said. "I'm not trying to be brave. I'm scared to death. They seem to be after you, but I think they're afraid of you, too. I'm counting on that fear to protect me. So, I'm afraid you're stuck with me. There's only one thing I want you to do."

"What? Talk you out of it?"

He shook his head. "No, although we can leave that option open. I want you to ask that Tolquen fellow for a *tzem* for me. It might not actually work, but I'd feel a whole lot better."

"It's a deal," I said. "I'd offer to share mine, but I don't think I could bring myself to take it off."

"I think yours is needed just where it is."

"Thanks," I said dryly. "You really know how to make a girl feel at ease."

Chapter 7

OUR ARRIVAL IN the camp was a major event for the bored scientists assigned to the dig. Several surrounded the truck the minute it came to a stop within the compound, while others peered out of lighted tents, straining to get a look. Because of the strict quarantine, the archaeologists were eager to exchange news of anything other than scientific consultation.

Emil ushered me out of the vehicle and into his tent, thwarting any attempt at conversation between the other members of the expedition and me. Once behind the concealing flap, he hugged me hard.

"Thank god you're alive."

"You noticed. What kind of greeting is that?" I squirmed and tried to break his hold. "You're strangling me. What the hell's the matter with you?"

"I was worried about you," he said, releasing me. "Where is it?"

"Where's what?"

"The book, damn it. I told you to bring the book. I've looked everywhere for a copy."

"I brought the book, but I don't carry it around in my pocket. Besides, you're already familiar with a lot of the material. It's an expanded version of my doctoral dissertation. And will you please stop that infernal pacing? You're giving me a headache."

He swore under his breath and strode to the flap of the tent. "Stay here. I'll be right back."

He returned with my bags. I was amazed that a man in his fifties could carry all five at once. He dropped them unceremoniously on the dirt floor and got down on his knees, opening the one closest to him. The moment he unfastened the zipper, the contents spilled out all over the floor.

"Who the hell taught you to pack scientific data?" he said irritably. "This material should be catalogued and banded together by category."

"Sorry. My luggage has been through a lot since I left Philadelphia. If you'll wait one minute, I'll get the book out for you. You're messing up my things."

"How can you tell?"

I picked up the carry-on and extracted the book. He pounced on me, snatched the book out of my extended hand, and took the prize into the corner by the lamp. I shook my head and started to put my papers back in the large suitcase.

"Organize them," he said.

"I will, as soon as I get settled in. Where's my tent?"

After flapping a hand toward the south, he ignored me. I studied him with affection while I stuffed articles, pictures, and papers back into the bag. Of sturdy build and unprepossessing height, Emil Larson looked more like a retired athlete than an eminent archaeologist. His face bore the gentle weathering of years spent under the tropical sun, and his beefy hands were twisted and scarred. Wrinkled khaki shorts displayed legs almost as battered as his hands. He never would wear long pants on a dig, despite snakes and bugs and the hard, sharp edges of the stone blocks he climbed. He hadn't changed much in the last three years.

"Where can I get something to eat?"

Emil looked up at me, the lenses of his thick glasses magnifying his hazel eyes. "You haven't changed," he said, echoing my thoughts. "I think you should stay here for the time being."

"I refuse to stand here and watch you read. I'm a big girl. I can go to the bathroom by myself, and I even sleep alone, without a night-light. I'm perfectly capable of finding my way to the camp kitchen and back. I haven't eaten anything but bananas since breakfast."

He regarded me, raising one of his callused hands to smooth the remainder of his thinning hair. "I never considered the possibility you might get lost. I'm concerned for other reasons."

"I appreciate that," I said, emulating his even tone. "But there're some things I'd like to see to. Besides, Rich was injured while we were on the road, and he needs to be treated before an infection sets in."

"How'd he get hurt?"

"That's a story that'll have to wait until after I eat."

"Very well. But I don't want you to talk to any other members of the team until I have a chance to fill you in. I mean it. You're not to speak to anyone yet."

"For crying out loud," I said, irritated. "I'm not an airhead, and I don't have any hot government secrets I'm anxious to impart. All I want to do is get something to eat."

He watched me over the rim of his glasses. "Promise you'll speak to no one."

"Oh, all right. I promise. Now, where's the kitchen?"

His attention was already back on the book. "Third tent."

I went out into the cool night air. I stood for a minute, allowing my eyes to adjust to the darkness. Here and there a light shone through the open flap of an occupied tent but, for the most part, the jungle darkness swallowed everything.

I heard the sound of voices from the third tent on the right, but I was no longer in any hurry to join them. Emil's attitude, together with the unexpected warning, put a damper on the relief I expected to feel at being in the proximity of people.

I hadn't known how much I needed to feel safe. The realization that I couldn't both depressed and unnerved me. By the time I reached the next pool of light I was almost running. I could feel them out there, watching my every move.

I was halfway to my goal when, out of the corner of my eye, I caught a slight movement between two of the tents. I looked for the nearest circle of light. When I saw that the closest was the mess tent, I sobbed out loud and doubled my pace.

"Marty."

I turned toward the sound without bothering to conceal my relief. "Rich?"

"Yes." He sounded like I felt.

We came together in the middle of the road, hugging each other.

"You're shaking," he said.

"So are you," I replied. "You felt them, too."

"They seem to be all around us. Waiting."

"Waiting for what?"

He shook his head and tightened his grip. "Maybe for word from that guy Tolquen. I don't know. But I don't think either of us should be wandering around out here alone, especially after dark."

"I don't think it makes any difference if it's dark or light," I said, my voice shaking. Nevertheless, we moved through the compound like a blur on the wind.

The minute we appeared in the doorway of the huge kitchen tent, an uncomfortable silence descended on the occupants. Some appeared surprised to see us, others were relieved.

I wondered which of them could be responsible for the malicious graffiti on the walls of the burial shaft. Keeping Emil's warning in mind, I decided to do a little probing.

Ignoring the stares and sniggers, Rich and I made our way through the line, filling trays with as much food as they would hold.

Then I took a deep breath and sat down with the disinterested scientists.

At first they resumed their conversation as if I'd never entered the room. I concentrated on my meal, shoveling food without regard for manners until the worst of the hunger pangs died away. It allowed everyone to get a good look without having to worry about catching my eye.

When my plate was clean, I sighed and looked up at the other occupants of the long table. Rich caught my eye and raised his eyebrows in inquiry. I winked.

"I'm sorry. I couldn't help it," I said to Rich in a loud stage whisper. "This food is wonderful. Donaldson never had a cook like this in the field."

Shocked silence from the other end of the table greeted my sheepish admission. I saw them glance at each other when I got up to refill my tray. I took my time, sampling the desserts, until I was so full I couldn't look at another thing. To keep up the act, I had to accept a generous slice of custard pie.

I sat down and ate the pie. No one said a word, and I was beginning to think they weren't going to, when the man on my right addressed me directly.

"You worked with Donaldson?" The question was curt and heavy with sarcasm.

I nodded, wiping my mouth. "Yes. As a graduate student, I was part of the expedition that excavated Kabah. Later, he moved me to Dzibilchaltun."

"Really?" someone farther down the table said. "Is that where you came up with your fairy tale?"

I let the laughter die down. "If you're referring to the terra-cotta dolls, number five did indeed depict a man with no heart. But the bones were far more interesting."

"I've seen them," the man down the table said. "They weren't all that interesting."

"The ones on display?" I said. "I agree with you. Aside from the date, there's nothing really remarkable about them. It's the other ones, the ones found beneath the church of much later date that I'm referring to. The data hasn't been published yet, since the university just finished validating them, but I have a copy of Donaldson's draft to proofread. Those bones were found split open lengthwise, and the marrow was extracted before they were dumped into the village garbage pit.

"It took me almost eighteen months to complete the field study of the finds, partly because of the vast number involved, and partly because of the unusual markings on each of the rib bones. Excuse me, won't you? I seem to be out of coffee."

I made as if to rise and refill my empty cup, but two of the men waved me back into the chair and a third motioned for one of the cooks to bring the pot to the table. I waited until I measured the cream and sugar into the mug before continuing with the story.

"You were about to describe the markings," one man prompted.

"They were most unusual," I continued. "Unique, as far as either of us knew at the time. At first, the bones appeared to be scratched, as if someone tried to draw on them without the proper tools."

A few nodded.

"Since we couldn't make out a definite design, I volunteered to take the artifacts into the lab and examine them under the microscope. The results were startling, and I had to call Doctor Donaldson in to verify my hypothesis. He measured the markings, looked at them under magnification, and came to the same conclusion. The odd scratches were the result of pressure on the bones from the jaws of an animal. But the bizarre thing about it was the size and the shape of the teeth. There was no doubt the etchings were created as a result of one human being gnawing on the bones of the rib cage of another human being."

I leaned back in my chair. Several of the scientists fidgeted but remained silent. Usually, that would have broken the ice, and a few would have countered with fantastic tales of their discoveries. The fact that it didn't happen disheartened me. After waiting several minutes, I decided they weren't yet ready to accept me. I drained my coffee cup and stood, nodding a friendly farewell. Rich accompanied me when I left the tent.

"Is that the truth? About the bones?" Rich said.

"It certainly is. I have pictures and documents to prove it, too."

"Where're you going now?"

"I've been ordered to report back to Emil as soon as I finished dinner," I said. "What about you? Did you get those wounds properly seen to?"

"Not yet, but I will. I'll be okay."

"As long as you don't go wandering around alone. Has someone assigned you a bed to sleep in?"

He nodded. "And there's even a tent surrounding it. I'll be fine."

He escorted me to the entrance of Emil's tent, pointed out the tent assigned to him, and bade me goodnight. I stood for a few seconds, watching until I saw him enter his quarters.

"Where the hell have you been?" Emil said when I entered his tent. "Didn't I tell you not to talk to anyone? Who was that fellow out there?"

I regarded him, hands on hips. "I'm capable of looking after myself. Besides, I have to work with these people, and I see no need to start by being rude. They already hate me enough as it is."

"They don't hate you. They're terrified of you."

I sank into the chair across from him and my face went pale. "Why? Because of the writing on the wall of the shaft?"

"How'd you hear about that?"

"Rich's friend R.J. He showed me the pictures."

"Damn. I told him not to."

"I know. But he thought it'd be better if I knew. And better if I didn't come here at all."

Emil licked his lips. "Why?"

I told him about my last night in Pennsylvania and the meetings with the mysterious Quentin and the man on the plane. The mention of the scales and the shell concerned him. When I finished, he sat there for some time without speaking. I got up to pace the length of the small enclosure.

"Do you think all this is connected in some way?" I asked when I could stand the silence no more.

"I don't know, but I think it must be, somehow."

"How?"

Emil shoved his glasses back into their proper place and shrugged. "On the surface, each of these instances seems to be unrelated, except for the two meetings with the man on the plane. The meeting with Quentin could be just as you at first thought, some kind of pick-up, except for the snake's scale. That ties the second man to him."

I nodded. "But where does the writing fit in? And how could ancient Egyptian, Latin, Mayan, and a bunch of other languages, half of which aren't spoken any more, get down there? Unless someone here wrote them."

"Impossible. The shaft was sealed under another building," Emil said.

"Then there's another entrance."

"I haven't been able to find one. I've had the shaft resealed until you could get here. So far, I'm the only one who's been down to the very bottom, and I found nothing to indicate the presence of another aperture. No air currents, no light sources, nothing."

I stopped pacing for a minute and tried not to look at him.

"You know I didn't write the threats," he said in a soft voice. "I'd never do anything to hurt you."

I nodded, accepting his innocence. "Then there has to be another way in."

"We'll see. That's the first order of business."

"Yes. If there's another way in, we have to access it. But either way, it'd still point to the fact that one of the members of your team is out to get me."

He looked at the top of his desk to avoid my eyes. "I'm not so certain. There's another possibility."

"Well?"

He tapped the book with an index finger and grimaced. "I'm not sure yet, but I think the answer lies in here. In the material you've uncovered." He raised his gaze to my face, then shook his head. "We'll check out the shaft first. Breakfast is at five-thirty. Be ready to work at six."

With that, he showed me to my tent. My bags already stood in the corner. Just before leaving he kissed me on the cheek.

It wasn't until long after I turned out my light, when sleep finally stole over my body, that I heard his retreating footsteps. I guess he decided I was safe for the night, and returned to his tent.

Chapter 8

THE BIRDS SQUAWKED at exactly five thirty-seven the next morning. The first harsh shriek sent me flying off my cot, into the soft folds of the mosquito netting. I untangled myself and went to the flap, intent on throwing my wind-up clock at the nearest bird.

I stopped at the open flap to stare. A spattering of gauzy pink clouds streaked the eastern horizon. Dark shadows retreated, fleeing before dawn's first golden rays. Around me, nocturnal animals abandoned the hunt to await the return of darkness. Hunted creatures burst into song, celebrating another day of life. I watched the new day establish its foothold. Then, calm and at peace, I went back into my tent to wash and dress.

In direct contrast to Emil, I struggled into a pair of jeans and a long-sleeved cotton shirt. Years of experience with the intense Mexican sun had taught me that a sunburn was neither attractive nor fun. Rich caught up with me before I entered the mess tent, and together we enjoyed a quick meal. After breakfast, I went to the ruins. I followed a marked, well-used path from the compound to the old temple. Standing at the base of the pyramid, I craned my neck to look at the top. I wondered how a ruin so immense had escaped the detection of archaeologists and explorers for over a thousand years.

After a strenuous climb, a survey of the surrounding terrain from the summit provided the answer. A small mountain range surrounded the ancient city, shielding it from casual view on all sides. Dense vegetation growing between the rocks hid even the tallest buildings from aerial view. Balancing my weight, I held onto the sheer face and took a look around.

The other members of the team thought nothing of the breathtaking height, as though used to it. They cavorted around the top of the structure as if they weren't 150 feet off the ground, with nothing to break their fall. After two years of laboratory work, the immense height made me dizzy, and the sheer face of the monument gave me the jitters.

I struggled to maintain my balance. Emil came over and pointed out some of the cleared areas of the site, explaining the excavation's progress. His soothing voice, coupled with the familiar scientific terminology, went a long way to relieving my anxiety. After several minutes my muscles relaxed. I listened to his explanations with interest.

"Unlike the Maya, who used their buildings as mere ceremonial centers while the people lived in huts on the outskirts, this area was used as a city, in Toltec fashion," Emil said. "In the partially excavated area to the west we've uncovered some fine stone houses, each brightly painted and decorated with animal motifs on the interior walls. There's a wonderful garbage heap on the other side of the pyramid. The Toltec were a thrifty lot, though. They didn't waste much."

"What about ceramics and metal tools?" I asked.

"Based on the types of ceramics uncovered, we've dated this city to around nine hundred AD, which would make it the contemporary of Tula, the Toltec capital. We already know the Toltec people could work metal by that time, in direct contrast to the other Indian groups of the area. Oddly enough, we haven't found any traces of metal yet, though we expect to at any time."

"The use of metal weapons is the main reason the Toltecs were able to defeat and conquer their neighbors," I said. "I suppose you've found evidence the people worshipped the plumed serpent, Quetzalcoatl?"

"Of course. There's an altar dedicated to him in almost every important building we've excavated, and most of the houses had drawings of the god carved into the walls."

"Did they use any pillars or idols of the snake in their architecture?" I asked, trying hard to make the question sound casual.

"That, too," Emil said. "In fact, the temple on the top of this pyramid is constructed of huge blocks of stone shaped into snakes, some of which have human heads peeking from the jaws of the animal."

He led me to the temple and guided me around it, pointing out the reliefs and paintings on the columns and the stone walls. The immense images of snakes, fangs, and scales were a little too realistic.

I turned away after a brief glance and pretended to study the construction of the walls. Luckily, one of the workers called Emil away, leaving me a moment alone. The almost life-like quality of the carved snakes reminded me of glowing yellow eyes and cold, scaly skin. I shuddered.

I turned my back on the images and opened my backpack to get at the equipment I'd need before we went any farther into the pyramid. I'd noticed the opening in the floor of the temple with its crude steps leading down into darkness.

It took several minutes of searching in my backpack before I had the equipment I'd need spread out on the floor of the temple. I picked up the small voice-activated tape recorder, inserted fresh batteries and a new tape, then clipped it to the waistband of my jeans. The microphone was on a headset with a padded mouthpiece, leaving my hands free for climbing, measuring finds, and taking photographs. I picked up my camera and gave it the same careful scrutiny.

"Are you ready?" Emil said, trying to sound patient and relaxed. He was neither.

I looked up to find the other members of the team watching my preparations. None of them looked the least amused. My cheeks glowing with embarrassment, I nodded and hastened to join them at the small opening.

Arriving at the man-made orifice, I raised my camera and took several shots of the surrounding temple to place the opening of the shaft for future reference. Besides the pictures, I measured the opening and its distance from the concealing walls, repeating the information into the recorder.

"Please describe the condition of the shaft at the point of discovery," I said.

Dr. Mark Andrews, the dig's physical anthropologist and one of the members of the board that had denounced my work, stepped forward. It was the first time I'd met him face-to-face. His age surprised me; in my mind I had pictured the board as a group of old fuddy-duddies with canes and hearing aids. His appearance shattered that illusion. He couldn't be much older than me - thirty at the most. His sandy brown hair had been bleached by the sun to a golden color that provided a pleasant contrast to his tanned face. He was handsome in a rugged sort of way, with a strong jaw and thick, bushy eyebrows that drew together when he was irritated or puzzled. I could tell by his attitude he didn't welcome my involvement. But he answered my questions with civility and allowed me time to collect all the data I wanted.

"The two blocks you see propped against the east wall were the original seals," Dr. Andrews said. "They fit into the lip of the opening just below floor level, creating a depression six centimeters deep in the floor of the temple."

I looked around the floor, noting that it was fairly even and spotlessly clean, except for traces of dirt in the corners. "How was this depression concealed? Stucco?"

"That's my opinion, though nothing remained except about eight inches of rubble and dirt that provided an excellent growing medium for jungle plants," Andrews replied. "The entire pyramid was covered with vines and broad-leafed bushes when we arrived. We did manage to find a few fragments of carved plaster, but they could've come from the walls or the floor."

"I'd like to get a look at them tonight, if I may."

He nodded reluctantly, his brows drawing together in an impatient frown. "If you're finished up here, I'd like to get a look at the shaft."

I wanted to take a minute to collect a few samples of stone from the walls and floor, but I didn't wish to cause any more ill will. Besides, I could get what I needed on the way out. I turned my back on the temple and accepted the large flashlight Rich offered me. We formed a line with Emil at the lead and began the steep descent.

I was near the end of the line. Dr. Andrews was the only one behind me. We both paused occasionally to study the condition of the passage. It was smooth, without carving or relief, which was not unusual. Like most cultures, the Toltecs expended most of their artistic energy decorating areas open to the public.

What was unusual was the occasional placement of a piece of jade or obsidian among the stone blocks. Upon closer examination, these fragments bore signs of abrasion, indicating a crude polishing technique in use at the time of installation. A thousand years in the dusty passage had not dimmed their beauty. They reflected the light of our flashlights, sending multi-hued bands of color shooting through the passage.

I paused beside a particularly large piece of jade, noting the clear perfection of the stone and the inlaid pieces of obsidian that formed an abstract mosaic. As I trained the camera lens onto the section of wall, Dr. Andrews, his dislike of me forgotten for the moment, focused his light to highlight the jewels. He then pointed out several others nearby which were part of the same obscure pattern.

"Have you ever seen anything like this?" Andrews said, waiting until I paused in the recording.

I shook my head. "Have you?"

"Unique, as far as I know."

"Can you make out what the design is supposed to represent?"

He hesitated, tracing the embedded stones with a short, stubby finger. I was amused to see that he bit his fingernails down to the nub. "It seems like I should know what it is, but somehow I can't figure it out."

I looked at him, startled to have my impressions put into words. He saw the look and grinned.

"We should catch up to Emil and the others," he said. "Maybe the photos will give us a clue when we get the film developed."

I nodded and continued down the narrow steps as quickly as I dared. The group waited at the bottom of the passage in an area that resembled an antechamber. The cavern continued level for roughly 30 feet, then ended at the mouth of a man-made crevice containing yet another set of stairs.

"The passage we're in is concealed within the base of the pyramid, and is contemporary with its construction," Emil said. "However, the next section and all of the area below ground level is much older, dating to the beginning of the Mayan era."

"On what information do you base that date?" Dr. Andrews asked. It was clear from his tone he was skeptical of the claim. "By your own admission you've been down here twice, and not for any great length of time. How could you date the structure based on a hurried glance?"

Emil held up his hand in a conciliatory gesture. "Perhaps I was a little hasty. I should've made it clear that it's my current estimation that the substructure is far older, based on the manner and type of construction. Ultimately, the job of dating the artifacts will fall to you and Doctor Murdoch, and that will help pin it down. We've uncovered the remains of earlier foundations under two additional buildings, and I suspect there may be more. This structure, hiding as it does the remains of a burial chamber, is by no means unique, although it isn't very common either."

"Like the pyramid at Palenque," Rich said. He, along with another local man, had been brought along to provide any necessary labor for clearing the site.

"Exactly. And the smaller one at El Rey on the island of Cancun," Emil said. "Enough chit-chat. Shall we go down and take a look?"

I took my place in the back of the line. I tried to focus on the solid wall of bricks surrounding the cut steps. We were below the level of the surrounding terrain and the air was cool and damp. Large slimy fungi grew in the cracks between the stone blocks, but the air in the passage wasn't stale or musty.

The steps ended at what must once have been the natural entrance to an extensive underground cave system. At some point, the builders lined the entire network with roughly-hewn rocks, but these were not cut with the same expertise as the ones lining the corridors.

While the party extracted ropes and other climbing paraphernalia, I took a few minutes to explore the cave, paying close attention to the rim of the fissure itself. Emil joined me at the opening to point out various rock formations, which grew just under the lip. He explained that the room beneath was sealed with the use of stones 10 feet long and two feet wide, wedged into the shelf. Next, the ancients spread rubble and wet mud on top of the stones and allowed this mixture to dry. Ancient workmen filled the entire series of passages with loose earth and pebbles up to the floor of the temple, 180 feet above where we stood. It had taken Emil and his crew almost five months to clear the debris.

R.J. found the scales in the first layer of loose dirt.

"They were practically on top of the caked mud," Emil said. "In the exact center of the opening. It was odd, for those scales were the only artifacts we found in the whole series of tunnels. We sieved every inch of the debris we brought up from here. There was nothing in more than one hundred and fifty tons of rubble except for three scales from some long-extinct species of reptile."

"You didn't find any evidence the snake had burrowed down through the tunnel?"

"No. I've no idea how he got in here."

I shook my head, as baffled as he. Emil prepared to make the final descent into the chamber by way of the intricate series of pulleys and ropes the men had succeeded in rigging.

The party grew quiet while we waited our turn to shimmy to the bottom. I knew they were waiting to gauge my reaction to the messages Emil found. I sighed. I'd have to examine the writing before the team would settle down to the task of excavation.

Eventually, everyone had taken the plunge except Rich and myself. I insisted he go down before me, joking he'd be needed at the bottom to help catch me when I fell. He smiled, then lowered himself into the void. The interior of the cave was so large that the voices of the men echoed through the corridor like a gunshot. They grew silent the moment I came into view.

Rich and Emil waited for me at the bottom of the line. The rest of the party moved a little farther into the cavern. With Rich on one side and Emil on the other, we approached the far end of the barrow where the unknown artist had rendered his threats in English. With my heart slamming uncomfortably in my breast, I took a deep breath and turned my light onto the wall. I moved closer to study the method of application to the damp surface.

It looked like paint. But it didn't feel like paint. Some of it came off on my finger and I rubbed it off without bothering to examine it. I quickly abandoned any idea of taking a sample.

"*Murdoch has seen the Incubus*," the wall read. "*The penalty is death. Exact the penalty.*"

After I'd had enough of that one, I went to stand before the slogan written in Latin. Chiseled deeply into the face of the rock, this inscription used the same application technique as the one written in Mayan text farther down the wall.

"*Tell the Murdoch that the Prophecy will be denied. Know ye that, wherever she is, the Nightmare will hunt her down.*"

The Latin word for nightmare was "incubus," so the word was the same in both inscriptions.

"You read Egyptian, don't you?" I said to Dr. Andrews, breaking the eerie silence. "Come translate this for me."

Andrews came forward, joining Emil.

"Well?" I said after allowing them three minutes of study.

"Come on," Emil said, complaining. "Petrie himself couldn't translate that fast. You know the Egyptians didn't write vowels. It could take us days."

"I could do it that fast," I said. "And I don't even know what the hell I'm doing. You already know what it says, so just save us all a lot of time and tell me."

The two men exchanged glances, which only made me madder. Emil threw up his hands in surrender and walked away, leaving me alone with Andrews. I met his level gaze.

"Are you certain you want to know?" His tone was surprisingly gentle.

"Yes, I do."

"Okay." He turned back to the wall and pointed. "This cartouche surrounds a name, your name. Since the cartouche is at the beginning of the message, we know the rest refers to you."

"Go on."

"Next, 'has'. Then 'betrayed'."

"Prophecy," I said in a tight whisper. "*Murdoch has betrayed the prophecy*. What prophecy?"

"I don't know. But whoever wrote this thinks you do. There's more."

"Please finish."

He nodded. "The next word I can't quite make out, so I'll skip it. After that, it says '*demands the heart*.' Ouch."

I found I was gripping his arm so hard my nails dug into his skin. I withdrew my hand. "What about the word you can't read?"

He pointed, indicating several symbols in the center of the message. "I can tell you what the sounds are, but I can't figure out what it's supposed to say. This one may be written in Egyptian characters, but its message is English. Someone took a sentence and transcribed it into hieroglyphs."

"I was meant to see this, and whoever wrote it wanted me to understand. But that doesn't make any sense."

"I agree. But there it is."

I stepped away for a minute, running my hands through my hair. "I guess you should tell me about the last word."

"The letters are pretty strange. N, k, b, s. Mean anything to you?" He turned back toward me. "My god, are you all right?"

"Incubus," I said tightly.

"Yes, it could be." Then he glanced at the wall. "Every one of these messages alludes to Incubus. But what does it mean?"

"I don't know." I looked around, noting the others crowded nearby.

"I don't know," I repeated in a louder voice, then stepped out of his supporting grasp. "I don't know who wrote these silly messages, but I intend to get to the bottom of this cruel hoax."

I turned away from the wall and made my way across the rough floor of the cave to the burial chamber. I knelt and prepared to examine the finds. Rich came up and gave me a reassuring pat on the back.

"I admire your courage, but do you think that was wise?" he said with a worried glance at the other members of the party.

"What choice do I have?" I whispered. "I can't let this mysterious adversary think I'm cringing. It's better to get it out in the open now and get this business over with."

"Somehow, I can't see one of these guys running around with glowing eyes and a can of brown paint. I just hope you know what you're doing."

"Didn't either of you notice?" Andrews said behind me. He, too, modulated his voice. "That brown stuff isn't paint. Those words were written in blood."

Chapter 9

ANDREWS FIRST reclaimed my attention and made me focus on the task at hand. After I left the wall he remained there for a short time, sniffing the air.

"If you need a tissue, I have one," I said when I could stand it no more.

He smiled, but continued to sniff. His brows were hunched so tightly he looked like he had a fuzzy caterpillar over his eyes. "Don't you smell it?"

"I don't smell anything except cave."

"Exactly. Remember A-ninety-four?"

A-ninety-four was the designation given to a mysterious grave discovered near Jericho. I joined in the sniffing chorus. Since I stood among the bones already, I leaned over and took a long whiff. "You're right. There's nothing here."

We got down on hands and knees to inspect the area, to the amusement of the others.

"Lose something?" It was Emil's cocky assistant, a man of my age who went by the name of Skeeter Owens. He had a look of superiority on his freckled face.

"No," Andrews said. I could tell from the curt response that Andrews didn't like him much either.

"Have you lost your senses, or is this some sort of anthropological ritual?" Skeeter said.

Mark Andrews ignored him and called to Emil.

"When you removed the seal to this room, did you happen to notice anything, well..."

While he fumbled for words, I went to the heart of the matter. "What did it smell like in here?"

"It smelled like a cave. Just as it does now. Why?"

Mark and I exchanged looks.

"No odor of decay?" I asked, watching his face.

Emil's brows soared to the area that his hairline once occupied. "Now that you mention it, no, there wasn't. With all these human skeletons, you'd expect the place to be rank from the decomposition process."

"That's the problem," Andrews said. "There doesn't seem to have been a decomposition process down here."

"What are you talking about? Of course the bodies decomposed," Emil said, getting down beside us on the rocky floor of the cave. "You have to look around the bones for stains and traces of bacterial residue. There's always evidence."

"We know that," Mark said with exaggerated patience. "Look around. Some of these skeletons are fresh. There's no discoloration, no stains from humidity, nothing. Not even on the oldest specimens on the bottom of the pile. And look at the rock and dirt surrounding them. It's clean, too."

Emil looked. He put out a hand as if to touch one of the artifacts, and Mark and I batted his hand away.

"Don't touch," I snapped. "I haven't photographed this section yet."

Emil flashed me a look of injured reproach. "So what are you trying to tell me?"

"We think this might be another situation similar to the grave at Jericho," I said, glancing at Mark. "If you recall from the literature, the material found in that grave is thought to have been placed there after decomposition took place, for lack of any evidence to the contrary. A re-burial."

Mark agreed. "But I think there's an even better parallel than that. Flinders Petrie, in his numerous excavations of Egypt, found several graves near Naquada that were disturbing because the scholars of the time couldn't find a reasonable explanation for the condition of the finds. The bodies were dismembered and the bones piled on the floor in heaps, similar to this situation. In a few of them, the ribs were cut away from the spine and the long bones split open. In some instances the scientists could see that the marrow had been scooped out."

He stopped talking and looked at me. His expression seemed to say, "You tell him. Everyone already thinks you're a crackpot, so what do you have to lose?"

Although I resented the implication, I couldn't deny the logic of his reasoning.

"Probably the most disturbing elements of the discovery were the grooves on the outside of the finds," I said, taking up where he left off. "Petrie noted they were gnawed, and later analysis proved that the markings were made by human molars."

"Like the ones you and Donaldson found at Dzibilchaltun?" Emil said.

"I think so," I replied. "Petrie's discovery took place in the first part of this century, but it's still not well-known," I said bitterly. "Scientists make a habit of forgetting disclosures that don't fit in with their preconceived theories. Since Petrie could never find a logical, rational explanation for what he found, the discovery's always been overlooked. It was forgotten by the rest of the scientific world."

Emil chuckled and looked at Mark. Mark blushed and tried not to look at me.

"You mentioned Petrie's discoveries in your book. I read that part last night," Emil said. "Fascinating. I also couldn't help but notice the shell you wear around your neck."

It was an obvious attempt to change the subject. With an amused grin I held out the shell so he could inspect it. "Yes, it's different, isn't it? It was given to me by the man at the airport."

Emil's hand closed around the shell, but he looked at my face. "Really? Do you know why these pendants were worn?"

"Rich tells me they were used as protection against nightmare."

It wasn't until after I said it, when I saw the shocked faces of Mark and Skeeter before they turned to stare at the wall, that I realized the implications and shuddered. Emil nodded.

"I was beginning to wonder if you were going to make the connection. Someone wants to protect you from Incubus, and Incubus is out to get you."

"But what is this Incubus?" Mark asked in frustration. "How can you protect someone from a dream?"

"Marty knows, don't you?" Emil said.

I couldn't allow myself to believe it. "The heart eaters. Is that what you're trying to say?"

"It makes sense. *Incubus demands the heart.* It's written right there. Carved in stone, as it were."

I glanced at the pile of bones, noting their split condition. Then I sat back on my heels and tried to think. I couldn't get past the fact that the ancient cult had somehow managed to survive into the present era.

Emil reached past me and extracted a glittering ornament from the mound. His hands shook when he studied the object. "I wouldn't rely on that shell too heavily for protection from these people."

I raised my eyes. He held a shell suspended from a thick silver chain. It was devoid of carving or ornament, but otherwise identical to the one I wore.

Around the neck of almost every visible victim hung the remains of various shells, very similar to the one Quentin gave me. No one said a word. Nevertheless, I couldn't quite bring myself to take mine off.

"It didn't seem to help any of them," Emil said, his face grim with concern.

THE OTHERS drifted away, leaving Mark and me alone with our bones. We worked in silence the rest of the day. We hurried through the tedious process of cataloguing the finds so we could finish and get out of the cave.

At midnight Mark threw down his equipment and called a halt. We stumbled back to the camp to eat a hasty meal. On the way to my bed I paused before Rich's tent, listening for a sound that would indicate he was awake. After several minutes I decided he was already asleep, so I went to my tent and stretched out on the cot. Before I could drop off, Emil pulled the flap aside and entered.

"You awake?"

"I am now. What's up?"

"I just wanted to fill you in on the latest news. We found another opening to the sealed cave."

Relief made me weak. "That's wonderful news. Tell me all about it."

"Don't get excited yet," he warned. He came over to sit on the foot of the cot. His demeanor prepared me for bad news. I pulled my knees to my chest and wrapped my arms around them.

"Tell me."

He took a deep breath and cleared his throat. "The cave containing the burials is the first in an elaborate series of underground crevices. Some are too small for a man to enter, but none of these openings indicate the presence of fresh air or outside light. After making sure, we moved on to the larger caves.

"Deep in the heart of the mountain, we found a huge cavern containing a subterranean lake. Since we were at the end of the line and hadn't found even the suggestion of an opening, Miles put on his diving gear and went down to take a look around."

"What did he find?"

"More burials. It looks as though the lake might have been used as a sacrificial well at some point in its history. We're going to have to see if we can dredge it out."

"That's interesting," I said in a guarded voice. "Go on."

"Miles searched underwater until he found the source of the water's flow," Emil said. "A narrow tunnel, just wide enough to allow him to pass, led deeper into the mountain. Knowing the dangers involved in exploring that kind of fissure, I made him wait until we could find another scientist experienced in diving. Luckily, Skeeter Owens is certified. He suited up and joined Miles.

"They entered the fissure this afternoon. They were gone for hours, and I started to get worried. Finally, they came back to report."

"What did they find?" I said again.

"The lake leads to another small, dirty *cenote* on the side of the mountain."

I leaned forward, excited. "That's it, then. Someone with a diving certification entered the cave through the lake and discovered the burial chamber. Why are you looking at me like that?"

He shook his head. "That's not possible. Both Miles and Owens tried to get through the opening. It's too small."

"Sure, for men with tanks strapped to their backs," I said. "What about a small swimmer?"

"No. I went to the *cenote* they found. The hole is visible just under the water. It's only about a foot wide. Way too small to admit anything except a small animal, like a beaver."

Or a snake. Neither of us said it, but the words were as tangible as if we had. "There has to be a way in you haven't found."

Emil shook his head. "We've been over every inch of those caves that a human can pass through. That's the only opening."

I stared at him. "Where does that leave us?"

"Right back where we started, I'm afraid," he said. "I'm more convinced than ever the answer lies somewhere in the material you've uncovered. All I have to do is find it."

He left me shortly afterward, but it was a long time before I could relax enough to drift into uneasy sleep. I dreamt of glowing eyes and slithering snakes until dawn broke over the mountain.

LATE IN THE evening of the second day, after we examined and removed about seventy skeletons, we came across material we could date where it sat, without sophisticated equipment. Mark removed a pelvic bone from the pile, the first intact large bone we'd encountered. There was an elongated skull beneath it.

Working carefully, we removed the surrounding artifacts to get a better look at the skull. It was old. It was also the first bone to display any evidence of staining from the damp environment of the cave's interior. The skeletal material of the cranium had darkened with age and humidity to a golden brown color.

It was a well-documented fact that the Paeleoindians of Central

America practiced cranial deformation during the apex of their civilizations. Only the higher reaches of society, the aristocracy, bore evidence of the odd torture. Deformation was achieved by placing the head of the infant between two flat wooden boards that were then tied into the desired shape. Babies remained in the mold until the plates of the skull fused together. The higher the rank of the child's family in the Mayan aristocracy, the sharper the cranial point. This one was steep and long.

"The cranial plates are rippled, probably as a result of pressure caused by the bindings holding the boards in place being secured too tightly," I said into my microphone. "This effect was known to occur only on the earliest examples of the process. In later years, padding was used to eliminate the graining effect. Based on this evidence, a preliminary date of six hundred to six seventy-five AD is reasonable for item number eighteen fifty-three."

Mark nodded. Using the dull end of his pencil, he pried open the jawbone to reveal two rows of sharply filed and bejeweled teeth, another hallmark of the upper echelons of Mayan society.

I walked around the object, taking pictures from various angles so we could later match the skull with its related skeletal material.

"It's a female, probably around seventeen or eighteen years old," Mark said, his pleasant voice quivering with emotion. "And, from the number and quality of the jewels in her teeth, I'd say a real important one."

I put the camera aside and joined him beside the skull. "Notice the extreme displacement of the cranial plates. What do you suppose she was doing in this area? The Mayan zone of habitation was miles from here, on the other side of the mountains."

Mark shrugged and grinned impishly. "Maybe she was dragged here by your hungry cannibals."

"Knock it off, Count Dracula."

We both laughed. For the first time in months I felt like part of a group.

"Do you think she might've been a prisoner of war?" Mark asked.

"Likely, considering the Toltecs' love of conquest. Maybe we'll get a clue from the condition of the rest of the bones."

Although we located the complete skeleton and several other individuals of Mayan ancestry, there was no indication of how these people had met their deaths - except for the teeth marks and splits on the bones themselves. Almost every example had severed left ribs, creating the question of just when the injuries occurred. We needed to spend a few days in the lab to determine if they were the cause of death. We also needed to send some of the samples to Arizona for accurate dating.

At midnight, after hauling the day's finds back to camp, we called it a day and climbed out of the cave. I was about to descend the steep slope when Mark put a hand on my arm to stop me.

"I'm sorry," he said, getting to the point at once. "I have no excuse for the part I played in the board of review Mathews initiated."

The subject was one I still found painful to discuss. "Okay."

"I took his opinions at face value, without bothering to investigate either you or the data. It's unforgivable, especially in view of the information I've gathered since then. None of us knew you were engaged to Mathews, or that you broke it off before the book was published. I wish we'd known."

"I understand how persuasive and compelling he can be. What most people don't understand is that he has a habit of twisting things to make you believe what he wants you to believe."

"You may be right, but it still doesn't excuse his behavior. I can't conceive of how he could do this to someone he was supposed to marry."

I laughed, long and hard. "That's because you don't really know him. He's incapable of love. All he wanted from me was a useful partnership that would reestablish his name in anthropology. He's been so busy with administrative work that he hasn't been out in the field for at least five years and hasn't published anything of importance. He's afraid the university will dump him when his contract expires next year. He saw a perfect opportunity to get his name back in print, and he asked me if I'd give him co-author status on the book. When I refused, he told me he'd ruin my career. I thought he was bluffing."

"So you published the material anyway, and he kept his promise. Why didn't you tell anyone?"

"Because I was stupid. I never thought he'd do it. When he convened the board, I believed the scientists would evaluate and investigate my data fairly. Most of the material was already on record in my name. Again, I underestimated Norman's ability to manipulate people. He convinced you and the others that the material, if published for wider review, would damage the university's reputation and its chances for gaining funds from the private sector. Once word got out that I was a mad scientist, no one in the field would talk to me. The only friend I have left is Shelley Peterson, but even she wouldn't dare expose Norman. The only thing I can do is prove him wrong, and that's one of the reasons I decided to make this trip. That, and the fact that Mathews didn't want me to come."

Mark chuckled. "Well, if it helps any, I want you to know you have one other friend in the field."

"Thank you, Mark," I said gratefully.

"Let's get down to camp before the cook throws our dinner to the jaguars." He took my elbow and walked beside me down the steep face of the pyramid.

After dinner, I felt a little restless, so I decided to go to the lab and take care of some work that had piled up. The first duty was to get some samples weighed and packaged to send to the Arizona laboratory.

We crated the material by layer, so gathering a gram or so of bone from each of the different periods was a simple matter. I broke off a tiny piece of rib from the remains of the Mayan princess and sent that off. I placed that piece into the box with the samples from the bottom of the pile and sealed it. I marked the box so the technicians would know to work on it first, then put it with the others due to leave at daybreak.

Because I was too restless to sit at the microscope, I toyed with some of the stucco samples gathered from the top of the pyramid's temple. Because the pieces resembled a giant jigsaw puzzle without color or design, I soon gave up. I carefully put the pieces back into order and brushed the dust off my hands.

It was time to quit stalling. Taking a deep, steadying breath, I grabbed a random pile of skeletal material and headed for the nearest microscope. This pitiful pile could either prove I was right all along, or relegate me to endless rounds of talk shows for the rest of my life. It was an unsettling thought. But I wasn't that selfish. Part of me needed to know the cause of death, regardless of my theory. Without any flesh or cartilage to aid the investigation, I didn't hold out much hope of finding an answer. Nevertheless, I selected a specimen and went to work.

The bone on the top of the box happened to be a right tibia from a male specimen. It interested me for several reasons. The bone was split in two and bore traces of odd scratches. Also, the person had evidently suffered from a mild fracture. From the amount of healing that had taken place prior to death, the injury must've been sustained within three or four days of the victim's demise. Perhaps the broken leg accounted for his appearance in the pile. It would have been impossible for him to outrun an adversary in that condition.

The next item was a left rib bone. I had to curb my excitement when I placed it under the microscope. To my naked eye, the broken end appeared clean, with no evidence of splintering. There was no trace of blood or any other dried fluid.

Under magnification, I saw splintered fragments of bone around the injury, indicating breakage as a result of pressure rather than cutting. The end of the bone near the jagged end showed gouges and scratches. I grabbed a set of calipers and measured the markings. The marks showed gnawing by teeth, and the size, depth and pattern of the gouges indicated human teeth.

I looked at the end of the rib. Minute traces of residual blood around the split revealed the injury occurred before the individual's death. Encouraged by this, I checked left rib bones from each of the boxes, starting with the most recent body and working my way down to the last person in the pile. They were all the same.

The ribs had been cracked open while these people were still alive.

I glanced around until I located the catalogue of pictures taken during the temple's excavation. Flipping through, I found a photo of the face of the pyramid highlighted by the afternoon sun.

The picture showed, in raised relief, the figure of a vanquished enemy lying on the temple steps. Priests in ceremonial masks bent over the prisoner's gaping chest. Blood poured from his wound and one of the priests held the prisoner's beating heart in the palm of his hand. The poor victim's face contorted with horror and pain. I stared at the picture for a long time. Then I turned off the microscope and sat back in my chair to think.

The damage to the rib bones would not be enough to cause death in any of these people. The chest opened before the heart stopped pumping, as the carving on the pyramid suggested.

Outside the lab, the jungle came alive with the noise of rustling foliage. Soon thereafter, a lone jaguar called from a place uncomfortably close to the camp. Although I knew the sound held no danger for me, my heart pounded in response to the feral call. I waited for several minutes but the cry was not repeated. The jungle resumed its normal rhythm.

I went back to my tent, wishing I had stayed out of the lab until someone else was in there with me.

THE NEXT DAY was Sunday, and our only day off. Most of the team took advantage of the rare opportunity to leave the compound for a few hours. Some of the crew piled into one of the trucks and made the trip into the nearest town, Teapa. They invited me to come along, which I took as an indication that they accepted me. After a brief hesitation I declined, feeling I needed to do some laundry and take a bath more than I needed a drink.

"Great idea," Mark said. "I have to work beside you every day and a bath would be much appreciated."

"I was hoping you'd take the hint," I replied. "That cave is beginning to have quite an air about it, and we both know it isn't coming from the bones."

Skeeter drove off before Mark could come up with a reply. I shook my head and went back to my tent, knowing they'd be much harder to contend with when they returned.

Rich caught up with me just as I was about to step through the flap.

"I've been meaning to ask you how your chest is doing," I said.

"Chest?" He looked blank.

"Remember the other night? You never got the doctor to look at the wounds, did you?"

"Oh, that. Of course I did. So much has happened that I almost forgot about it."

"I guess it doesn't bother you too much, then. All the same, I'd feel a lot better about it if I could make sure the wounds were healing for myself."

"Thank you, but it really isn't necessary."

"You're holding out on me, aren't you? Into the tent and off with the shirt."

"This is silly. Besides, they're fresh bandages. The camp doc just put them on an hour ago. It's sweet of you to be concerned, but I'm okay."

I tried unsuccessfully to stare him down. "Well, if you're certain..."

"Positive," he said. "What would you say to a nice long swim?"

"I'd say let's go."

"Great. I found a clean *cenote* that's only about ten minutes away."

"Give me five minutes to get my things and change."

He nodded and hurried off while I dashed around the tent, filling my carryall. Then I struggled into my bathing suit and, shouldering the bag and a clean towel, wandered out into the compound. Sounds of revelry emanated from one of the tents, so I went over to see what was going on.

The sight that greeted me was surprising, to say the least. Down on the floor, just inside the tent, was the distinguished leader of our scientific expedition, his rear end pointed up and his face on the floor. He, like the others, shouted and cheered.

In the center of the dirt floor two identical wooden mazes stood side by side. A small iguana was in each, and the men took bets as to which of the reptiles would find his way to the end of the course first.

Emil looked up, then waved to me. His fist was full of colorful peso notes. "Want to lose some money? So far, my iguana has won every race."

"Congratulations," I said. "It must be your lucky day."

He cocked his head to one side and regarded me with the mocking look I remembered from my childhood. "I take it you don't approve."

"Don't be silly. It sounds like fun, but I have a date to go swimming with Rich."

Emil looked past me and nodded toward the door. "There he is. Don't you know better than to keep the man waiting? Have fun."

I kissed him on the top of his balding head. "And don't you lose too much on that lizard. He looks good out of the gate, but I don't think he has the stamina to go the distance."

"Never trust a woman who can't pick a winning iguana," Emil said, turning back to his maze.

I laughed and ran to join Rich. Together we walked out of the camp and into the outlying fringes of the jungle. I looked forward to a few hours of interesting conversation, relaxation, and a refreshing swim.

Chapter 10

RICH WAS RIGHT, as usual. The pool was one of the clearest I had
ever seen, and I couldn't wait to dive in. I managed to curb my
enthusiasm until I washed my laundry and draped it over the bushes to
dry. Then I took the plunge.

The *cenote* was almost perfectly round and composed of natural
caves that flooded as a result of pressure from underground streams.
The sides consisted of rocky walls rising twenty feet above the surface
of the water. Along the perimeter I saw small fissures, probably the
remains of dried-up subterranean rivers. Only one of the clefts still
produced, sending water over the edge in a rippling cascade that sent
sparks of glistening drops into the sun-drenched air.

Rich, who couldn't come in because of his injuries, sat on the
bank and played lifeguard, an open book propped on his legs. After a
few minutes of quiet reading he removed his shirt. The picture wasn't
an unpleasant one, but I concentrated on washing. I had learned long
ago not to mix business with pleasure. If I had to live with him for
months on the dig, the situation could become complicated.

When I was as clean as I was going to get, I pushed away from
the side and swam some laps. Since the *cenote* was at least thirty yards
across, it provided ample room. In the end I just let myself float,
enjoying the feel of the hot sun on my body and the cool water
underneath. Overhead, lazy white clouds sauntered across the sky. I
amused myself for a while by watching them form recognizable shapes,
then shifting to form others.

I don't know how long I floated there, but eventually I turned
over and dove to get a look at the rocky bottom. The pool wasn't as
deep as I thought but, at about 15 feet, it was still deep enough. The
water was clear and I could see to the bottom if I stayed close to the
perimeter.

While I was diving in the area farthest from Rich's perch, I
spotted the first bone. I had to make several dives before I could be
sure.

I knew the peoples of Mesoamerica once used these *cenotes* as
sacrificial wells, but the majority of pools reserved for the purpose
were slimy and dirty. If this well had been used for such a function, the

stench would be unbelievable. It was more likely some unfortunate animal had fallen over the side and drowned. Treading water with my back to Rich, I decided to take a longer dive and see if I could determine if the bones were human or animal.

I went under, following the rocky wall to the bottom. I used the stone to help propel me down until I was within grabbing distance, then surfaced with the prize in my hand. I crossed the pool to a little ledge and hoisted myself out, gasping. It was a human femur. Judging from the size, it came from an adolescent or small adult.

"Rich," I said breathlessly, shaking the water from my eyes. "Throw down the rope. You won't believe what I found."

After a short delay, Rich's shadow appeared over the rim of the pool, obscuring the sun. I could tell he didn't have the coil of rope, and I laughed when I realized I had roused him from sleep. He was probably still a little groggy.

"Sorry to disturb your nap, but do you think you could throw the rope down."

I studied the bone, noting for the first time the break in one end. The break allowed someone to scoop out the marrow inside, just like the bones in the cave. I could find no sign of scratching. It appeared that the end had been cleanly severed using a sharp implement. My heart started pumping with excitement.

Rich hadn't tossed me the rope. He stood at the edge looking down, his shadow falling squarely over my body. Something was wrong. I turned back to the silent silhouette and put up a hand to shade my eyes from the glare.

That's when I noticed the figure wasn't tall enough to be Rich. I glanced around, all too aware that my ledge didn't offer a convenient means of escape. I was trapped like a fly in a spider's web.

"Who are you?" I asked with more courage than I felt. "What have you done with Rich?"

"Your companion is unharmed." The voice was familiar.

"Tolquen?"

"It is I."

There was so much I wanted to ask him, yet I realized I didn't really want the answers. I'd be happy if I knew no more about Tolquen and his mysterious followers than I already did.

"I've changed my mind about our little chat," I said. "How about if we call a truce? I'll leave you alone, and you call off the dogs. Everyone happy."

He laughed, and the sound went a long way to ease the tension.

"We both know that would never do. Your destiny is too closely linked with ours. We could never let you go, and you could never allow us to rest. It has begun, and it is beyond our power to change the course of fate."

"Are you referring to the Prophecy?"

"So, you know of it."

"No, I don't. And I don't want to know of it. Just tell your friends to stop writing it all over the bathroom walls. It gives me the creeps."

"The creeps? What are these?"

It was my turn to laugh. I felt the urge to cry at the same time. I took a few controlled breaths. "You know as well as I do that I'm not your people's answer to anything," I said when I grew calmer. "I'm just a scientist who wrote a book about burial customs. Believe me, if I could undo what I've done, I would, but I think you guys are overreacting. No one takes the book seriously."

"But you know differently."

"Only because of what's happened in the last week. If your ghouls hadn't started following me around, I'd still think the cult died out almost three hundred years ago."

"But we are not a cult."

My head snapped up. "Then what are you?"

"That is what I have come to explain. He has decreed it."

"The Macadro?"

"You are quick. After our first meeting, I had my doubts. Come, give me your hand."

He leaned over and reached for me. I looked at his small build, hesitating. "There's a rope. It should be just over there."

I could see his face. He looked amused. His eyes twinkled and his lips curved to display perfect teeth. I found myself smiling back as I extended a hand.

He was stronger than he looked. He hoisted me out of the *cenote* and onto the rim. He led me around the pool to a sheer vertical cliff. The fascination I felt at our previous meeting returned. I followed.

A damp rocky ledge no more than a foot wide followed the outline of the cliff and went under the waterfall. Its well-trampled appearance gave testament to frequent use. Once we were past the *cenote,* I found myself watching Tolquen.

The first time I saw him, as a shadowy figure in jungle twilight, I thought him to be about Emil's age. In the light of day, he looked no older than I was. Maybe a few years younger. It was only around the eyes that the illusion of age persisted.

He was short. I estimated he stood only five-six, which put him right at my height. Muscular and rugged, his build resembled that of a weight lifter. There wasn't an ounce of fat on him.

I studied him so hard I failed to notice the direction we took when we left the *cenote*. Made up of sharp rocks and pebbles, the path he chose hurt my bare feet, forcing me to step carefully. The blood from a small scratch flowed from my heel, making my foot sticky. I'd just noticed the cut when Tolquen stopped, sniffed the air, and closed his eyes. His entire body stiffened.

"What's wrong?" I asked.

The look on his face was a curious mixture of rapturous delight and agonized strain. Small beads of sweat broke out on his brow. "Do not come closer." His voice sounded shaky and thick. He opened his eyes and turned toward me. "You have cut yourself. Stay away."

My blood bothered him. Fear returned and I backed away. "What are you?" I asked for about the hundredth time.

He took a reflexive step toward me, then stopped dead when I poised for flight. "Do not be alarmed. It is not my fate to harm you. But you must cover the injury, and quickly."

"My boots and clothes are back by the *cenote*." If I could get him to go back for them, I might be able to escape.

Then I looked around. I didn't know where we were, and I hadn't the faintest idea of how to get back to camp. I cursed myself for not paying closer attention to the path. Straining my ears, I couldn't even hear the crash of the waterfall. I decided to chance an escape, then froze when I felt that other presence. Mycerro and friends were somewhere close at hand.

Considering what else might be out there, Tolquen was definitely the lesser of two evils.

"I'll wait for you here," I said.

As soon as the promise was given, he was gone. It wasn't until then that I got the bright idea that the Incubi, if that's what they called themselves, might have rigid rituals around which they performed their ceremonies. For all I knew, Tolquen might be taking me to some holy place for the express purpose of extracting my heart while the other members of the cult danced about my prone body. I shivered despite the hot sun and hugged my knees to my chest.

Chapter 11

BY THE TIME Tolquen returned, the foot had almost stopped bleeding and I was in a much better frame of mind. The threatening presence had lessened somewhat, and I took that as a sign that Tolquen had chased them away. My curiosity returned. I wanted to know more about him and his extraordinary cult. I made myself look upon his staunch refusal to approach me as amusing rather than sinister.

He stood ten feet away and tossed me the bag containing the shell I removed before my shower, along with all my clean clothes. He even stopped to dampen one end of my towel so I could use it to remove all traces of blood. Upon close inspection, I found the wound wasn't deep. I donned a thick pair of socks and my work boots, then nodded. We resumed our walk. Tolquen even allowed me to come up beside him on the narrow path.

"Where're we going?" I said. In the distance I spotted the outlying structures of the ruins.

He flashed me a charming smile, but I wasn't quick to respond. The incident with the blood bothered me.

"You wished to see the old city, so I thought a tour would be in order."

"I've already seen most of it. Emil gave me a tour just the other day. There isn't all that much to see, since they've only cleared about a tenth of the entire area."

"The Toltec city, yes." He dismissed it with a wave of his elegant hand. "There is nothing there worth bothering with."

"Really? Then why show me around?"

We arrived at another of the small cliffs that dotted the terrain. Vines and wildflowers covered its sheer surface, just like most of the others I'd seen.

Tolquen turned to walk parallel to the incline, smiling at me with an odd mixture of condescension and disbelief.

"You are delightful."

He raised an arm and lifted a section of tangled vine to reveal a small opening in the cliff. It was just large enough to allow me to pass through without bending. Tolquen followed me in, then let the vine fall back into place. The darkness inside was complete. I couldn't make out even the outline of my companion until he struck a match and located a natural rock shelf overhead. He extracted a battery-powered lantern and switched it on.

Tightly fitted man-made blocks lined the walls of an underground passage. The floor, like the one in the cave containing the burials, consisted of natural stone chiseled smooth. Tolquen led the way through the narrow tunnel, and it wasn't long before we emerged into a chamber. A series of intricate paintings covered every inch of wall space. The room was small, measuring only ten by eight feet. It resembled one of the tombs in the Egyptian Valley of the Kings except that the air was wonderfully fresh. A cool breeze wafted through the corridor, cooling my body after the long walk.

The artwork was free and alive, lending a lifelike quality to the animals and people. I wandered the perimeter of the room while Tolquen took a seat on one of the numerous benches lining the perimeter. He watched me in comfortable silence.

Here and there I recognized a few of the animals portrayed. At one point I stopped for some time to marvel at the whimsical depiction of a woman caught for eternity in the act of beating her clothing against a rock. Another picture centered around a by-gone battle. The opponents squared off to face each other across a deep chasm while snakes and jaguars waited at the bottom with gaping jaws. The work was so fine I could see the terror in the eyes of the combatants. The king sat on a throne, well away from the threat of injury, with several young women beside him.

I turned to survey the rest of the room. The ceiling was low and it, too, was covered in drawings and reliefs. Along the four walls were crude stone benches, and there were several more in the center of the room surrounding a blackened stone pit that I took to be either a hearth or ceremonial altar.

"What is this place?"

Tolquen placed his lantern on the floor and sat, gesturing for me to join him on the bench. To keep a little distance between us, I sat on the one opposite, which only served to increase his amusement.

"It is the place Doctor Larson seeks. It is Tamoanchan."

"Tamoanchan is widely regarded as a mythical place, built by the ancestors of the Olmecs. Why should I believe this is Tamoanchan?"

"Because it is. A group of adventurous nomads discovered this valley, which at that time was teeming with every type of game. Since the place was ideally situated for natural defense, they decided to settle here and make use of the abundance of fresh water. The climate was much different then. It took little effort for the tribe to turn to agriculture, once they learned they could spread the seeds and let nature do the rest."

"It's believed that development of an agrarian society is a gradual process. You make it sound as if it happened overnight."

"But it did, once the priestess showed us the way. Soon after our arrival we had immense fields of corn to tend while we worked to build the city."

I let that comment pass. "Arrival? Evidence points to the fact that the American continent was populated during the last Ice Age, when various Asiatic groups crossed the frozen Bering Strait."

"The people who put forth that theory have never been to the Arctic for any length of time," Tolquen said, smiling. "What were these intrepid wanderers supposed to wear?"

"As far as we can determine, they wore animal skins."

"Exactly. Have you ever tried to walk thousands of miles through sub-zero temperatures wearing nothing more than a few animal skins? And what were they supposed to eat along the way? Polar bears? Have you ever tried to kill one?"

I had to bite my tongue to keep from laughing. "Okay. What's your theory?"

"I have no theory. I have facts."

"Give me the facts, then."

"It is quite simple. Thor Heyerdahl has done it, just as thousands of people before him."

"So you're saying the peoples of the Pacific Islands came here first, over the seas."

"Among others, yes. They made up the major groups of refugees, but they were by no means the only ones. We are a true melting pot of primitive cultures. Anyone who could build a seaworthy craft and had the courage to set out into the unknown eventually landed here. Most of the groups wandered off to the north or the south and were never heard of again. Others stayed. The more intelligent and industrious settled here, to await the coming of the One."

I forgot to be afraid. His comments were thoughtful and logical. I still regarded him as a bit of a fruitcake, but at least he was an educated nut. "How did they know the One was coming? And how did they know that others existed?"

"It was foretold to us, just as your coming was foretold to us."

I stood up and paced the room. After several minutes of internal debate, I stopped before him, holding out my hands to make him understand. "I'm not your savior or your goddess, or whatever it is you think I am. I'm just a person, like you."

His laughter interrupted me.

"I can't see what the hell is so amusing."

"Please forgive me, young one. It has been so long that I nearly forgot—"

"Will you stop calling me 'young one?' You can't be much older than I am."

He didn't exactly laugh, but his eyes were shining. He turned his back to me for several minutes, and when he did speak it was with a voice that wasn't quite steady.

"Shall we continue our tour?" he said, lifting the lantern.

Curiosity won out over pride and I followed him to the far wall. At first glance the surface appeared to be solid stone. When we drew nearer, I noticed that the corner section was made of fabric decorated to match its surroundings. A series of concealed weights held the tapestry in place.

I felt a cold draft and asked Tolquen for a minute in which to don more suitable clothing. He agreed and, after handing me the lantern, stepped through the curtain. I slipped a pair of jeans and a sweater over my bathing suit and joined him in the hallway.

The feel of the fabric curtain was like nothing I'd ever handled before. I paused, running my hands over the cloth while admiring the fine weave. The intricate design wasn't stiff or coarse. I bent closer, trying to see the painting technique. Then I knew. The vibrant colors were woven into the material to match the surrounding murals.

"It is beautiful, is it not?"

"It's exquisite. Wherever did you find something this fine? The person who worked this is a true artist."

"I did not find it. It was made to hang here by the woman of this house. There are many such tapestries here, and most are as good as the one you see. Some are better. Weaving was something the women of the city took great pride in, especially toward the end."

"The end of what?"

He took both the lantern and my bag and led the way farther into the mountain. "The end of the occupation here. From the beginning we knew this place was nothing more than a brief stop for our kind. We waited to see who among us would be chosen by the Others, and who would perish so the rest might live. I was the only one who chose to remain here. The rest are scattered, but that, too, shall end. They grow closer by the day."

"You're the only one of what who chose to stay? I'm growing tired of your constant riddles. You haven't answered a single one of my questions."

He sighed. "I know it is frustrating for you, and I am trying to explain. To me has fallen the task of allowing you to know what we are, as well as relating a small part of our history, and in that I cannot fail. It is the wish of the Macadro."

I was so intent on listening to what he said that I didn't pay much attention to my surroundings. He held open another of the hanging tapestries, allowing me to precede him. The chamber was ten times the size of the first, and the artwork was far superior. However, I gave the room no more than a hasty glance and went to sit beside Tolquen on one of the many stone benches.

"Who is this Macadro, and what does he want with me?"

"You must understand there is a certain amount of information I am allowed to give you, and other topics I am forbidden to discuss. The Macadro, and all concerning the elders, is among the forbidden."

"Then what are you allowed to tell me?"

Tolquen waved his hand to indicate the room in which we sat. "I have permission to discuss anything you wish to know regarding this city, our purpose here, and my life, except for the very beginnings of my existence as one of the Incubi. I cannot tell you how the transformation took place."

"You're an Incubus?" I said, wondering why he didn't frighten me. "But I thought the Incubi were a cult of heart-eaters."

"As I already told you, we are not a cult. We are a race."

I laughed. "Do you really expect me to believe that?"

"I understand it is difficult for you, but it is the truth. When I first landed here, I was not so. I was mortal then, with all the fears of your kind."

I gasped, springing up from the bench. I stared at him with wild eyes. His comments were becoming more ludicrous by the minute. "You were mortal then? What kind of nonsense are you trying to feed me?"

I started for the doorway, but he was there long before. I hadn't seen him move.

"Let me out of here. I swear I'll leave you alone."

"I cannot let you leave yet, and I promise you will not be harmed in any way. But you must listen to me."

"Why? What you're telling me is insane."

"If you will sit down, I will show you it is true nevertheless. Trust me."

"Trust you? You have to be out of your mind."

"Give me five minutes to prove what I say is the truth. If I fail to convince you, you are free to go. Just five minutes."

I searched his face for some external sign of madness. He returned my stare, and his eyes were pleading and desperate.

"I can assure you the city is surrounded," he whispered, gazing at the far wall. "Can you not feel them out there, waiting? If you leave here now, without a sign from me, you will be dead before you can walk a few feet. I am asking for five minutes to prove what I say is true. Is the help I have given in the past not worth five minutes of your time?"

I sat down on my bench and looked meaningfully at my watch. "Five minutes, then I walk."

He let out a long, unsteady breath, then placed my bag and the lantern on the floor. He crossed to a small rucksack in the corner and withdrew a dagger. I was off the bench in an instant, poised to run if he decided to attack. While I watched in growing anxiety, he raised the knife and brought it down on his own body.

My shout had no effect. I watched the blade connect with his left shoulder, bend a little with the strain, then penetrate. I closed my eyes, sickened and shocked.

"Marty."

The whispered word had the impact of a cannon shot on my reeling senses. I forced my eyes to open.

I was halfway across the room, my gaze glued to the wound on his shoulder, when I stopped. Tolquen stood as he had before, except that the dagger was back in its sheath. His shirt, parted so I could see the area of impact, displayed no traces of blood. I expected to see blood pouring from the shoulder. Instead, the wound was . . . closing.

Less than two minutes since the blade made contact, there was little more than a scratch left to mark the spot, and even that knitted itself while I watched. In another few seconds, the wound had healed. There wasn't even a scar.

I reached out a trembling hand to touch the spot, then recoiled at the cold, clammy feel of his skin. I touched him again and noted the scaly oiliness under my fingers. Raising my eyes, I studied his face. Part of me was satisfied to have my worst nightmare confirmed, the other part was disgusted.

I stared into his glowing yellow eyes and fought the urge to be sick. "What are you?" I said again. "You can't be human."

He laughed. "You wondered how races separated by thousands of miles and eons of time could develop in the same way. I am the common link you seek, dear Marty. I and my kind are the piece of the puzzle no one before you unearthed.

"I am the Nightmare. I am the burden which cannot be borne. I am Incubus. I am a mere fledgling in the reckoning of my kind, for it has been but six thousand years since I was made. We have roamed the earth for over twenty thousand years, waiting for the Prophecy to be fulfilled.

"The waiting is past. For good or ill, you are the one whose coming was foretold in the dark days of our beginning. You have it in your power to either end our line or increase it so we may enter our next Golden Age."

I felt like I was going to faint. The room spun around me, out of control. I had to grab for the wall to remain on my feet.

"Be warned," he continued. "There are some who welcome your arrival and some who do not. It is beyond the power of any to change the path designated you by Fate."

"Do you honestly expect me to believe this shit?" I said in a weak, strangled voice.

He broke the tension by laughing again. "I see you are not convinced, but you are at least ready to listen. Sit and let me tell you the history of this place. After that, I will show you proof."

"And what will happen after that?"

"My task will be completed, and I can make it known to the elders. What happens next is up to you."

Tolquen took me by the hand and led me back to the bench. "Sit. Be comfortable. It is a long story."

Chapter 12

"IT WAS ON market day that I first met him," Tolquen began. He had a dreamy, far-away look on his face that almost made me forget the incident with the knife. "I was young, not yet ten. We were met by one of the village elders the moment our canoe landed, and he told us an outsider had come from across the sea. The man was white from the hair on his head to the tops of his feet. Stranger still, the visitor was dressed in long, flowing garments.

"I was bending over to place a fish into a basket when a strange shadow fell across my path. The people of the islands, men and women alike, usually went around wearing nothing but a skirt made of leaves from the palm trees, which we called a *pareu*. Never in my life had I seen a shadow that had no shape. It was straight from the shoulders to the feet.

"I gathered the courage to glance up. Standing four feet away, looking at me with eyes the color of the sea, was a man with hair so bright it hurt my eyes to look at it. I looked away, then glanced around to see the reaction of the others. Most of the children and all of the maidens followed him, but the stranger did not seem to notice. He stared right at me. Within his eyes I saw a deep chasm that went to the very depths of the earth.

"How can I describe the feeling that slowly washed over me? It was as if I knew his thoughts. In the depths of those eyes I saw into his mind. Does this make sense to you?"

I remembered the incident on the plane and nodded. "Perfect sense."

"I felt the stranger call to me, knew that he asked me to trust and to follow. I was one of the Chosen. He inspected the nets on display. In the end, he ordered several woven vessels for transporting liquids and gave orders to deliver them the following day. In return he offered a fine canoe of unusual workmanship, bigger and better than any I had ever seen. We could travel to the farthest islands on such a craft. When my father hesitated, I stepped forward and arranged to meet the stranger the following day.

"'Very well,' he said. 'I shall meet you here at the rising of the sun. If the vessels are as good as the ones you show here, the boat shall be yours.'

"I rowed to the big island just as the first touches of gray streaked the sky. Usually the quiet time before dawn was the nicest part of the day, a time when I could swim or fish. But that day I was far too impatient at the prospect of seeing the stranger."

Tolquen laughed and winked at me. "You know how it is?"

"I imagine it's like the first day with a new puppy. You can't wait to get home to make certain it's all right," I said.

"In a way, but the pull I felt was much stronger than that. I wanted to be with him constantly. I was ready to follow him anywhere."

"After one meeting?"

"Yes." Tolquen strolled over to the wall. "Have you never been in love?"

I dropped my gaze. "I thought I was, once."

"Then you cannot know the feeling. You will soon. I arrived at the island early, long before first light. At first I saw no sign of the man and my excitement crumbled. I had not realized until that minute how much I longed for the meeting. I waited and waited, but still he did not come. I wanted to sit in the bow of my boat and cry, so deep was my disappointment.

"Then I told myself to act like a man. I knew people would be about to check the fishing lines and cast nets. I did not want to be caught crying, so I got up and made ready to launch my boat.

"'Hold there,' a voice cried out from across the sand. 'We had a man's bargain. Have you come this far only to change your mind?'

"It was the white stranger. He had not forgotten. The knowledge made me almost giddy with happiness. I showed him the vessels I brought and he accepted all, telling me he had not seen such fine workmanship in all his travels.

"The man gathered up his baskets and prepared to leave. I offered to help carry them, but he refused. Then, terrified he would forget me, I begged him to take me across the sea.

"The stranger paused, then closed his eyes and laid his hand on my chest, over my heart. After several minutes he smiled and withdrew his hand.

"'You will cross the ocean, Tolquen,' he told me in a gentle voice. 'But the time is not yet nigh. Do not despair. One day soon I will call to you, and you will follow the path I now must tread. Until then, keep the canoe I have given you. You and the others will need it so that you may come to me. Do not forget you are chosen.'

"With that he walked away across the sand and I watched him go.

I was sure I would never see the strange white man again.

"Several years past but I could never dismiss the stranger from my mind. I grew, but my mind dreamt of new worlds to see. I sat in the canoe the stranger had given me, staring at the unending ocean. Needless to say, this behavior worried my mother.

"My mother then took me to the head Priestess, which was exactly what I wanted. The pull of the sea was growing so strong I could think of little else."

"How old were you?" I asked Tolquen, loathe to interrupt yet anxious to know the details.

"I was approaching my sixteenth year. It is easy to remember because that is when the males of our tribe were supposed to take a wife. Peloni, my mother, grew concerned because I did not show interest in any of the maidens she brought for my inspection."

I laughed. "Surely there was one who caught your eye."

He seemed a little embarrassed.

"Are you blushing?" I teased.

"We do not blush."

"Then what is that pink color I see in your cheeks?"

He cleared his throat and sent me a dampening look. "Arrangements were made and a day set aside for the trip. I could not hide my interest at the prospect of going to another island and Peloni watched me anxiously. Maybe she was afraid I would try to leave on my own. She was wise The pull grew too strong to resist, but finally the day arrived. Against my wishes, Peloni insisted on making the trip with me. We climbed into the stranger's canoe and set out.

"We spotted the tiny island just before midday, which was almost unheard of. Normally, the trip would take all day. We sailed to the far side of the island. When I rowed the canoe into the mouth of the inlet, the little bay was packed with people.

"There were canoes of all shapes and sizes assembled, and I recognized the markings of several different tribes. I greeted many of the young men when we sailed past. One boat, however, made me stare. The boat was identical to the one I sailed.

"Straining my eyes against the glare of the sun, I was able to make out the markings of the Doliki tribe. The Doliki lived on an island far from mine. Only once before had I ever seen one of their boats."

"Didn't you wonder what all those people were doing there?" I asked.

Tolquen shrugged. "I took it for granted they were there for the same reason I was."

"You think they'd all met your mysterious stranger?"

"I think they were all summoned by him," he said.

"Summoned?"

He sighed and looked at his feet. "I told you, the pull was strong. I knew I had to be there. I assumed it was the same with the others."

I nodded.

"I beached my boat and looked down at Peloni, feeling an odd mixture of pity and excitement. I knew I would soon leave, but I wanted to make it as easy as I could for her.

"She placed her hand on my arm and tried to pull me back toward the canoe. 'You cannot go. I forbid it. You are behaving foolishly.'

"'Do not make me ashamed of your cowardice, woman,' I told her softly. 'Do not make me sorry I brought you here.'

"Peloni had no choice but to follow me when I turned to join the stream of pilgrims making their way through the woods to the small hill in the distance. We were all silent, yet I felt excitement in the air. Ahead was the silhouette of the Priestess in ceremonial gear. We climbed to the top of the hill and took our places on the ground at her feet.

"'Members of the Chosen, I bid you greeting,' the frail Priestess said. 'The time has come for some of you to assume your places beside the One Who Calls. The road you choose is perilous, and most of you will not prove worthy. Only those who have heard the True Voice should consider this. Let those among you who doubt leave now.'

"The Priestess turned her back to allow those who wished to leave to do so without fear of reprisal. The rest of us closed our eyes. When we opened them, less than half the men still remained.

"'It is good,' the Priestess said.

"She then moved among us, meeting each man's gaze when she passed. One or two turned away, and these men left. In this way, she managed to decrease the number to about twenty.

"When the woman at last stood before me, I met the watery old eyes with unflinching conviction. She stood for a long time. When she turned away, a small smile curved her puckered old lips.

"The Priestess resumed her place before us. 'There is much work to be done before preparations are completed for the great journey. Each of you will be assigned certain tasks to perform. They must be done with skill, for your survival depends upon each man completing his duties. The crossing of the sea is dangerous, and not all will make it to the other side. You may rest until the sun sets below the horizon, at which time the work will begin. The boats must be ready to leave with the rising of the third moon. Those who cannot complete the tasks will be left behind. It is the will of the One.'

"I found my mother among the banyan trees and kissed her for the last time. One of the retreating men agreed to take her home. I stood on the sand, waving until she was out of sight."

Tolquen stood in silence, his finger tracing the figure of a woman painted on the wall. I waited for several minutes, then reached out to touch his arm.

"You never went back to the island?"

He shook his head. "In the beginning, there was too much for me to do here. Later, after I became immortal, it was too late. It is better so."

"Did you miss your mother, your family?"

"No," he said after a moment's hesitation. "I met someone who filled the gap. I am part of a larger family now."

My heart filled with pity for the boy he had been. Despite his words, I sensed a deep emptiness that had never been filled. I didn't want to feel sympathy for what he had become, so I turned away and walked to a bench on the other side of the room.

"For the next three days and nights our little colony worked under the watchful eye of the High Priestess," Tolquen continued. "She was a demanding taskmaster, overseeing all preparations to ensure nothing was left to chance. She taught us how to lash two of the small canoes together to form a catamaran, then instructed us in making a platform between the two which she called a deck. Food, water, and other necessities were stored in the wells of the canoes, and we could stretch out inside to rest when the weather was calm.

"She taught us how to steer the boats by the lights in the sky for sailing at night. For daytime navigation the instructions were simple: In the morning, we were to head straight into the rising sun. In the afternoon, we were to sail away from it.

"Finally, the third day arrived. Late in the afternoon the Priestess called us together for a final meal and some last-minute counsel.

"'What I must tell you is this: None of you may interfere with the destiny of another. Each crew must work together, but no one individual may have obligation toward another. If one becomes sick, he must be cast into the sea. If one boat falters, the others must turn their backs and sail on. The promise is not made to each individual, but to the group as a whole. You will succeed only if you heed this warning. From our seed will spring a race that will live forever.'

"'You are coming with us,' I said.

"The Priestess nodded. 'I was called, last night while you were at work. I ride on the third raft, and we will sail with the rising of the moon. Each man has but a short time in which to make his own offerings to the god.'

"One by one the men left the clearing to see to final preparations. I decided to wander the small island for a last look at my home. I kept close to the shore, walking swiftly around the headland. I thought of my mother and my village. My heart whispered a wish that all would stay well with them and that they might hear news of me.

"Without knowing why, I increased my pace and ran across the beach. The image of the white stranger entered my mind and I stopped, spewing sand. My head turned and I knew I was no longer in possession of my own body. Something guided me, controlled me, but I felt no fear.

"Looking up, I beheld a bright light streaking across the sky, and I recognized the face of the stranger in the center of the vision. The glare from the apparition lit the night and made the sea seem to boil. In a moment it was all over, and the bright ball fell into the sea. For several minutes the water continued to boil. Finally, all was again calm.

"I was about to turn and go back when again my body was seized. My feet took me to the waters edge and I waited. Eventually, my searching eyes were able to make out a floating shape under the waves. A few minutes later the object was close enough to touch.

"Under the rippling water, I saw a shell of great beauty. As it lay upon the beach, the shell started to glow. The soft blue light inspired no fear. Rather, an image of warm blue eyes came to my mind, and the eyes told me to take the shell. I obeyed.

"The shell felt cool and smooth. The blue light faded, then died out. Only then did I regain my senses enough to note that the moon was rising. I was late. Without stopping to examine the shell, I turned and ran across the sand, arriving just as the first of the three boats was launched.

"With a brief apology for the delay, I took my place with the crew of the third boat and helped to shove away from the shore. Our boat was the last to go. We used long poles to push into open water. Once the poles were no longer needed, we tossed them overboard. Then we raised the sails and maneuvered them until they caught the wind.

"The boats sailed in a tight convoy to combat the loneliness we felt whenever we looked at the vast open space around us. Since I elected to work the night watch, I slept while most of the crew worked.

By the time I was called to my turn at the tiller, the Priestess was already asleep.

"By the fourth day at sea I still had not told her of the shell. I grew anxious to share the vision with someone, but I hesitated to mention the wonder to the other men. So, on that fateful night, I relaxed at my station and I let my mind wander, trying to picture our new land. Without warning, the boat lurched to the right with such force it wrenched the tiller from my hands. I made a wild grab for it and managed to regain control just as another large wave rolled over us. The wind freshened and the stars retreated behind threatening clouds.

"'Take down the sail. A storm is upon us,' I shouted.

"I could see no sign that the others had heard. In fact, I saw nothing but another large wave looming up to wash over the deck. When the wave broke over my head, it almost took me with it. I fought to keep my place at the tiller. I knew I could not leave it. If the boat turned sideways we would capsize.

"I tried to shout, but the water swirled up and filled my mouth. I grew desperate enough to consider leaving the tiller to see to the sail myself. Either way, the little boat would be doomed, but we stood a better chance of remaining in one piece without the sail.

"'Take down the sail,' I cried, making one last effort to rouse the others to action.

"The lightning flashed, showing a tall figure crawling toward the boom. I almost sobbed with relief and fought the tiller with new courage. The next thunderbolt lit the deck and showed me a silhouette attempting to lower the sail. I knew the minute he succeeded. The ship stopped shuddering and settled into the water. The figure almost reached the stern of the boat when the full fury of the storm was unleashed. He fell flat and resumed his careful crawl across the deck.

"The storm continued to blow for what seemed an eternity. I barely managed to regain control of the rudder when another swell crashed over us, wresting the tiller from my bleeding hands. I looked for some sign that the storm was winding down, but I could see nothing in the darkness. There was no sign of the man who had come to my rescue.

"My strength diminished. The strain of keeping the boat pointed into the swell made my tense muscles ache. The wooden tiller cut the palms of my hands, leaving deep splinters. I was so cold I could no longer feel my toes."

Tolquen stopped talking and moved to one of the benches

surrounding the pit in the center of the room.

"What happened?" I asked. I couldn't believe he had stopped there. "How did you make it through the storm?"

He smiled and shook his head. "Come here and lie on this bench," he said after a few minutes. "You will be much more comfortable."

He refused to continue until I did as he asked. I got up and took the seat, sensing his need to have someone near. The shattered look in his eyes told me the memory was still a painful one. I felt the first stirrings of pity that he was unable to say so.

I suppressed the unwanted emotion and asked him to continue.

"Rising up out of the ocean was a huge wall of water," he said. "The wave poised to break over the boat. The next flash showed the wave had grown in the intervening seconds and moved closer. I braced for the impact, certain I had met my fate.

"Strange visions filled my sight. I saw the Priestess and tried to tell her how sorry I was that I could not live up to her expectations. The image of the Priestess stayed with me. I thought I saw her lips move. The Priestess in my mind chided me, 'Remember the shell.'

"I took one hand off the tiller to touch the shell under my *pareu*. The moment my bleeding fingers made contact with the smooth surface, I almost fell overboard. It was warm.

"Perhaps warm is not the right word," Tolquen said with a shake of his head. "It felt much as it had before, but a soothing sensation tingled in the tips of my fingers. I felt calm at once. My courage came back, and I knew what to do.

"Gripping the tiller with hands that no longer felt like weights, I found I could anticipate each movement of the violent surf and steer the boat around the worst of the swells. All I had to do was ride the diminishing waves for a few more minutes. The lightning, far in the distance, crackled less frequently. I saw one star struggle out of the dense layer of blackness, then another. Soon the night sky returned to normal, and I was elated to discover I had managed to keep on course despite the storm.

"I remembered the shadowy person who had risen to my rescue, and scanned the deck to locate the figure. I managed to pick out a large lump lying a few feet away, then breathed a sigh of thanks when the form rolled onto its back and tried to sit up. It was the Doliki tribesman, Dokulu. After several minutes he staggered toward me.

"'You are unharmed?' he said in his deep voice.

"'Yes,' I said. 'You?'

"'Yes.'

"I should have known better than to ask," Tolquen said with a reminiscent smile. "It was a matter of honor among the Doliki not to admit to physical discomfort. They are a people of few words.

"I asked about the others." Tolquen sighed, then looked at me. "They did not survive."

"I'm sorry," I said, reaching for his hand. "I rather liked the old Priestess."

Tolquen nodded. "It was too dark then to search the boat. The courage provided by the shell soon wore off, causing my body to shake with reaction. I felt exhausted, but would rather die than say so in front of Dokulu. Still, I think he knew. He offered to take the helm while I rested. I agreed after a few polite denials, then sprawled out on the deck. I was just about to drift off when I remembered the odd peace the shell had given during the worst of the storm. Touching it filled me with the same inner peace as before. The shell was definitely warm. It pulsed with life.

"Turning away so my movements would not be seen, I unfastened the shell from around my waist and cradled it in the palm of my aching hand. The shell grew warmer and throbbed, like the beating of a heart. The palm of my hand started to tingle. I forced myself to relax and let the thing do what it would.

"The cuts on both hands ceased to bleed. The minor scratches faded and healed. Soon only the deepest of the cuts remained, and they closed in a matter of minutes.

"I lay on the deck, unable to believe it. The shell glowed with a soft blue light, emanating from its center, shifting and waning with each pulsation. I fell asleep, the precious shell still cupped in the palm of my hand. Dokulu woke me at sunrise and offered me a dipper of water. His unusually grim countenance forewarned me that bad news was coming. I joined Dokulu and the High Priestess in the stern, relieved to see the old woman had survived the storm."

"That's wonderful," I said, squeezing his hand.

His mouth curved in an affectionate smile. "She is a hard one to kill. She offered me a piece of dried fish when I tried to hug her, so I ate. When I finished, she knelt beside me.

"'Give me your hands,' the Priestess said. She studied them for several minutes, then nodded. 'They are healed. It is good.'

"I was startled. I asked how she knew they were hurt, but she shrugged and refused to answer. Instead, she turned to look at the surrounding ocean.

"'What happened to the others of our crew?' Dokulu asked.

"'I warned you there would be some who would not make it. The god has a way of choosing his own. It cannot be helped, and his will may not be altered.'

"'But what of the other boats,' I asked her. 'Surely there are some who made it through.'

"Mother nodded. 'Some are out there still. It is up to them and the One who calls whether they follow or not. I cannot see their destiny. I only know it is no longer linked with our own. Do not be afraid. The worst has been done, and we have proved ourselves deserving in the eyes of the god. Gentle rains and smooth seas will be our path. We must trust the god of the shell to bring us to the other side.'

"'You saw the light in the sky,' I said.

"'Dokulu saw it, too, though he would not believe the evidence of his own eyes,' Mother said, chuckling. 'It was you the light was meant for, and you are now the keeper of the sign. The others are beyond our help. We must go on.'

"She took the tiller while Dokulu slept," Tolquen continued. "And so the journey continued, with just three where there had been many. While I worked my hand would often stray to the shell. A brush of my fingers across the smooth surface always calmed my nerves. I believed in its power and felt confident knowing it was there."

Tolquen paused, and I reached for my knapsack. The shell Quentin gave me nestled on top of the clothing. The star over the bull reflected the light of the lamp.

"What did your shell look like?" I asked.

"They are identical, except for one thing," he said, looking down at the object in my hand. "Mine did not have the star."

"Then it isn't the same one?"

When he spoke, his eyes avoided mine. "Mine was destroyed. Do not look so frightened. It served me well before the end."

I slipped the chain over my head and settled back on my bench. "Well, don't just sit there. Finish the story."

Chapter 13

"I WAS NEARING my seventeenth birthday when we spotted land off the port bow. It happened late in the day, just about sunset. I shouted and the others came at a run. We stood for a long time, staring. I do not think I have seen anything so beautiful in my entire life. On the advice of the Priestess, we drifted with the tide through the long night.

"When the sun at last peeked over the eastern horizon, we awoke. The first crimson rays showed the outline of a hazy blue mass floating on the rippling tide. Dokulu and I, anxious though we were, waited for the Priestess to give the sign that we were free to approach the beach. She sat for some time, staring at the shoreline, rocking to and fro. Finally, the old woman ceased her meditations and bid me raise the sail.

"The Priestess steered the boat closer to the shore. The land was covered with strange new plants, most of which I did not recognize. I was happy to see some familiar ones here and there among the scraggly pines. A delicious scent pulled at me, and it was all I could do to keep from pushing the Priestess aside to take control of the tiller. Just when I thought she would take the boat ashore, she turned us back to sea.

"I thought the long voyage had at last addled her wits," Tolwuen said, "and I said so. But she just shook her head and said this was not the right place for us. Dokulu agreed.

"'It calls to me, but it is not the place we came to find,' he said.

"'It is for some of the others. Not for us,' Mother said.

"'I am tired of sailing, and of this boat,' I said. 'What harm could there be in putting into that small cove just to walk for a few minutes and gather some food?'

"I was skeptical, but Mother was firm. She bade me let the shell settle the question." Tolquen laughed and rolled his eyes. "I hesitated before pulling forth the shell. For a short while the thing lay quiet in my palm, but I noticed it growing heavier. Soon it started to pulse in time with the pounding of my heart. Within seconds a dim light appeared deep in the center of the shell, and it gradually increased until it hurt my eyes to look at it. Still, I could not make myself turn away.

"The shell started to shake. It convulsed with such force my body quaked. My knees buckled and I sank to the deck. It was all I could do to avoid being cast into the sea. Through the corners of my eyes I saw Dokulu and the Priestess holding on, fighting the pitching of the boat. There was nothing I could do to help them.

"The light within the shell changed color. What started out as a bright fiery yellow mellowed to a strange brownish glow. The shell continued to tip and buck, succeeding in flipping itself over until the pearly inside faced up. The unrestrained pitching grew more fierce. I thought the boat was going to capsize or fall apart under the strain. Not even the horrible storm we endured had buffeted us with such violence. The timbers and lashings squealed in protest.

"Just when I knew the boat could no longer withstand the punishment, the shell in my hand gave a final, brutal lurch and the light burst forth in an explosion that blinded me," Tolquen said. "The explosion flung me backward, and the back of my head collided with the deck. I managed to keep a terrified eye on the ball of slithering brown light. It oozed across the deck, moving toward the Priestess.

"The light resolved itself into a huge serpent, complete with scales and dripping fangs. The beast coiled itself into a tight ball and reared up, its head held three feet off the deck. It bounded forward until it reached the tiller. The sharp yellow fangs closed on the wooden pole just as the Priestess moved out of range. The sail swung about and caught the wind. As soon as the boat changed course, the snake relinquished its hold on the rudder and reared up once more. It emitted a horrible roar that caused the beams to shake.

"Then, almost as quickly as it had formed itself, the thing dove over the side, into the water. It swam ahead for a few yards, then raised its head and repeated the deafening sound.

"I moved first, realizing what we were supposed to do. As quickly as I could I sprang to the swinging tiller and wrested it back into the position the snake had indicated. Then I collapsed into the stern. The thing from the shell settled into the water to swim ahead of us, its pace leisurely.

"Where did it come from?" I asked when Tolquen paused.

"It came from my shell. When I looked, the carving of the snake had disappeared, and only the bull remained."

I swallowed hard. "You're joking."

He shook his head. "The shell is an instrument of great power, Marty. It is a force to be reckoned with. Even the Priestess, the wisest woman I have ever known, could not comprehend its secrets. That is why I urge you to keep it close."

I looked down at the ornament and the spell his words had spun shattered. It was, after all, only a shell. "Right. Go on."

I think Tolquen knew I wasn't convinced, but he continued nevertheless. "With the snake to guide us, I questioned Mother about the new land we had reached. 'There seems to be a struggle for power going on,' I told her. 'I sense that now. Not all who were called were drawn here by the same entity. The place we just passed was not the place we set out to find. Rather, it is not the place I set out to find. Some who made this voyage were called by one side of the conflict, while the others were summoned by the opposite side. As close as I can determine, the three of us were chosen by the one who sent me this shell. It is my guess we will soon join others drawn by the same voice.'

"The Priestess nodded.

"'Then who calls to us, and what do they want?' Dokulu asked.

"'I do not know,' Mother confessed, her tone heavy. 'I only know this is where I must be.'

"And so we followed the serpent. It bore a tall, erect plume of bright white hair on its head, reminding me of the stranger I longed to see. Its movements seemed almost erotic as it sliced through the water, and I could hardly take my eyes off the lustrous scales. Such an animal could not possibly want to hurt me, of that I was certain.

"As if it sensed my growing fascination, the beast paused and turned to look at me. The eyes glowed with the strange yellow light, but I was not afraid. Rather, the light seemed to bathe me with comfort and security.

"After three days, the snake lead us to a beautiful cove with sandy beaches and dense green foliage. He slithered onto the sand, bending his long body until it looked like he beckoned us to come ashore. We followed, jumping into the shallows. It was such a joy to be back on dry land that I forgot about the snake. We collapsed on the beach and ate fruit until we could eat no more.

"The beast coiled its long body into a tight ball, as if waiting. When I had eaten my fill, it unwound itself and slithered across the sand. Following its unspoken orders, I took out the shell and placed it on the sand beside me. No sooner was the shell pointed at him than he increased his speed. He closed the distance in a few seconds and melted into the shell. When the last of the tail disappeared, I picked up the shell and turned it over to study the etchings.

"Just as I knew it would be, the image of the serpent again rested beneath the legs of the bull. I smiled and put the shell back on the cord around my waist."

I sat up on my bench, watching Tolquen's face. "I hope you

realize your story is growing more absurd by the minute," I said.

"I am telling you my shell contained a snake," Tolquen said. "I do not know what may be inside yours. "Anyway, we settled in that place for a time, gathering other wanderers into our group. When the Priestess thought the time was right, she led us inland to this place and told us we would settle here. I stayed for several months, until the colony became well established. Then I knew I had to leave.

"I wandered for almost five years before I felt the time had come to return to the Priestess. After a long journey I stood at the top of the mountain, looking down through the driving rain. At first I could not believe I was in the right place. Three days without sleep played havoc with my senses and I could no longer trust my mind to show me actual fact.

"Standing in the center of the rocks was one of the most curious objects I could imagine. What appeared to be a round slab of stone turned out to be a head carved from a huge block of rock. After several minutes I inched a little closer. The head looked familiar. It was meant to be a replica of my own features. I rubbed my eyes and looked again.

"There was no doubt about it. I stared at an eight foot monument to myself."

I sat up straight and grabbed his arm. "You're telling me one of the Olmec heads is carved with your features?"

He nodded, eyes twinkling.

I got up to pace off some nervous energy. I looked at him with a sly smile. "There's one way to prove what you say is true. One of my bags contains pictures of all twenty-three known Olmec heads."

Tolquen stepped into the hallway. He returned in a minute carrying my duffel bags.

"I left those in my tent," I said.

"I had them fetched so you would not have to go back to the camp. It is becoming far too dangerous," he said. "I knew you would want to refer to your photos."

I cast a wary eye in Tolquen's direction and, circling him, retrieved the notes. The comment about danger reminded me who I was with. He had given me no reason to trust him, a fact I had better start remembering.

I flipped through the stack of pictures until I found the Olmec heads. Then my knees gave out and I sank to the ground.

"Personally, I do not think it a good likeness, but I will let you be the judge," he said, laughing. "The nose is too broad."

The carved features belonged to the man standing before me. The style was primitive and the design crude, but Tolquen's almond-shaped eyes and heavy lips were unmistakable. For the first time I considered the possibility Tolquen's story might be true.

I cleared my throat several times. "Most scientists believe the Olmec heads are no more than twenty-five hundred years old. You're saying they're at least twice that age."

Tolquen chuckled and shook his head. "On what do they base this? How can you date stone?"

"Of course you can't date stone," I said. "The date is an estimate, based on material found in nearby tombs."

"I see. Because someone gets buried near a cave, that automatically means the cave and everything around it belonged to him."

I stared at him, a hand rubbing the tense muscles of my neck. "But those tombs are the only tangible evidence we have to go on. Given the circumstances, the assumption was a logical one."

"You are so young. You have many things to learn, and the first is the most important."

"And what's that?" I said, irritated.

He sighed. "The most important thing to remember, especially in your line of work, is that nothing remains the same through time. Have you ever stayed in one place long enough to see the changes brought about by the passing of time? I have seen cities and races and people come and go. But one thing remains constant through it all. Do you know what that is?"

"No."

"It is the space beneath your feet." He tapped the stone floor with the heel of his boot. "This ground, this dust, has seen the passage of more life than even I can imagine. It is the space where countless animals and people have met their deaths. It has been here since time began and it will be here when time is no more, yet few of the entities who tread it will leave any indication of their passing.

"If I were to scratch my name upon it now, today, some future scientist will think the writing is the same age as the room around it. That is the saddest thing of all. As a race, humans have no concept of the intricate relationship between time and space."

"And you do?"

"Yes, I do," Tolquen said with more feeling than I had seen him display. "But only the merest concept, the slightest breath of an idea. Perhaps one day I shall really know. That hope is what allows me to keep going through the centuries. That and the thrill I get from being one of the few who are able to laugh at the passing of time."

He approached me until his nose almost touched my cheek. "I need to see what comes next. I need to understand the complex relationship between time and space."

I swallowed audibly. "I need to understand what comes next in your story."

Tolquen backed away, laughing. "Very well. Where was I?"

"At the carving of your face."

"Ah, yes. After a while the rain came down heavier, so I pressed on. Soon I was drenched and miserable. I could not feel my feet or hands. I looked up from the muddy path and saw another of the huge boulders. This time, it was Dokulu who stared at me with hollow, sightless eyes.

"I reached out to trace the granite features, marveling at the skill required to reproduce his countenance. The beauty and accuracy of the head made me impatient to see what they had done to Mother's city.

"At last I saw the soft glow cast by hundreds of lamps. The valley looked like a section of the heavens fallen to earth, nestled between the mountains. Shadows moved about within the buildings. The sight was so beautiful I paused to stare, despite the rain and wind. I was just about to enter the city when a voice rang out of the darkness.

"'Halt, traveler. Who tries to enter Tamoanchan after nightfall? What business have you here?'

"I turned toward the sound of approaching footsteps. 'I have returned after long travels to speak with the Priestess. Perhaps you can tell me how to find her.' The guard hesitated, and for the first time I considered the possibility that the Priestess might be dead. However, the sentry's reply assured me she yet lived, though she would see no one. He added she was awaiting the return of a traveler named Tolquen. When I told the guard I was Tolquen, he laughed in my face.

"'Sure you are.' The guard took on a tone of bitter sarcasm. 'Why is it always my fate to deal with those who claim to be Tolquen?'

"I did not know how to react to his words. I only knew I had to get somewhere warmer. 'Is there not some place we can go to get out of the wind?'

"The guard hesitated, then signaled for me to follow. He led the way to a small building on a narrow ledge cut into the hillside. The guard lit a lamp and gestured for me to be seated on a long wooden bench. After studying me for several minutes he came closer.

"'You do resemble the altar dedicated to Tolquen,' the guard said. 'But I need proof to best decide what to do. Mother will not be pleased if I awaken her at this hour and you are not who you claim to be.'

"'What manner of place is this when a man's word is doubted without proof he is a liar?' I grew tired of the guard's caution. I asked how he knew of me.

"'Everyone knows of Tolquen,' he said. 'Many come to our gates claiming to be him. They have been put to death for the deception, along with the foolish guard who allowed them to pass.'

"The incongruity of the situation struck me and I laughed. 'Why on earth would anyone claim to be me?' I asked the guard, and he replied: 'It is rumored that the Priestess holds a talisman of terrible power, which will make the user a wizard of great skill. Many come and try to force the Priestess to surrender the talisman, but it is said that only Tolquen may wield the magic.'

"I sobered, realizing they were trying to get the shell. It throbbed in my hand. I saw faint yellow light escaping the gaps between my closed fingers. The guard did not seem to notice.

"'Does Dokulu still reside here?' I said. 'Get him. He will confirm what I say is true.' The shell grew heavy. The strain of holding it out caused my arm to quake, and I dropped my hand into my lap. I felt the snake draw closer and cursed the foolish guard. I felt sorry for him. He was about to get the proof he demanded.

"'Dokulu is the captain of the guard,' the guard said. 'I cannot awaken him.'

"His attitude convinced me I would get nowhere. My hand tightened on the shell, then opened. The man's eyes fell to my lap and widened in fright. A fraction of a second later, the head of the snake emerged and lunged toward the guard, fangs dripping. The poor soul fell off his stool and put his arms up to ward off the apparition.

"I felt a surge of pity for the guard and got to my feet. He did not deserve to die that way. In the seven years since the shell first came to me I had never tried to stop it from doing what it wanted. I searched my mind for special words to make the serpent withdraw. Nothing brilliant came to mind. In desperation, I yelled the first thing that popped into my head.

"'Halt,' I commanded, just as the hissing jaws were about to fasten on the sentry's neck. I think I was more surprised than the guard when the serpent stopped in mid-lunge," Tolquen laughed. "The glistening head hung in the air, as if suspended by invisible rope. The jaws opened and closed in a nightmarish parody of chewing, saliva collecting in a puddle on the floor.

"'Is this the proof you sought?' I asked the guard. 'Now will you take me to the Priestess, or shall I let him finish the job?'

"'In the name of the god, Tolquen, call him back. Please!'

"I looked at the snake, wondering how on earth I was going to get it back in its shell. The only thing I could come up with was 'Come,' and I uttered it in a stern voice. The snake wound itself back into the shell while I held it in my hand. It was my first experience with the sensation of the snake returning to its home. Like the other movements of the shell, I found it carnal in its intensity, and if it weren't for the presence of the babbling guard I could have derived a great deal of pleasure from the experience. I had to be content with the burning look in the snake's eyes when it slithered inside. Every movement of the long body excited me. I had to close my eyes and turn away.

"When the snake disappeared, the shell gave one last movement, a wonderful nudge against my palm, that made me want to call the snake back. Instead, I reattached it to its chain and folded my wet cloak around it. Only when it was covered did the yearning pass, allowing me to focus on the terrified guard.

"To my horror, the man groveled at my feet. 'Forgive me, lord.'

"'Come, man,' I said. 'Stand and be comforted. I attach no blame to you if you have told the truth. But, if I find the tales of impostors to be false, I shall seek vengeance.'

"'I spoke truth, lord. Ask anyone.'

"'I will do just that,' I said. 'Now, I would consider it a favor if you would show me to a place where I might spend a comfortable night.'

"He took me to his own house nearby. I stumbled to the guard's door, too tired to look at anything beyond dry clothes and a comfortable bed. Once he had seen to my needs, he resumed his post at the gate. My hand crept to my waist and felt around until I found the shell. As if it knew I needed comfort, it nestled into my palm. It emitted a warming glow that crept up my arm, spreading throughout my body. Satisfied the snake wanted to remain with me, I slept.

"The bright light of morning and squawking macaws woke me," Tolquen continued. "It took me several minutes to figure out where I was. Thankfully, the guard had thought to spread my garments before the fire. They were dry and ready to wear. I refused to appear before the Priestess as a beggar, wearing another man's clothes.

"When I was ready, I stepped through the doorway and paused on the threshold to look at the city before me. With the strong light of the sun beating down, I had to shield my eyes from the reflection of thousands of polished blocks. Each building resembled a finely cut jewel. The sight was every bit as thrilling as the Priestess predicted.

"I turned away, intent on finding a small animal to satisfy my hunger. I surveyed the terrain and saw that the guard's dwelling marked the edge of the occupied area. Beyond the shack, dense vegetation provided ample hunting."

Tolquen hesitated, then glanced at me. "My eating habits had become...eccentric...in the intervening years. I don't want to alarm you with the details, but I had developed a taste for the hearts of small animals."

I swallowed hard. "I take it you mean uncooked hearts?"

Tolquen smiled. "Is there another kind?"

"I'm a scientist." I tried to make my voice even but I couldn't stop the blood from draining all the way to my toes. I think he noticed my pallor. "If I'm going to understand you, I need to hear all."

"Very well," he said with a laugh. "Let us say I broke my fast well and continue."

"Go ahead and give me details. I can take it."

"Remember, Marty, you asked for it." His expression turned pensive, as though he recalled a pleasant memory. "I caught a groundhog and pressed it to me. Startled, it scored my chest with its claws. The smell of oozing blood excited me. Inspired by the smell, I tore its chest with my teeth and pressed the wound to my scratches, allowing the blood to mix. Then, running my fingers through the gore, I brought them to my waiting mouth. The taste was exquisite. It was the first time I had tasted myself, and I found I could distinguish between my blood and the gamy flavor of the groundhog. I buried my face into the animal's chest, seeking its heart.

"I pulled the pumping heart into my mouth," Tolquen said, his deep voice dropping even lower. "It gyrated against my tongue, causing my built-up passion to explode in dizzying waves of gratification. Just at the height of orgasm, when my body was tense and alive, I brought my teeth together hard, severing the arteries.

"The muscles of the tiny heart, still pumping against my tongue, brought on a second climax more satisfying than the first. I groaned in delight, then opened my jaws to maneuver the morsel into position. I brought my teeth together and felt the explosion of blood against the roof of my mouth.

"I lay for sometime, enjoying the warm afterglow, before I remembered the Priestess. I rearranged my clothing to cover the scratches on my chest, then looked around for a place to bury the carcass. In the wilderness I did not bother. But now that I was close to people, I thought it wise to hide the evidence of my odd feeding habits."

I shuddered and looked at my feet. "Why didn't you just finish it?"

"It had been a long time since I bothered to consume the remains of my victims," Tolquen said. "The heart and the blood were all I wanted. Are all I want still."

For the life of me I couldn't resist the urge to gather my sweater tighter across my torso. Tolquen noticed and shook his head.

"You are safe from me, dear Marty," he said with a devilish smile. "But be warned. Not all Incubi will abide by the Macadro's edict."

"Yes. You mentioned a struggle. I take it that conflict continues?"

He grew serious; the sparkle in his eyes dimmed. "It not only continues, it intensifies. But let us not speak of that just yet. It grows late and I must finish my tale."

Chapter 14

"WHEN I REACHED the one modest dwelling in the heart of the city, I paused to look around. The people followed and watched my every move. I resisted the urge to yell something threatening and turned back to the small shack.

"I raised my hand to knock, but the flimsy door opened before I could strike. The old Priestess stood before me. She had not changed in the five years of my absence, except perhaps to grow a little shorter. She leaned heavily on her cane. My eyes misted over when I saw her, and I stretched out my arms to give her a hug.

"'You are late,' she said. 'I have waited since sunrise for you to get down here.'

"I chuckled. 'I should have known you would hear of my arrival. I suppose Nanol has been to see you.'

"'I do not need Nanol's ridiculous gossip to know what is happening. I have known for ten moons you were on your way back. You took your time about it, too,' the old woman said.

"To my surprise, the Priestess pushed me out the door with a strong hand. She followed, grabbed my arm for support, and used her cane to indicate the direction she wanted me to take.

"'You should not have stopped to eat,' she said. 'Now we will have to wait that much longer.'

"'Wait for what?' I said. 'Where are we going?'

"Instead of answering, she increased her speed. The top of the hill was littered with little paths that ran in every direction, and the Priestess chose one that looked rarely traveled. The foliage was so dense in places I was forced to draw my *u-kab-ku* and hack away at the underbrush to clear a path wide enough for Mother to pass."

"What's an *u-kab-ku*?" I said, interrupting him.

"Literally translated, it means 'Hand of God.'"

Tolquen went to a far corner of the vast room. He returned a few moments later carrying a flaked stone knife that he handed to me.

The knife was about eight inches long and only about an inch wide. The blade was lashed to a long piece of basalt carved with the images of snakes and jaguars.

"I've seen these before," I said. "Excavators have uncovered several smaller ones throughout Mexico. They were ceremonial knives, weren't they?"

"Some were used during rituals, but most were just knives," he said. "Why must you anthropologists assume everything you find has religious significance?"

I flushed. "We didn't think the average citizen would use such beautiful implements just to clear fields."

"Well, we did." He reached out for the knife. I reluctantly returned it.

"Eventually we came to a tiny valley between two small hills," he continued. "At the bottom of the valley the ground was rocky and treacherous, with boulders sticking up at all angles. Thick grasses and brilliant flowers grew out of the dust. Nothing moved in that little hollow except the bugs.

"I wanted to pause for a while and let the serene beauty of the spot quiet me, but the Priestess refused to allow it. After a brief look around to get her bearings she was off again, dragging me behind her as she hobbled to the far corner of the valley. The hill rose up to its highest point, casting long shadows over a bare patch of dusty soil.

"The Priestess walked directly to the sheer face of the rock, then paused, running her hand over its surface. I was amazed when part of the cliff swung out, revealing an opening large enough for me to pass through. Mother entered first, then looked back at me. I had no choice but to follow.

"Once inside, I discovered that several lamps, carved right out of the stone lining the sides of the interior passage, were lit to illuminate the tunnel. The dusty floor of the passage sloped down at a gentle angle until it was lost from view. The surrounding walls of stone were smooth, yet I could detect no marks indicating the hall had been chiseled out of the hill.

"'What is this place?' I said. The resulting echoes hurt my ears and I had to cover them.

"The Priestess looked at me and winced. 'I am not deaf. You must speak softly here. It is a place of reverence and worship, sent by the god.'

"'You did not make it?'

"The Priestess chuckled and shook her head. 'Such construction is beyond our power. Come, the others are waiting.'

"I wanted to ask who the others were, but she gave me no time. We hurried down the passage. A solid wall of stone glittered in the dim light, indicating the end of the tunnel. I glanced about, looking for some sign of the other people. Not even a footprint could be seen in the hard-packed earth of the floor. My uneasiness grew until I doubted the sanity of the old woman.

"One look at her face was enough to confirm my suspicions and make me want to retrace my steps. The old woman stood before the wall, hands resting on the head of her cane. Her eyes were shut and she muttered unintelligible words. Soon thereafter the rock floor started to shake. The force of the quivering increased. My hand flew to my waist, thinking the shell responsible. My fear grew tenfold when I found the shell cold and still.

"The entire hill quaked. I glanced at the rocky ceiling, wondering how long we had until the hillside collapsed upon us. The urge to flee was strong. I took a step backward, then another. My eyes grew wide with fear when the heavy curtain of rock at the end of the passage moved. Torn between the need to save myself and the urge to grab the Priestess, I sobbed aloud and retraced my steps.

"Grabbing the old woman around the waist, I hoisted her onto my shoulder. I turned back toward the entrance. I took three paces before the rocky ceiling collapsed, blocking any hope of escape. A large piece fell on my head, knocking me to the ground. Waves of dust and debris swirled up to choke me.

"The Priestess, still deep in the clutches of her trance-like state, seemed unaware of our doom. I lay her upon the ground in despair.

"Oddly enough, the acceptance of death brought with it a sense of peace and tranquillity. I recalled memories of happier times, which caused me to focus on the shell. I no longer needed to touch the ornament to feel its power. It was there around me like a security blanket, enveloping me and the unconscious Priestess. The larger pieces of debris fell around us.

"In a few minutes the deafening roar ceased. The resulting quiet was far more frightening. Realizing I had closed my eyes, I opened them and surveyed the damage. I was surprised to discover that, despite the noise and flying fragments of stone, the ceiling of the chamber above my head remained intact. In fact, there was little damage.

"The stiff wall of rock that moments before had marked the end of the tunnel now lay upon the floor, splintered into fragments of dust that swirled at my slightest movement. Behind me, the corridor we had passed through was blocked. I leaned over the old Priestess, then laughed in relief when I saw the gentle rise and fall of her chest. I stood and tested my muscles. The bruise on my neck was small but painful, and I winced at the thought of carrying the Priestess back down to the village.

"I walked toward the cave-in. All hope of escape by that route faded when I saw the impenetrable wall of rock. That left the new doorway. I hesitated to take that passage, unwilling to attempt to negotiate the unfamiliar tunnel in total darkness.

"As I stood undecided, my attention was held by a weird glow within the opening. The blue light grew in intensity, reflecting off the clouds of dust until the cave filled with blue mist. The Priestess moaned and stirred. I backed away, dragging her with me, until my spine was against the rubble blocking the tunnel. The blue light advanced. I bit back a sob of terror and closed my eyes.

"At my waist, the shell awakened," Tolquen said. "I felt the first stirring with relief and groped for it, intent upon freeing the protector so it might aid in our escape. With shaking fingers, I succeeded in untying the tether, then placed the shell on the ground and backed away. A quick glance toward the glowing fissure told me I did not have long to wait, for the light had grown stronger until it filled the entire chamber.

"On the ground in front of me the shell bucked with a force that caused the swirling dust to form a funnel, sucking dirt and debris into its center. The shell glowed with a blue light of its own that joined with and then reflected the luminescence from the doorway. The gyrations grew stronger than any I'd witnessed before. I watched with a mixture of satisfaction and dread as the crust of the shell splintered, then exploded into a thousand fragments.

"One of the pieces hit me just above the eye, cutting the skin. I felt no pain. My attention focused on the loss of the shell I'd carried for so long.

"After a few minutes the dust cleared a little. I glimpsed the horror on the floor at my feet. Lying among the splintered remains of the precious shell was a heaving, undulating mass of glowing slime. While I watched, the mass seemed to spread, then pull back to its original size. It lay still for a while, then expanded again. It grew larger, and bluish tinge of the mass grew stronger. Within minutes the slime was almost as large as the Priestess. It put off a source of light equal to the glow from the tunnel ahead. I felt panic build inside me. The destruction of the shell had taken my last hope.

"The slimy mass at my feet changed. In the awful light I saw a piece rear up and break away. The gelatinous sludge pulled itself into a thick coil, then formed scales and fangs. It was the snake, and I writhed in disgust when I remembered the sensual satisfaction I had derived from intimate contact with it. As soon as the snake was formed, the beast uncoiled itself and slithered toward the opening. The remainder of the pulsating muck grew bigger. I guessed I was about to witness the emergence of the bull.

"It only took a minute to complete the transformation. I fell to my knees when I witnessed the last of the pulsating goo form into a huge creature with horns upon its head. After opening its foul mouth and letting out an awful sound, it started in the direction of the blue light.

"I summoned the last of my waning courage and forced myself to stand and face my doom. I took two slow steps forward, squared my shoulders, and made my eyes look upon the apparition filling the narrow fissure. Though the harsh light hurt my eyes, I would not allow myself to look away.

"I saw the snake from my shell. It wrapped itself around the lower extremities of the thing in the doorway. The giant beast stood just behind. It was several seconds before I could force any sound out of my dry, cracked throat.

"'Do what you will with me, but spare the old woman,' I said.

"Ahead, the brilliant light dimmed and the unfaithful snake detached itself from the thing and slithered back to me. It started to wind itself about my legs and I tried not to enjoy the contact.

"Yet I still welcomed the familiar feel of the serpent next to my skin. I shuddered, disgusted with myself, and ordered the reptile away.

"Across the chamber, the blue light dimmed a little more, allowing my eyes to make out the shape of a man. 'Forgive the serpent for his apparent defection,' the man in the doorway said. 'He is so happy to see us reunited that he forgets where his loyalties should lie.'

"'Who are you, and what do you want?' I called, with more bravado than I felt.

"Incredibly, the man in the doorway made a sound that sounded like a laugh. 'Do you not know me, Tolquen? It has been a long time, but I expected you to remember.'

"At the sound of the deep laugh, the snake slithered back to the man in the doorway and again coiled around his legs. I wanted to do the same thing. It was the white stranger. The one who had given me the magnificent canoe. The man I had waited for all of my life. I almost ran into his outstretched arms. He folded me close and I returned his eager embrace. I cried out in agony when the stranger at last let me go.

"'Do not worry,' the white stranger said. 'We will have all the time in the world to be together. Come, let us begin.'

"The man walked over to the unconscious body of the Priestess and lifted her onto the back of the bull from the shell. The snake wriggled up my body and nestled around my shoulders. The cold head caressed my neck and the forked tongue softly brushed the underside of my chin. Once the Priestess was settled, the stranger turned toward me and held out his hand.

"I accepted the man's hand, then walked beside him through the door and into the caves under the hill. Behind us, the splintered wall of rock reformed itself and closed again, sealing us in and the rest of the world out.

"I was never certain how long I stayed in the caves below the hills with the man I came to know as the Macadro. It could have been as little as one hour or as long as a year," Tolquen admitted.

"Didn't you try to figure it out?" I asked.

"Time ceased to matter to me. The passage of days and even years was of no consequence when I considered the span of eternity stretching before me."

"What happened in the cave?"

"While sealed in the underground cavern with the Macadro, I, of my own free will, underwent the ancient ceremonies that turned me into one of the immortals."

"And those ceremonies consisted of what?"

He smiled and shook his head. "That subject is forbidden."

"You can give me a little hint, surely."

When the silence continued, I decided to do a little probing. "What about the snake and the bull from the shell? What became of them?"

"You might say they played a part in the transformation, an integral part."

"The Priestess told you there were three others in the cave when you arrived. What happened to them?"

"Only two of us emerged as Incubi. The others became absorbed."

I didn't want to know what he meant by that. "Let's move on to Dokulu. Listening to your story, I couldn't help but like the man. What became of him?" I grimaced, fearing he had become an Incubus as well.

"Being an Incubus is not as bad as you seem to think," Tolquen said, reading my thoughts. "How can I make you understand the feelings involved? I remember when the Priestess brought me my first human. It was after we had been in the caves for a while. The Macadro had passed his judgments and made his selections. The other new

Incubus and I were recuperating from the initiation ceremonies. We lay together on the floor of one of the caves when she entered, bringing the men with her.

"I could tell the minute they entered the room. The smell of their marrow, the wonderful sound of their hearts pounding. I could feel it, even from across the room. I was so enamored I closed my eyes and let the scent fill the room."

I shivered at the naked lust in his voice. He spoke of them as though they were prize cuts of meat.

"I approached the newcomers. I was close enough to touch them when the Macadro walked in with the third man who had failed to pass the test. It was almost more than I could stand. My body shook and my hands trembled. I wanted to pull one of them to me and just press the body against my chest. I had to close my eyes to keep from ripping them apart to get at their hearts.

"The Macadro noticed my infatuation and chuckled. He bade me pick one of them. Each had begged to be offered as a sacrifice to the new gods. I looked into their eyes and I knew what he said was the truth. The Priestess seemed to want me to choose her. She considered it a great honor to live forever within the body of a divinity. Since it was forbidden for women to be initiated, she had decided long before that this was the only way she would be allowed to share in the adoration of the deities she helped create.

"I approached and held her watery eyes in my gaze for a long while. She returned my stare with unflinching determination, her head held high. I asked her what she truly wanted. I reminded her she could live out the rest of her days in comfort as the adopted mother of a god on earth. I saw her eyes cloud with love, but she remained firm.

"When I hesitated, she argued. 'You know I have the sight. Think about the advantages you will have by joining with one so strong. The Macadro has told you to choose well, as each heart brings with it the attributes of the living person. I beg you, grant me this in appreciation for any help I may have given you.'

"After one last look in her eyes I gave in. Partly because the scent of her was driving me wild, and partly because I needed her inner strength. How can I describe for you the heady intoxication associated with the act of feeding? When we give up mortality to become an Incubus, we also give up most of the physical pleasures we enjoyed. The only way to again feel erotic stimulus is to feed. The feel of a warm, beating heart in my mouth is the greatest aphrodisiac I have ever known.

"I drew her unresisting body closer to mine. Under my hands I felt her pliable flesh with the thick blood surging just below the surface. I saw her heart beat through the thin skin. I stood with my arms crushing her to my chest as I breathed in the intoxicating aroma. When I could stand no more of the exquisite torture, I lowered her to the ground and tore open her neck with one nip of my teeth.

"Under me, the old Priestess moaned in ecstasy and embraced my shoulders. I made myself take her gently. Please remember that I had no desire to hurt her. Although it may sound brutal now, I assure you I felt the utmost reverence for her."

I nodded and rubbed my own neck.

"The blood flowed from the gash, and I pressed my lips to the spot, then sucked the blood to fill my mouth. Soon I could feel it thundering through my veins, mixing with my own. I opened my mouth to moan and felt my muscles tighten with pleasure.

"I raised my head and looked into the watery eyes of the Priestess. She was barely conscious, and the gash at her neck had slowed. I licked the wound with a loving tongue and her lips parted in a contented smile. I bent to press my own to them in appreciation.

"When I had drained her of as much as I dared, I moved my body over hers and parted her concealing garments. Her chest beckoned me. I could no longer hold back the need I felt. I pressed my face to her breast and tore into her with gnashing teeth. The skin parted to reveal the rib bones. The delicious aroma wafted up as soon as the skin was broken, making me moan again.

"Snapping the bones was a simple matter for me. I was amazed that they broke at the slightest pressure from my jaw, and I paused for a second to taste the paste inside. The taste was even better than the smell. I closed my mouth around the break and sucked until there was nothing left. I discovered that the marrow was far more delicious than the blood. It is considered a delicacy among us.

"A moan of delight from the Priestess beneath me brought me back to the business at hand. I pressed against her in hopes of increasing her enjoyment.

"Her contented look made me happy, yet humble. I kissed her again, then turned my attention to the hole I had torn in her chest. The smell of the blood and the marrow, the sound of her heart pumping drove me wild with need. I placed my hands under her shoulders and raised her chest to my mouth.

"I took her heart, savoring the feel of the pulsing muscle until it exploded in my mouth. My body tensed and waves of pleasure washed over me, giving me the most explosive sexual experience of my life. The thought of her once-pounding tissue coursing through my body heightened the experience. Almost instantly I sensed her wisdom and strength meld with my own. She was a part of me, and I placed the hollow shell back upon the rocky floor of the cave."

THERE WAS A long, uncomfortable silence. Tolquen sat on his bench, smiling over the memory.

"What did she mean by that bit about each heart bringing with it the attributes of the living person?" I asked after clearing my throat. The vivid description of the feeding, together with the obvious pleasure he derived from the act, left me nauseated. It was all I could do to remain seated.

His descriptions also excited me, but I did not want to think about it. I wanted to hear the rest of the story and get the hell out of there. I wasn't quite so certain I found the idea that revolting. And the thought terrified me.

"It is quite simple, really," Tolquen said. "Each time we eat, we gain from the person consumed. We gain their life spans, their intelligence, and their talents. In certain ways we also gain a small part of their personalities. That is what she meant when she mentioned the Macadro's warning to choose wisely."

"What do you mean you gain their life spans? I thought you were immortal."

Tolquen nodded. "We are, as long as we continue to feed. When an Incubus is made, he assumes the longevity and, to a lesser extent, some of the strength, of the one who made him."

"Then the Macadro isn't the only one who has the power to make these horrid creatures?" I paused, flushing. "Sorry, Tolquen, I didn't mean—"

"It is all right," he said. "I have been called far worse than that. To answer your question, the Macadro is not the only one. Each of us has the ability to make others of our kind, but the creation has its price. For each new Incubus we make, our power diminishes. The strongest of our kind are the ones who bestow the gift sparingly, if at all."

"Then this Macadro must not be strong," I said.

"Wrong again. The Macadro, to my knowledge, has only given the gift twice."

"That's impossible. You and the man with you here already made two. Are you trying to tell me you've made all the rest? I've traced the existence of these people back at least twelve thousand years. There's no way one individual could be responsible for all of it. Not unless he also has the ability to be on five different continents at the same time."

Tolquen got to his feet. He crossed the room and leaned against the polished stone. "No, he does not have that ability. I see I am going to have to tell you some of our history to make you understand."

He was silent for a minute. "The man you know as the Macadro is the oldest of our race, true. He was made a long time ago, and there is no one who knows how the miracle was brought about. There are rumors and legends. Most of them are pretty fantastic and I do not believe them. The Macadro himself has never said how the thing was brought about, but I imagine it was different from the way I was made.

I settled back against the wall and looked at him expectantly.

"Long ago, the Macadro stalked a large beast and somehow managed to get separated from his kinsmen. After several days spent following the creature, he found himself in a small valley surrounded by steep cliffs. He managed to wound the animal and followed the trail of dripping blood to a deep cave in the cliffs. He finished off the suffering beast, then set to work on the carcass. Once the pelt was removed he cut off a piece of the meat and ate without bothering to wait until a fire could be kindled.

"As he chewed the tough meat his eyes grew accustomed to the dim light. He saw that the walls of the cave were painted with the images of beasts and other magical signs. He figured he had stumbled upon a sacred place. Since he assumed their beliefs to be closely related to those of his own people, the young man saw no harm in exploring the inner reaches of the cavern.

"He wandered around inside until the sun grew dark, then ate another piece of the beast and prepared to rest in one of the smaller crevices of the cavern where the pictures were large and numerous.

"Someone entered the cave while he slept. Before he could stand and protect himself he was overpowered and forced to drink a foul concoction of bitter herbs. The potion rendered him senseless, and soon he lost track of everything except the pictures on the walls.

"The Macadro drifted in and out of consciousness for an interminable time. His waking hours were filled with images of beasts, and after a while he thought he saw them move. The delusions increased until he thought he was going mad. He saw serpents detach themselves from the ceiling above his head. They slithered down the walls. They would coil themselves around his head. He lost consciousness, only to awaken to the same nightmare.

"Finally, when he thought he could no longer stand the torture, his tormentor appeared and announced he had passed the test. After that, he saw images of the beast he had killed and eaten on the floor of the cave. In these dreams the animal rose up to confront him with what he had done. While the Macadro watched, the creature split open its own abdomen and offered him any one organ to eat. The Macadro, after what seemed like weeks of watching the same dream, finally broke down and chose the heart.

"In the dream he reached out to take the organ, but his fingers never made contact. Just when he thought the prize was within his grasp, the giant animal dissolved into the image of the priestess of the cave, the one holding him prisoner.

"The Macadro fell to the ground in despair when he realized the food he craved was only an illusion. Between the harsh sounds of his own sobs he heard the laughter of the woman. The young hunter, tortured beyond endurance by the cruel treatment of the demented Priestess, swore to exact vengeance upon her and her kind for all eternity.

"His angry words, spoken with all the conviction of a man who knows his death is imminent, seemed to frighten the old woman. She backed away. He repeated the curse as he rose to his feet. She shrieked and ran from the cave.

"The Macadro, too long without food and water, collapsed to the floor. He lay there, his mind weakened to the verge of madness, while delirious visions tortured him with promises of sustenance that always went unfulfilled."

Tolquen was silent for several minutes and I squirmed impatiently. I felt pity for the Macadro. The treatment he suffered at the hands of the crazy old witch brought a lump to my throat. I realized the Macadro did not need pity from me.

"How did he come to be the father of a race of ghouls?" I said. "And where'd the ring come from?"

"I do not know," Tolquen said. "No one knows. He never told me. When he finally emerged from the cave, he was changed. Some of the changes were awe-inspiring. Others, disturbing. Because of his long ordeal his hair changed from black to white. I believe he gained possession of the ring while in the cave, but that is mere supposition. Perhaps one day he will tell you."

"Don't count on it. I don't intend to get to know him that well," I said, holding out my hands. "You said he underwent awe-inspiring changes? Like what?"

He smiled at me and gestured toward the smooth skin of his chest.

"Our ability to heal. Our tissue is continually rejuvenating itself. It is impossible to injure us."

I looked at his chest. "Would you mind if I had a look at that knife you used?"

Tolquen gestured to the bench across from me. The blade and its sheath rested on the smooth surface. "You are always the doubter, are you not?" His twinkling brown eyes invoked an answering smile.

"I guess I can't help it. I was trained to be that way."

I picked up the knife. A moment's careful scrutiny convinced me the weapon was real, and extremely sharp. If he had used deception in cutting himself, it had not been with the knife.

I glanced at his chest through lowered lashes, my fingers still working the blade. He noticed and laughed harder.

"Come and be sure."

I walked toward him, my gaze glued to the area just above the parted shirt. The bronze skin of his chest was perfect. There wasn't even the slightest hint of a scratch to show he was mortally wounded a few hours before. As I drew nearer to him, I noticed for the first time that his torso wasn't moving at all.

"You don't breathe," I said, putting my hand over his left breast. "Your heart beats, but you don't breathe."

His skin felt smooth and glossy to the touch. "You're not cold, either."

My eyes raised and locked with his. Something in the brown depths held me immobile, my hand still caressing his skin. I caught just a flash of emotion before he lowered his eyelids and one of the brown hands came up to cover mine. I stepped a little closer, my free hand rubbing the shoulder under his thin shirt.

"Are you alive?" My voice wasn't quite steady. My eyes fixed on the little spot at the base of his throat where I could see the ghost of a pulse beating. Under my hands his skin had grown almost hot.

"I suppose that depends on your definition," he said, his voice thick. "I exist, but I cannot be killed by mortal hands." His mouth moved to rest against the hair at my temple. I couldn't feel any movement of air through his lips when he spoke.

I pulled away. I rubbed my hands against the fabric of my jeans and moved to the other side of the room. He stayed where he was, but I knew he watched me. I paced off the nervous energy that had surged up within me.

"I could not touch you even if it were not forbidden," he said.

That got my attention. "Forbidden? By whom?"

His gaze slipped from mine. "Not by anyone. It is impossible for us to have physical relations of the sort you crave."

My cheeks flamed red and I couldn't look at him. "I see. You can't be killed?" I said, changing the subject. "What about fire?"

"It has no effect upon us."

"Sunlight?"

"You have seen for yourself that I can walk by day, even under the hottest tropical sun."

"Crosses? Garlic? Wolfsbane?"

He went to a bench and eased his body down. I appreciated his thoughtfulness in avoiding sudden moves.

"We are not vampires. In fact, vampires are off-shoots of the dark one's folly."

"What? I thought they were mythical creatures," I said, surprised.

"As we are mythical? No. They are as real as we are."

"What do you mean they're offshoots of folly?"

"We have waited a long time for fulfillment of the prophecy," Tolquen said on a heavy sigh. "During that time, the elders have sometimes mistaken other females for the one we await. In trying to convert these unfortunates, we have created a living aberration, an unholy nightmare. They were all mistakes."

"Who could make such a mistake, and how?"

He ignored the first part of the question and went on to the second. "Our blood has an addicting quality to it that we do not understand. It also has powers over human flesh that is frightening, even to us. If a human drinks it, they thirst for more. The craving becomes all-consuming. We found, too late, that if we deny them they seek to quench the thirst by taking from their own kind. This mix of mortal and immortal blood makes them stronger, but they have to pay a high price. For some reason, their bodies change and sunlight affects them.

"With us, it is the opposite. It is not the blood we crave, although we drink it because it tastes good. We need the hearts. Without them we would die. But that is the only way to kill us, and it would take thousands of years to accomplish. We assume the life spans of those we consume. If I were to stop eating today, I would begin to use up the time I have accumulated. However, since I enjoy the act of feeding and do it often, it would probably take fifty thousand years or so until I started to age. If I did not feed in all that time, I would live out the rest of my life span as a normal man."

"Do you have to feed daily?"

He shook his head. "We have to eat every fifty-two years, but we prefer it much more often."

"Fifty-two years? Interesting. Is it coincidence that number corresponds with the *xiumolpilli*, or Mayan century?"

"This is what we get for allowing an anthropologist to discover us," Tolquen laughed, delighted. "No. It is not coincidence. The people who worshipped us developed the calendar in question. It corresponds with our cravings. Every fifty-two years, the people offered thousands of sacrificial victims to keep us happy."

"Then how on earth have you managed to escape detection? I'd think with all those bodies laying around, someone would ask questions."

"We do not leave bodies laying about," he said. "We are not monsters. The first thing we are taught is how to escape detection, and the most important way is to ensure there is nothing left of our meals for anyone to find."

I shook my head, uneasy. "If that's true, how do you account for the body left behind in Pennsylvania? I take it an Incubus was responsible for the murder?"

Tolquen's expression darkened. "I believe that unfortunate victim was left as a warning to you. Have no fear, though. The Macadro was on hand to see nothing happened to you."

"That thought doesn't exactly fill me with a feeling of well-being," I admitted.

He laughed, then grew serious. "Have you ever heard of the chosen women—the *Mamacunas*?"

The abrupt change of subject threw me. I had to pause to think. "Of course. They're a cloister of virgin women who tended temples throughout South America during the time of the Toltec influence, about nine twenty-five AD until the invasion by Cortes. Their job consisted of weaving fine textiles for garments worn by priests. Occasionally, when the aristocracy ran out of slaves and prisoners to sacrifice, the *Mamacunas* would be offered to the gods. Why?"

Tolquen leaned back and stretched his legs out. "Very good, but with one important correction. The *Mamacunas* existed long before nine twenty-five. There are cells which have managed to survive undetected until the present day."

I turned to him, my eyes wild with disbelief. "Are you trying to tell me the Chosen Women were—and still are—your clean-up crew?"

Tolquen chuckled. "It is their job to dispose of the flesh the gods would prefer not to eat. They have existed in America for almost six thousand years, but they also exist in other parts of the world. There have been times, of course, when their services were not needed."

I nodded, sickened despite my interest. "Like during the time of the Maya, when the people ate the remains of human sacrifices after the heart and blood were offered to the gods." I stared at him in shock.

"Very good," he whispered.

"You really are a god."

He nodded and relaxed a little. "I was known to the Aztecs, the Maya, the Inca, and the Olmecs as Tolquenahuaque, 'the lord that is always near.'"

He turned to regard me for several seconds. "Do not worry. I gave up my delusions of grandeur long ago. Now I am a simple man."

"If this is your idea of simple," I said in a weak voice, "please, don't ever show me complex."

Chapter 15

"I STILL DON'T understand this business of making," I said. We'd been together for hours, yet I still had more questions than answers.

"That is only natural, since I am forbidden to go into detail," Tolquen said, bracing his hands behind him on the bench. He sounded as frustrated as I felt.

"I wasn't referring to the ceremonies or rituals involved with turning a person into an Incubus," I said, roaming the room as if the walls could provide the answers I sought. "I do want to know about those, of course. But I suppose I'll have to wait until your Macadro decides I'm ready. What I want to know right now is how in the world there could be so many of these things running around if the oldest one only made two others. And one of them was created six thousand years ago. According to the evidence I've uncovered, the race goes back at least three times that many years. Intact graves discovered from the Upper Paleolithic period show someone was around back then, eating hearts. I've visited these sites, and I've viewed the remains."

The thrill of being with someone who could shed some light on the mysteries of the past made me a little giddy. I stopped roaming and stood before Tolquen, my arms flung wide to emphasize my words.

"You admit these creatures exist. Hell, you claim to be one of them. I need to know how many there are. I swear I won't publish any more information about you and your friends. I'll leave you and your kind alone after this. But I need to know. If the Macadro didn't make the creatures who came after me in the woods, then who did? And you mentioned the dark one's folly. Who is he?"

Tolquen reached up a hand to rub the muscles of his neck, then walked around the perimeter of the room. He stopped before the lamp and checked the battery level. I could tell he stalled for time in which to collect his thoughts. When he straightened his face wore a look of bland acceptance.

"Barghest," he said, answering my last question first. "Remember when I told you the story of my arrival here? I mentioned the first place we saw was not the one we were meant to visit."

I frowned. "Yes. The Priestess and Dokulu had the strong impression the place was evil."

"Yes. But the place was not evil. The presence was."

Weary, I sank down on the nearest bench. "Can't you please just answer my question?"

"Can you not see I am trying?" he shouted, frustration finding an outlet. "This is not easy for me. The Macadro wants you to know only certain things, yet I am supposed to convince you we exist without revealing anything of the elders. Give me a break."

"Temper, temper," I said. I was beginning to understand the awkward position he found himself in. On one side he had the Incubi and their interests to consider, on the other my constant badgering. It was no wonder the man was torn.

Tolquen wheeled around to face me, his expression murderous. Then he caught the grin I struggled to suppress, and his teeth flashed in an answering smile.

"Sorry, honey."

The unexpected endearment warmed my soul, but I don't think he was aware he'd said it.

I decided to offer a compromise. "Suppose you tell me what you can and I'll try to curb my inquisitive nature until I meet your Macadro. Then I'll tie him to the rack and make him talk."

He sat beside me. "Are you sure you do not want to wait until tomorrow? We have been here for a long time. You must be tired. And starved."

"I wouldn't be able to sleep until I'd heard everything. I guess you don't have any food hanging around down here?"

"No. No one is hanging about the place. I make it a habit to always clean my plate."

I blushed, then stared at him. "You don't eat regular food?"

His relaxed laugh made me feel foolish. "Even the thought of eating cooked flesh is enough to make us sick. If we are unfortunate enough to ingest some of the stuff, we are careful to cleanse ourselves of the impurities as quickly as we can."

"But what about vegetables or fruits?"

He shook his head. "Our diet is strict. Nothing else will do."

"I guess I assumed the Incubi ate hearts occasionally. Like for rituals and religious festivals."

His eyes twinkled with amusement. "We have no religion. We, who have been worshipped by mortals, believe in no god. Would you, in our position?"

"Of course," I said, ignoring his last comment. The talk of Gods stirred my dormant memory. I grabbed his arm. "Barghest was the name of an ancient god of the Sumerians. We didn't know of his existence until a few years ago, when excavations began in what later proved to be the land of the Canaanites. Their chief god, Baal, was mentioned in the Bible as the god of the phallus, but we had no written evidence that more gods existed until the archaeologists uncovered temples dedicated to Barghest. We still aren't certain just what he was supposed to be the god of."

Tolquen offered only a knowing glance.

"He was rumored to be brutal," I said, thinking aloud. "The legends about him are scarce and degrading. It's believed he betrayed his maker and was forced to exist in isolation, damned for all eternity. From the few artifacts we've uncovered, he had a huge following of believers who'd stop at nothing to bring about the will of their god. His followers were the misfits of society, yet everyone knew his name, and each house contained an altar dedicated to his worship."

I looked Tolquen straight in the eyes. "Are you telling me Barghest was a person? I've seen a few of the statues and totems attributed to his worship. Each portrays a brutal, almost heathen, aspect of human nature. One is especially savage. Standing only eight inches high, the statue depicts two children, maybe brothers, engaged in mortal combat over the dying body of a woman presumed to be their mother. Each grasps a part of the woman's heart while they pummel the other. The limestone was painted to show blood spurting from the wound in the mother's chest, covering the bodies of her offspring. Because of this statue, and several more like it, we believe Barghest was the Canaanite god of betrayal, death and destruction."

"Not exactly." Tolquen hesitated. "Since you know that much, I cannot see any harm in telling you the rest. Barghest is a heart-eater, true, but he is not an Incubus. He is an elder. He was the first one the Macadro made when he emerged from the cave. To be precise, the Macadro did not make him. Barghest took the gift, by force."

I stared at him, my hand still clenching his arm. "Took it? How is that possible? I saw the way the blade of the knife bent just before it penetrated your skin, and you told me that the Macadro is the strongest of your kind."

I stood up, grabbed the knife, and placed the point of the blade on the top of the stone bench. Leaning all my weight on the handle, I couldn't get the thick shaft to sway even a fraction of an inch.

Tolquen watched. "The Macadro is strong and, after six thousand years of being, I, too, have gained strength. But we are not always thus. In the beginning we are little different from mortals. Our strength comes from feeding. I am strong because he who made me was strong. And because I have guarded the gift. Do you understand?"

I shook my head.

"As I said, no one knows how the Macadro was altered. When he came out of the cave, he was much the same except for several vital differences. The first was the dramatic enhancement of his sensory abilities. He could hear a human heart beat from miles away. He was quicker than before, and could outrun even the fastest animal afoot.

"He followed the scent and sound, and soon he encountered a tribe of hunters who had set up camp in the hills. He joined their group and, using his skills, succeeded in bringing down enough meat to feed the entire tribe. But the meat did not interest him. He could not get his mind off the smell of the people around him.

"While the others cleaned the kill, the Macadro watched them from a distance, waiting for one to separate and approach. A young woman brought him a piece of the beast. He accepted it, then tried to make her go away. Her proximity drove him crazy. When she would not leave, he lost control.

"When he returned to his senses, the girl was dead and he was more satisfied than he had ever thought possible. Still, he felt guilty about what he had done. He tried to bury the remains. When he looked up he noticed he was in plain view of the tribe, and he could tell from their horrified faces they had witnessed the clumsy feeding."

"Oh my god," I said, weak with shock. "Did they try to kill him?"

"No. They worshipped him." Tolquen's grin was sheepish. "You must remember this happened almost twenty-five thousand years ago."

"The Macadro is that old?"

"Yes. But consider the humans of that time. Successful hunting was rare, and most of these primitive people died from starvation. A man who could provide a tribe with enough meat to feed the population was divine. They granted his slightest wish without question. Of what consequence was the life of one female when compared to the well-being of so many?"

"I see your point."

"The Macadro stayed with the tribe for a while. He noticed that each feeding made him a little stronger and a little faster. He also noticed one of the men of the group started to follow him around. This man, known as Barghest, watched the Macadro and came to the conclusion it was the humans that gave the Macadro his unnatural strength and amazing speed. Barghest waited until the supply of food ran low, then went out hunting on his own. He managed to bring down a small antelope, which he dragged back to camp and dumped next to the fire. When the grateful group gathered round, he demanded a dying child as payment. The tribute was paid, and Barghest took it into the hills as he had seen the Macadro do. The meal did nothing to enhance his skills as a hunter, so he became angry and reclusive. He bided his time until the Macadro's next feeding, then jumped him just when he was entrenched in the stupor of pleasure.

"Barghest, murderously jealous, tore out the heart of his rival and swallowed it whole. Then, when he looked down at the mutilated body lying in the dust, he ran into the hills, screaming in tortured agony. The Macadro found out, many years later, that the heart had given Barghest the same abilities he possessed. Like himself, Barghest did not grow older with the passing of the years. Instead, time and frequent feeding combined to increase his strength and abilities."

"Wait a minute," I said. "You mean the Macadro wasn't dead?"

"Of course not. When Barghest discovered the Macadro had not died, he grew frightened, expecting the one he had wronged to repay him in kind. In consequence, he surrounded himself with others of devious temperament, and he found a way to make them immortal. As the years passed, the Macadro found that each time he fed his strength grew. He soon learned that young people gave him the greatest bursts of power, but wisdom and fortitude could only be gained from the hearts of the old.

"But it was not so for Barghest, we fear. He and his followers make it a practice to feed upon the young. Their victims are chosen only for the strength they bring. They also choose those of weak character. For this reason, the followers of Barghest are feared and hated by the rest of us. They have forgotten what it is to be human."

"But I don't see how Barghest can be all that strong," I said, fingering the blade of the *uh-kab-ku*. It was almost as sharp as a razor. "You said each time one of you make another, the new Incubus gets some of your strength in the process. How on earth can he be as strong as the Macadro, and why doesn't the Macadro just destroy him?"

Tolquen grinned as if I were his prize student. "We are not certain how many of the others Barghest himself is responsible for, and how many were made by his offspring. We do know, however, that his strength grows by the hour, and that the time is not yet at hand for the inevitable confrontation. But each hour that passes draws us closer, and each Incubus must choose with which elder he will stand for what may prove to be the end of our existence."

"Which brings us back to the Prophecy, and you aren't allowed to tell me about it," I said.

"No, young one, I am not," he said. "But do not fret about that. I have a feeling you will soon know more about us than the little I have been able to tell you."

There was a long silence.

"Why did Barghest think the Macadro was dead?" I asked, offering the hilt of the blade to Tolquen.

He accepted it and replaced it in its sheath. "What would you expect someone to be, after you ripped their heart from their body? After we give a heart, we fall into a deep sleep. Since we do not breathe, the condition resembles death. It is the only time we need to take rest, and only in order to give the body time to generate a new heart."

"You can regenerate a heart? How can that be?"

Tolquen shrugged. "We can regenerate anything. Most of the time we are unaware it is even happening. With the heart, it is different. In order to repair it, our bodies must go dormant. At such times, we are vulnerable—we do not know what is happening, and anyone may approach. For that reason, most of us hesitate to do it."

"But if you can't be killed, what difference does it make?"

"We cannot be killed by mortals," he said, stressing the last word.

"Then you could be killed by another Incubus?"

"The possibility exists, although it has never been done. That is why there is fear among our kind, and why the Macadro and Barghest are selecting followers to stand beside them."

"You can't mean they still hold a grudge against each other after twenty-five thousand years," I said. For a brief moment, I thought of Norman Mathews. "Well, maybe they could."

Tolquen shook his head. "The current struggle has nothing to do with that old feud. There is a much more important matter, long forgotten, that now threatens our existence."

"We always come back to that stupid Prophecy, don't we?"

"Yes," he said in heavy tones. He looked at me with a stern expression. "And do not even think about wheedling any more information out of me."

"Who, me? I wouldn't dream of it," I said, trying my damnest to look innocent. "Besides, there's still a lot I don't understand about the Incubi."

"Like what?"

"Well, for one thing, why are women excluded? Is this Macadro some kind of sexist?"

I wasn't prepared for the speculative glance he threw my way. "It is not a matter for the Macadro to decide," he said. "The time of their making is not yet at hand."

"That tells me a lot."

His eyes warned me not to pursue the subject.

"You still haven't told me who made the other Incubus in the cave with you," I said, relenting. "If it wasn't the Macadro, who was it?"

The satisfied smile on his face was answer enough. "You?" I said in disbelief. "Why?"

Before he rose to return the dagger to his bag, I caught a glimpse of his face. The sadness in his brown eyes brought an unwilling lump to my throat.

"Because I could not bear to go through eternity alone. Even with his presence beside me, forever is a lonely place. I do not think I could have made it this far without him, when the Macadro is rarely with me."

"Then Dokulu is one of the Incubi," I breathed. The lump disappeared, to be replaced with anger. "How could you do that to someone you loved?"

"He asked me to," he said. "He was my friend. How could I deny him the gift that was his by right? The Macadro could have chosen him over me. He should have chosen Dokulu. Dokulu was, and is, everything I wanted to be. How could I refuse him? It is much better to see him walking beside me, to hear his voice. What kind of friend could bear to watch while the body slowly shrivels with age, yet do nothing to help?"

"But he was your friend—"

"How dare you judge me," Tolquen said in a choked voice. "If you could stand by and watch someone you loved grow sick with plague or pox, you are the fiend. Worst of all is old age. It robs us of the only thing that sets humans apart from the trees and the birds. Dignity. Could you let that happen, even though you had it in your power to stop it? If you could, you are much more inhuman than I."

He strode out of the room, letting the thick tapestry swing with the violence of his exit. I looked at my hands and sighed.

I stretched my cramped muscles, wandering about the room. The bright, colorful paintings on the walls drew my gaze, but I stood before them for a long while without really seeing them.

I turned away and started to pace. I liked Tolquen. In another place and time, we could have been friends. He was gentle and kind-hearted. Hardly the attributes of a ruthless murderer. He wasn't responsible for what he had become any more than a lion was responsible for bringing down his prey. Both did what they had to do to survive.

Tolquen was what he was. I didn't make him, but neither did he make himself. He was a pawn in the larger game begun by Barghest, and waged with equal gusto by the creature he called the Macadro. If I lived long enough to cross paths with either of them, I decided I'd do whatever I could to bring about their long-overdue destruction.

But first I had to apologize to Tolquen.

I walked to the table, picked up the lantern, and started for the tapestry door. Just before I could reach it, Tolquen drew it aside and stepped into the room. His face held a guarded look, as if afraid of his reception. We just stood for a minute, staring into each other's eyes.

I realized that I'd consider it a favor if he'd allow me to call him my friend. For the first time since my father died I looked at a man and felt affection without the messy complication of physical attraction.

"Forgive me?" he asked. His vibrant voice sounded wary, unsure.

"For what? Do you forgive me?"

The broad shoulders relaxed a little and he held out his hands. "For what?"

I guess I dropped the lantern. It wasn't in my hand when my arms went around him a moment later.

The comforting cocoon of his embrace was another new experience. It felt good to be held by someone who wanted nothing more than I was willing to give.

The thought of friendship called to mind another face. I remembered Rich. The last time I saw him he lay on the rock at the *cenote.* I grimaced and stepped back.

"Rich," I said. Then my eyes narrowed and I regarded my new friend with malice. "What did you do with him? I swear, if you hurt one hair on his head, I'll—"

His wide eyes and loud laughter stopped me in mid-sentence. "I could not hurt your guide even if I wanted to, no matter how much he might deserve it."

"Deserve it? He hasn't done anything wrong. I owe him my life. If it weren't for him, your friends in the woods might've found me first, and then where would I be?"

"It may seem that way to you, but if the Macadro ever finds out about that little incident, your guide will be in deep trouble," Tolquen said, still laughing.

While I watched, dumbfounded, he pulled aside the tapestry and beckoned to someone in the outside corridor.

I watched the first long leg appear through the doorway, then the second. Then I saw nothing but the sheepish, smiling face. It was Rich.

In that moment, I knew I had been betrayed. The guard I'd trusted to protect me had been in league with Tolquen all along. It was two against one, and the thought that the next few minutes would be my last sent me over the edge. My temper blew. But they wouldn't take me without a fight. I launched my body toward the door.

Gripping the front of Rich's shirt with my hands, I pulled until the thin fabric tore with a violence that nearly knocked me to the ground. His chest showed no sign of injury. I stared at the perfect brown skin for a minute while the knowledge of his treachery gnawed at me.

"How long have you two plotted this?" I said in a voice that shook.

Tolquen and Rich exchanged looks. "What?"

"I was right. You brought me here for some kind of ceremony," I said. "I'm going to be your next meal. You bastards. I trusted you. Both of you."

My rage exploded and I raised my right hand and struck Rich's face with all the strength I possessed. The sound of skin connecting with skin filled the room.

"You conniving son of a bitch," I said, furious. "I was worried about you. I liked you, and now I find out what a monster you are. I hope the Macadro does find out about the mistake you made. I've half a mind to tell him myself."

I was so mad I stepped closer to him and started to pound his chest with my fists. The blows bounced off him without doing any damage, but at least he had the sense not to laugh. He just took it.

"How could you let me think you were my friend?" I shouted. Tears of rage cascaded down my face, but I was beyond caring. I let them fall. "No wonder Tolquen laughed at me when I was worried you might be hurt. You two must've had a wonderful time, laughing at me. I hope you've had your fun."

"It wasn't like that," Rich said.

I continued to flail at him, even though my hands were numb and my shoulders ached. If this was to be the end of me, I determined to kill one of them before I died.

"Don't give me any more of your damn lies, Rich," I said. "Or perhaps I should call you Dokulu. But what difference does it make? You're contemptible and hideous, whatever name you go by. Just the sight of you makes me sick."

Behind me, Tolquen placed a hand on the small of my back and tried to draw me away. "For the love of god, calm down."

"You appeal to the love of god? What kind of god would allow something like you to exist?"

I pulled away, then turned to include Tolquen within the blanket of my wrath. "Don't touch me," I shrieked. "To think I let you hold me."

Rich took an uneasy step forward, his expression one of frightened concern. "Calm down. The shell. You don't know—"

I lunged for him again, intent upon killing him. I only wanted to hurt them the way they had hurt me. In allowing me to think they cared what happened to me, I had fallen into the trap. More than that. I had come to like them. The discovery of their duplicity wounded me to the core of my soul.

I stepped toward Dokulu and the shell at my breast gave a shuddering leap. I watched, horrified, while the shell disgorged what appeared to be a revolting mass of glowing slime. I tried to run for the door, convinced the apparition had come to kill me.

The ball of slime followed me and dipped around my shoulders. I whimpered and held up my hands, trying to hold it off. It circled several times in rapid succession, then hurled itself straight at Dokulu. He screamed and tried to beat it off with his fists. It attached itself to his chest. Above the sound of his terrified cries, the sound of ripping skin and snapping bones echoed off the cold stone walls.

The glowing ball burrowed deeper into the flaying body of Dokulu.

The sickening sounds paralyzed me. My knees turned to mush. I sank to the ground with my hands to my ears. Tolquen yanked me to my feet. He held me off the ground, shaking me.

"It feels your anger," he shouted. "It knows your feelings. It is going after his heart. Call it back before it kills him."

Across the room, Dokulu lay on the floor. His skin, once beautiful and glistening, turned a ghastly gray. The slime sucked his blood with audible gulps. I could only stare and shake my head. The slime grew larger while Dokulu grew weaker.

After a few futile moments spent trying to mobilize me, Tolquen let me go with a heart-wrenching sob. He turned his efforts to the dying body of his friend.

I landed on my knees. To terrified to stand, I crawled away until my back met the stone wall. I bowed my head and closed my eyes against the monstrous entity that sought to exact its judgment within a few feet of my cowering body.

Chapter 16

TOLQUEN'S PLEAS for help finally penetrated the fog of fear that surrounded me. I looked around the room. Dokulu was losing the struggle with the mass of slime attached to his chest. The sight of the shapeless ooze made me want to turn away. But the look in the poor bastard's eyes when they locked with mine helped me to remember that Dokulu had helped me in his own way. I stood slowly.

"Call it back," Tolquen shouted in desperation.

The absolute last thing I wanted was to have that thing come anywhere near me, but I couldn't watch Dokulu's painful demise. His agonized screams quieted to a whimper. I took a cautious step closer to the melded forms on the floor.

"Halt." The single word erupted from nowhere. I shrank from the sound. It was several seconds before I realized it had come from my own lips.

Incredibly, the harsh sound of my voice seemed to have some effect on the sludge. It hovered over Dokulu, poised to resume the onslaught.

Dokulu remained on the floor, his body still. Whether he was alive or dead, I couldn't tell. The important thing was to get the slimy organism away from him. While I stood there, the oily globule shifted and changed shape. I took an involuntary step backward.

The glowing ball pulsed with inner life. Its greasy form continued to generate gray light, and the hatred it emitted was tangible. I felt the emotion fill the room. It tried to persuade me to let it finish the task it had begun.

"Shut it out," Tolquen shouted. "Control your wrath. It feeds on your feelings. Remember it is part of you."

Part of me? I shivered again and made a conscious effort to get control of my anger. The thing was ten times stronger than the entity I'd met on the plane, and it took all the willpower I possessed to keep my mind closed to it. The struggle only lasted for a few seconds, but it felt like hours. I felt my strength ebb away. I fought my own repugnance and panic.

Finally, I felt the ball's stifling animosity begin to waver, then cease altogether. The mass stopped its disembodied pulsing. Finally, it sank to the ground. Its inner light faded to a soft, gray glow.

Tolquen rushed to the side of his friend. He bent over the carcass, seeking some sign of life. I felt the first bubble of hysteria break over me. I struggled to keep the laughter from erupting from my dry, cracked throat.

I wondered how to tell if a zombie is still alive. From where I stood, I saw there was no longer a heart left to beat.

Dokulu's torn chest lay open, eaten away by the ball of slime. Nothing remained of the internal organs that once nestled under the ribs of the left side. I caught a glimpse of cauterized arteries and fragmented bone before I turned away to wretch in a forgotten corner.

I closed my eyes and tried to rationalize what I'd witnessed. I took several deep breaths, but I couldn't stop the shaking that racked my body or the bile that rose up in my throat.

When I opened my eyes again, Tolquen had removed his shirt and bent over the remains of Dokulu. I stared, incredulous, thinking he was about to administer CPR. The hysterical laughter welled up inside me again, but I made no attempt to control it.

Across from me, the shriveled blob of slime lay motionless on the floor. I watched it for some time, but it didn't move. It appeared to be as dead as Rich. I made myself inch closer to it in order to get a better look. When I bent over to study it, the thing gave a convulsive lurch and leapt off the floor. It attached itself to the *tzem* around my neck and tried to crawl back inside.

I screamed through the entire process. I fought with fumbling hands to get the disgusting receptacle away from me, but the thing was too quick. It was back inside by the time I succeeded in raising the chain over my head.

Without touching the shell, I grabbed the chain and threw it as far from my body as the enclosing walls of the room would allow. I rubbed my hands across the seat of my jeans and hurried over to Tolquen. If I didn't touch something familiar soon, I knew I'd go insane.

As soon as I was within reach of his crouching form, I put out a hand to touch Tolquen's back. The rippling brown muscles were a source of protection for me. I sobbed and pressed my hand to his glistening skin.

Then I pulled away sharply, shocked at the unnatural texture and temperature I felt. He was cold and clammy. His skin had a rough texture to it that reminded me of a reptile. Specifically, a snake.

Unable to tear my eyes from the only recognizable thing in the room, I backed away until I was once again in my comforting corner. I placed my hands against the cold damp wall, grateful that something still felt and looked the way it should.

I slid to the floor, my wobbly legs no longer able to support my weight. I brought my knees to my chest. If my hands hadn't touched all the disgusting things I'd handled in the last few minutes, I probably would've sucked my thumb.

Dokulu, his body still and motionless, lay on the ground, his feet almost touching my own. His chest gaped open. His skin looked parched and burned, as though it had dissolved through contact with acid.

Tolquen bent over the body, watching for some sign the tissues were alive. From my position on the floor, I saw no evidence. It looked as though the impossible had finally happened: An Incubus had met his death.

I felt no satisfaction. Revolted by the entire proceeding, I registered the knowledge, then looked away.

"Get me that knife," Tolquen shouted.

I couldn't move.

Mumbling angrily, Tolquen grabbed the blade from the bench and returned to Dokulu's side. While I watched in numbed terror, he drew the sharp edge against the flat of his wrist. The blood seeped out. I stared at it, shocked to see it was as bright and red as my own. When the first drops appeared, Tolquen pressed the wound to the hollow mouth of his friend.

This action so repelled me that I surged to my feet. I launched my body at Tolquen with the vague idea of stopping him from desecrating the body. I attached myself to his arm and pulled with all my might, but it had no effect. His free hand came up and brushed me away as though I were a fly.

I landed hard against the face of the rock and sat there, too shocked to move. Dokulu's lips, lifeless and dead a moment before, closed themselves around the wound on Tolquen's wrist. Inside his gaping chest cavity, I saw the red liquid flow and swirl. His skin changed color. The tissue began to mend.

I put my hands over my ears to close out the awful noise that filled the room. The sound was my own shattered screams.

Dokulu's rejuvenated skin, almost closed within a few seconds, was transparent. Underneath its smooth iridescence I saw erratic beats of a tiny new heart struggling to develop. The muscle grew larger until it threatened to break through the fragile barrier encasing it.

Meanwhile, his skin filled in and thickened. His greedy lips sucked at Tolquen's wrist. Finally, when Tolquen's flesh puckered, he pulled his wrist away, breaking the suction with an audible pop.

Dokulu gasped and tried to pull him back, but Tolquen jumped out of range. Dokulu emitted a great sob of anguish and then paused, sniffing blindly at the air. His eyes glowed with an evil yellowish light and he turned in the direction of the corner where I cowered.

Tolquen moved to block Dokulu's path. "Get out of here," he said over his shoulder. "He smells your blood. He needs it in order to heal. Please, move. I cannot hold him much longer."

Moving as quickly as my numbed legs would allow, I edged along the wall toward the door. I searched Dokulu's yellow eyes for a hint of humanity, for any semblance of the Rich I had come to know, but found nothing. I shuddered and lowered my gaze.

"Take the shell," Tolquen said, as I was about to duck through the doorway.

I froze. The thought of going anywhere near that gruesome slime was more than I could stand.

"Can you not see it is the only protection you have against any of us?"

That was a convincing argument if ever I'd heard one. I sidled over, picked up the farthest end of the chain, and held it on the tip of my outstretched finger, as far from my body as I could.

"And do not try to get rid of it on the way back to camp," Tolquen said. "Be careful. I hope I will see you again some day."

Without another backward glance, I squeezed through the narrow doorway and started to run. I hoped I had seen the last of Tolquen. Or any of the Incubi, for that matter.

After several minutes I realized I'd come without a light, and I sobbed again.

The thought had barely formed when the shell at the end of the chain in my hand started to emit a warm, bluish light. I gulped back a sob of revulsion. Holding the thing even farther from my quivering body, I used the faint light to try to determine my location.

Soon, I recognized the section of tunnel. I pulled aside the nearest tapestry and looked at the murals. It was the first room Tolquen showed me.

Breathing a little easier, I stumbled along the dank corridor until I reached the entrance. My free arm reached out to pull back the heavy curtain of tangled vegetation, then stopped before I made contact with the natural door.

More Incubi waited outside. I felt their presence, read their thoughts. They knew where I was. I considered retracing my steps. Tolquen would surely help me.

Behind me, in the long corridor that stretched into the mountain, I heard the scuffling sound of footsteps. I took a couple of steps in that direction, then froze. The hair on the back of my neck stood up with the realization that I was not alone. I'd forgotten the thing that was Dokulu.

I hesitated for several seconds. When I heard him slavering and sniffing, my paralysis shattered. Dokulu caught the scent of my blood.

I pulled aside the vines and stepped out into the night air. In my hand, the glittering gold chain grew heavy, but I was afraid to look at the shell to try to determine the cause. The glowing light grew more intense, bathing the immediate area in a soft bluish illumination that reminded me of Christmas lights.

My arm involuntarily moved to cast the beacon away, then stopped. My hand—of its own volition—brought the chain up and over my head in one quick, decided movement. I watched, my mouth hanging open.

All around me, the things with the glowing eyes closed in, tightening the circle. The light from the shell attracted them.

I saw the first one, ten yards away, and then the second came into view, just behind him. Soon the entire area brightened with the eerie yellow radiance of their eyes. I looked about wildly, hoping to find a path still open. Everywhere I looked, I saw a pair of glowing yellow eyes.

I placed a shaking hand on the warm shell dangling from my neck and sobbed a prayer of gratitude that its friendly blue light enveloped me in a tiny pocket of comfort. Whatever else it had done faded into insignificance. I gripped it a little harder and felt a seed of misplaced courage return.

The things stopped and stood in a half-circle, cutting off any hope I may've had of escape. Between the twelve pairs of yellow eyes staring in front of me and the reincarnated hulk lurking in the tunnel at my back, I was surrounded.

Under my trembling hand, the shell gave a small, reassuring lurch. I didn't care for the realization that the thing might be able to read my mind, but some natural instinct for survival warned me to remain silent and wait.

My hand dropped away from the shell. The blue light started to pulse, and then to change in a kaleidoscope of flashing color that encompassed every tint of blue in the spectrum. If the situation had been a little less frightening I would've enjoyed the show.

After several minutes of staring at the brilliant light, I was able to raise my head and force myself to meet the yellow eyes of the Incubus who stood in front of me. The creature looked at the shell and backed away.

All of the things in the line of illumination from the flashing shell retreated, as if afraid. The Incubi on either side, however, pressed in a little closer.

Barely had the observation registered when the shell shuddered against the skin of my breast. Then, with a force that ignited tremors in the pit of my stomach, the shell doubled its energy. The thing pitched and twittered. The light erupted from all sides in blinding stabs of blue that resembled lightning.

I recalled Tolquen's account of the violent action of the shell just before the snake emerged on the deck of their boat. I knew he hadn't exaggerated. It was all I could do to remain standing when the bucking grew stronger.

And yet, I felt no pain. The wild gyrations seemed almost caressing. I closed my eyes and tried not to enjoy the feel of the shell's gentle touch as it moved against my chest.

I knew the reaction was nothing more than a sympathetic response to the undeniable yearning in Tolquen's voice when he described the incident. I hoped I'd look back on these feelings with disgust and embarrassment. If I survived that long. But I couldn't deny a feeling of unity with whatever lurked in the shell.

The Incubi retreated. Behind me, in the tunnel hidden by the vines, Dokulu approached. My heart leapt with renewed fear. If he came out of the passage to attack, I knew nothing could save me.

I took a tentative step forward, and the Incubi around me retreated. I took a deep breath and walked forward, my head held high, my gaze glued to the small path they made for me. I saw this was another way of getting me into the open so they could surround me. I heard them close the gap from behind the minute I stepped away from the cliff.

I made my cautious way onto open ground with the tight circle of Incubi following. The shell at my breast gyrated, spewing forth its threatening light. The hulk that had once been Rich burst out of the tunnel behind me and paused, tilting its head back to sniff at the night air. I shook my head and groaned, wondering what he had done to Tolquen. In his weakened state, he was no match for Dokulu's mindless fury. I pushed the worry away with an effort.

No sooner had Dokulu burst forth from Tolquen's prison than I thought I heard a sound. At first, I thought the voice was Tolquen's. But then the call came again, closer, and I lowered my head in defeat.

"Marty? Where the devil are you?"

Emil's shout split the night, causing the yellow-eyed horrors around me to turn toward the sound. I heard them slobbering. They waited, bodies tensed in expectation.

I felt tears drip down my cheeks and my shoulders shook. The last thing on earth I wanted was to be the cause of death for someone I loved.

I opened my mouth and tried to shout, but no sound emerged from my constricting throat. I could only stand and watch him advance, helpless to warn him of the danger.

He topped the summit of a small rise and paused for a minute, surveying the scene. I saw his eyes narrow against the amazing sight before him.

"Friends of yours?" he asked.

I sobbed and sank to my knees. While I watched, six pairs of glowing yellow eyes turned in his direction. Even from behind I saw the light sharpen and focus on his tall frame.

One of the fiends took a slow, deliberate step toward him, but he appeared not to notice. His level gaze held mine. I read desolation and resignation in the depths of his aging eyes.

Worse, I could read the love he felt for the only child of his best friend, and the sacrifice he prepared to make in the name of that love.

Chapter 17

"I TAKE IT YOU found your lamias," Emil said, glancing around the clearing. "Not a very talkative group, are they?"

"No," I said in a hoarse voice. I stood, praying the demons around me couldn't see my knees quaking. "Not very cordial, either. And, just to be precise, they're not lamias. They're Incubus. Or is it Incubi?"

"Excuse me," Emil said with a tight smile, bowing from the waist. "I didn't know there was a difference."

"A big difference," I said. "A lamia's a vampire and, therefore, dead. Incubi aren't dead. They're something worse. You wouldn't call a flea a louse, would you?"

"Not without risking insult to the louse. But what could be worse than a vampire?"

I flashed him a weak smile, grateful for his calming presence. "You wouldn't believe me if I told you. I don't suppose you brought the cavalry with you? Or any great ideas about how we're going to get out of here alive?"

"Sorry. Somehow I failed to foresee this particular problem. However, the light these fellows are producing just might attract a little attention our way – if any of the crew are still awake to see it."

"What time is it?" I said in surprise.

The look of amazement Emil flashed in my direction informed me I picked a poor time to ask the question. It also told me he was nowhere near as cavalier about our situation as he tried to appear.

The Incubus closest to me took a step forward. "Enough."

Both Emil and I jumped. I felt fear return to knot the inside of my stomach. After such a long period of non-threatening inactivity, I'd hoped the Incubi wanted only to scare us; that they had no intention of harming either me or the man who just happened to wander by.

One of the things standing behind Emil grabbed him without warning. I managed to gasp a caution, but I was too late. My cry came an instant before the rest of the pack went into action.

While the circle moved to surround Emil, I noticed more closing in on me. My attention focused on the Incubus closest to me, and I trained the most malevolent look I could muster on him.

He smiled and kept right on coming. He looked into my eyes and laughed. The yellow glow he emitted grew stronger, until it seemed to radiate through me from all sides. I felt heat when the rays penetrated my skin. The heat intensified until I felt my entrails broiling inside my body. I doubled over, clutching my stomach, and tried to back away. They kept on coming, closing the gap. I stopped and forced my spine to straighten.

The shell at my neck still sent soft blue pulses of friendly light into the night, strobing in rhythm with the frantic beating of my heart. The heat inside me died away, but the piercing looks of the surrounding Incubi did not. They ignored the shell and kept coming.

When the fiends advanced close enough for me to reach out and touch them, the wild gyrations of the shell took on a new urgency that almost sent me to my knees. I locked my wobbling legs together, determined to remain standing.

The lead creature brushed the bristling hairs of my arm. I shuddered. I swallowed and forced myself to stare past them.

As if it knew of my repulsion, the shell gave another lurch that made me stagger, causing me to make contact with the creature at my back. The feel of the cold body was more than I could stand. I screamed.

Something leapt, not fully formed, from the pendant. The creatures around me jumped back, all except the one who'd spoken. I assumed he was the leader. He seemed to have some power over the others. He remained beside me, but he appeared transfixed by the apparition that leapt from the pendant.

All I saw was a blinding flash of grayish light. The fireball sprang out of the pendant and hovered three feet off the ground for a few seconds. It circled my body, slowly gaining momentum with each revolution. After several seconds, the ball made a lunging dive for the Incubus remaining at my side.

The ball of light fastened on its chest, just above the heart. I covered my ears to shut out its screams, but I couldn't turn away. The other creatures turned to watch their leader sink to the ground, drained, while the gray-blue ball grew larger and stronger.

When the last screams of the dying Incubus ended, the ball of light rose into the air, hovered for a second, then split itself into two parts with a loud crack. Each ball twisted and turned until it singled out two more Incubi, then moved in to attack. They lunged straight for the nearest, most threatening pair of fiends and tore open their chests. In seconds, the Incubi lay motionless and the balls resumed their hovering flight. One of the remaining creatures looked about with a nervous glance, then sauntered away.

I risked a quick glimpse to determine how Emil fared. The circle of yellow light around me was so strong I couldn't see beyond it. I opened my mouth to shout, but a hulking shape loomed up out of the darkness and went in Emil's direction. It was Dokulu. I let him pass, thankful my presence didn't concern him. Between the spheres of light, the glowing Incubi, and concern for Emil, I didn't have room for more fear.

The balls from the shell divided again. When all four had selected a fresh victim and maneuvered into striking position, they moved in for the kill, looking and acting as one. They caught two of the Incubi trying to flee. From the jungle some distance away I heard their agonized cries. The shell seemed to have the situation under control, I noted with satisfaction.

Some of my fear evaporated. I looked around the clearing, happy to see more Incubi on the ground than not. Remembering Tolquen's words, I took the shell into my hands and peered at the drawings on the surface. The light produced by the spheres was just enough for me to distinguish the carved outline of the bull, with the snake reposing at its feet. Neither my fingers nor my squinting eyes could find any sign of the star.

Lost in contemplation of this further evidence of Tolquen's veracity, I failed to pay attention to the battle going on around me. Something grabbed me from behind. The attack was explosive and came without warning. A clammy hand fastened on my shoulder, sending me flying through the air. I landed hard on my arm. Pain shot through my body and the bone broke with an audible, sickening snap. I gulped for air to keep from passing out.

I forced my mind to block out the pain. Almost as soon as I hit the dirt I was up again, shielding my useless arm. I scanned the area for an escape route, but there was nowhere for me to go. The balls of light, numbering at least six, chased the Incubi around the clearing. While I watched, another creature's eyes grew dim while the fiery sphere fixed to its chest grew larger. I couldn't trust the flames to distinguish between my attempt at flight and that of the Incubi.

I heard the attacker approach behind me, and I whirled around to face it. A cry of terror escaped my lips. Ghastly red light shone from every orifice of his twisted face. It was the color of fresh blood, and his eyes and nose and mouth swam with it. I turned to run, heedless of the danger.

He caught me before I'd taken two steps. I looked into the

unmerciful glow of his eyes and screamed again. The creature laughed. Its tongue and teeth still bore the tattered remnants of flesh from its last meal. Its breath smelled like a decomposing body. Bile rose up into my throat, threatening to suffocate me, but I made no attempt to swallow it. I was too tired to fight the pain and fear any longer.

"Your friend was delicious," the creature hissed. It sprayed my face and neck with blood. Emil's blood. "I'm sure you're going to be even better."

I swooned. Misery overwhelmed me. I saw the creature bend over me. It opened its mouth and lowered its head toward my chest. I felt the slimy lips on my skin. I screamed until I was hoarse and out of breath. My hand, pushing against the creature with all the strength of desperation, had no effect. I raised my knee and rammed it into its groin. It laughed again and lowered its head.

Its mouth opened and its sharp teeth grazed the skin beside my left breast, cutting open the flesh. I felt its questing tongue penetrate the gaping wound.

It fastened its lips over the cut. I felt its drawing suck. I tried to knock it away, but my blows did nothing. The creature groaned—a deep, sensual sound—and pulled my body closer.

Gradually, I accepted the inevitability of my death and ceased to struggle. Soon, the mouth so close to my breast felt pleasurable. I closed my eyes and gave in to the sensation. My hands rose to wind themselves into the reeking hair of the creature.

The beast at my breast fused itself to me. I felt its pleasure when the blood drained from my body. With each passing second, I became more aware of its thoughts and feelings. I shared the ecstasy of the feeding. It was more carnal than anything I'd ever experienced. I echoed the Incubus' soft moan of contentment, bent my head back, and relaxed into his embrace.

In answer, he immediately became more tender. His bruising grip softened to a lover-like embrace. He pulled me closer. I felt his tongue push past the ragged tear in my chest, forcing its way through the muscles covering my ribs. I didn't feel pain. Instead, I felt the tip of his tongue divide, split in two. Each half sought entry on a different side of my heart.

The creature's body shuddered with pleasure. He pressed more intimately against me, grinding his hips into mine. I spread my legs and sighed in satisfaction, all the while feeling the pleasure build. He brought me to the brink of orgasm. I clutched his bucking hips, urging him on, and heard his gurgling laugh of triumph.

From out of the surrounding darkness a figure appeared. I assumed one of the fleeing Incubi had returned to help his kin destroy me. I welcomed the newcomer and peeled back the remnants of my shirt to offer him the other breast.

Then the feeding stopped.

Instead of joining in, the newcomer bent over and grasped the feeder by his neck. The newcomer was Dokulu, and he looked murderous. With one swipe of his powerful arm, he threw the creature from me and followed it into the dust.

I cried out when he pulled the creature away. Its tongue took forever to exit my body. I felt it withdrawing even when I saw his body hit the dirt seven feet away. I looked down, caught a glimpse of it, and screamed.

It was long and thin and forked. I screamed again and tried to turn away.

Looking down, I felt a burning pain in my chest and vomited when I saw how much blood there was. My blood.

I shook away the last of my momentary infatuation and pulled my tattered shirt closed. Then I squinted through the swirling dust to get a glimpse of the writhing figures.

I watched the fight, hoping Dokulu would win. It didn't take long. Dokulu leapt onto the creature, his head seeking the other's chest. Rent fabric and torn flesh filled the air surrounding them, then Dokulu opened his jaws. The crack of splintering bone reached my ears, followed with the creature's scream of pain. Dokulu's body tensed and his head burrowed deeper into his victim's chest. Blood poured out, spattering my face and clinging to my clothes.

The thought that the creature almost succeeded in killing me finally washed over me. Worse, I let him do it, almost begged him to do it. My head started to spin and the clearing around me went black. I lay back with a whimper and let blessed oblivion claim my remaining senses.

WHEN I REGAINED consciousness, my broken arm throbbed painfully. It took a while, but I managed to sit up without my head spinning. It was a while longer before I regained the strength to open my eyes and look around.

Everywhere I looked, the gaping hulk of an Incubus lay on the ground, lifeless. The gray globes of light circled the perimeter of the jungle. Shadowy figures went from body to body. I thought I recognized Tolquen leaning over one mutilated Incubus near the mouth of the woods.

The creature that attacked me lay close beside me in the dirt, his chest ripped open and empty. I gagged when I remembered the delight his mouth had given me. Unable to keep my stomach from rolling, I collapsed in the dust and wretched. I took deep breaths until the dizziness past.

I leaned over to inspect his empty chest cavity. The wounds were identical to the severed ribs I'd studied in the camp's laboratory.

I scanned the foul-smelling corpse for a sign of life, but found none. The body was dry. It looked as though all the blood had been drained from the tissues, causing the skin and organs to collapse. Even the eyeballs appeared cracked and sunken. Extending a shaking hand, I touched the carcass. The skin felt like unprotected leather left under the sun for too long.

The Incubi could be killed.

The warming thought sent a fresh wave of adrenaline through my body. I sat up and looked around, trying to control the elation I felt.

I counted eight bodies in the dust, and each had a hole in its chest. None of them seemed to have a heart. I bent once again over the mutilated body of my attacker, and felt the elation die.

The corpse was coming back to life. The exposed inner wall of the chest grew pink and slick. A tiny sac formed, no bigger than the nail of my thumb, and beat with a weak, erratic rhythm.

I scuttled away and screamed. The heart, growing at a rapid pace, settled into a stronger beat. It was almost as large as my ear and just beginning to turn red when Dokulu approached. He glanced at me with vacant, glowing eyes and threw my body out of his path. I stifled another scream and cowered in the dust at his feet.

Dokulu looked at me for a second, then turned away. I pondered his odd attitude. He bent over the Incubus beside me. With one savage movement he lowered himself to the ground, took the tiny organ into his gaping mouth, and bit through the connective tissues. Dokulu swallowed with an audible gulp, got quickly to his feet, and strode into the darkness.

It was some time before the nausea dissipated enough to allow me to stand up and take notice of what else was happening around me. Of the twelve original Incubi, only one still stood. As I watched, one of the gray-blue balls swept down on him. He did not get back up.

A brief flash of movement on the other side of the clearing drew my attention. I flinched against attack. In another second, the figure moved into the light cast by one of the gray spheres. I recognized

Tolquen, bending over one of the lifeless hulks that littered the clearing. He, like Dokulu before him, bent and ate the heart that struggled to form within the creature's chest. They continued checking the bodies for signs of reanimation. I sank to my knees.

After a time the two met along the perimeter of the clearing and paused for several seconds in what looked to be deep debate. I glanced about the clearing, but couldn't catch a glimpse of the bodies. The immediate area filled with a greenish, sickly mist that hovered just above the ground.

The gray spheres of light converged on the spot where the two men stood. One by one they melded into a single gray globe. Dokulu gestured in my direction several times while Tolquen nodded. They approached, the gray ball following at a leisurely pace.

The curious band drew close to the corpse of the creature who still lay beside me. I saw yet another tiny sac struggle to form inside the mutilated chest. I stifled disgust and tried to crawl away.

Dokulu and Tolquen ignored me. They studied the creature on the ground. Only the gray ball acknowledged my presence by swooping to hover over the elbow of my broken arm. I sat still, so as not to provoke the light to attack.

"We might be able to get him to tell us, if we allow him to rejuvenate," Dokulu said in a doubtful voice.

Tolquen shook his head. "He could not tell us anything, even if he were willing. Barghest guards his counsel much too jealously. I guess they were sent here without much information. Otherwise, they would not attack so openly, and with so weak a contingent."

"That's what bothers me," Dokulu said. "Barghest isn't foolish. He should've known they'd fail."

"I think he did," Tolquen said. "I cannot fathom his purpose, but I know he sent them for a reason, all the while knowing the outcome."

"Perhaps it was meant as a test. Maybe he wanted to determine our loyalties."

Tolquen shook his head. "I think he had something different in mind. If only I could guess what it was. Oh, well, it is something more for the Macadro to ponder. You have taken him twice?"

"Yes."

Tolquen smiled. "Then finish him. I will allow you the honor."

Dokulu lowered himself to the ground and took the developing heart of the creature into his mouth. Once Dokulu consumed the sac, the body of the Incubus withered, then sent up tiny fingers of steam from the recesses of the chest. Soon the greenish steam came from the entire corpse, and it wasn't long before the circle filled with tendrils of noxious gas. I put my hand over my nose to keep from gagging, and stepped back a pace.

Within minutes the flesh turned to swirling vapors. The bones, standing out white and brittle against the dust, turned brown and dissolved away, leaving nothing but a faint outline of lighter dust to mark the creature's existence.

The green cloud hovered for a few minutes, then dissipated into the night air. I raised my face to the breeze, letting it wash away the stench of the decaying entities around me.

It was over, and I had survived.

Chapter 18

TOLQUEN TURNED TO face me over the swirling mist. "About Emil
Larson. I want you to know how sorry I am. He was too far gone.
There was nothing else I could do—"

"Please," I said. To talk, to even think about Emil would break
my fragile shell of self-control. I turned away from Tolquen and gave
myself a minute to gain possession of my emotions.

The demise of the Incubi had eliminated the immediate threat. But
I sensed this was only the beginning of the conflict. More Incubi would
come. In the meantime, my broken arm and loss of blood were
problems with which I had to contend. Although it was obvious that
physical force alone would have no effect on the Incubi, I would've
felt a lot more confident if I'd been in the best possible physical
condition. It was going to take weeks, maybe even months, to mend the
bone and get back my strength. I knew I didn't have that kind of time.
Every second counted.

True, I had discovered a weakness I might be able to exploit. But,
in order to do that, I had to know as much about the entities as I
could—far more than Tolquen had told me.

I put my good hand up to rub the tears out of my eyes, then turned
to face him. "How was it possible for the two of you to destroy twelve
of these creatures?" The ball of light at my side dipped nearer to my
arm, and I took a step backward. "With the help of the shell, of
course."

"It would've been difficult, if not impossible, if they had any
strength at all to them," Dokulu said in a voice dripping contempt.
"Barghest sent fledglings against us. He isn't normally that rash. I
don't know whether to be flattered or insulted."

"Fledglings?" I repeated.

"Not one of these Incubi was more than a month or two old, and
we think most of them were made within the last two weeks," Tolquen
said, his deep voice thoughtful, "specifically for this attack. The one
that managed to get to you was the oldest of the lot, and Dokulu thinks
he might have been created two or three months ago."

"According to what you told me, recently made Incubi don't have
much strength," I said, studying Tolquen with narrowed eyes. "The one

who attacked me was strong. I couldn't even scratch his cheek."

Dokulu laughed. "Strong to you, but not to us." He was still a little high from the night's feasting. His eyes glowed and his white teeth flashed. "Compared to Tolquen or me, he was as pliable as a wad of chewing gum. I didn't have to use any pressure at all to rip him open."

"You can tell how long an Incubus has been around by how soft its skin is?"

"Their strength, which we acquired when we took their hearts, was only a little more than what we would expect to gain from a mortal of the same age," Tolquen said. "The power we got from the second taking was even less—"

"How was it possible for them to keep generating a new heart?" I asked. "And how did you finally stop them? What do you mean by power?"

"Of all the females in the world, we had to get stuck with a scientist to fulfill the prophecy," Dokulu said with a tight grimace.

"What's that supposed to mean? I'm not going to fulfill anything."

Tolquen and Dokulu exchanged wary glances. For the first time I saw no sign of hilarity on either face. Dokulu turned and walked away. He disappeared into the passage under the cliff, letting the tangled vines swing back into place with a soft sound.

Tolquen watched him until he was out of sight. "You are tired," he said. "Dokulu has gone to get you some food and to prepare a place for you to rest for the remainder of the night. But first I think it is time we did something to fix that arm and heal those cuts." His eyes flashed and I caught the ghost of a smile on his lips. "The smell of your blood is driving us crazy."

I backed away a pace. "I know your blood is supposed to have great restorative powers, but I don't want to risk becoming dependent on it," I said, shuddering. "Vampire was never on the list of things I wanted to be when I grew up."

"I cannot blame you there," he said with an infectious grin. "I had something else in mind."

"What?"

"Trust me."

I rolled my eyes but allowed him to take my arm. "I do feel weak. But if you think this is going to get you off the hook, you're dead wrong. I'm sick of your evasive answers."

He held up his hands. "Do not worry. We have decided you need to know certain things for your own safety until we can return you to the protection of the Macadro. But the taboo on the Prophecy still stands."

"Agreed," I said, sighing. "I came to the same conclusion. But the rest had better be informative."

He took my arm and escorted me under the cliff, into the underground city. The gray ball of light followed close behind. Loss of blood had left me weaker than I realized. Without his support, I wouldn't have been able to walk more than a few paces.

We walked along the narrow corridor until we came to the large room where Tolquen had told me his story. The drapery covering the portal moved aside and Dokulu's head emerged. His eyes locked with Tolquen's for a split second, and Tolquen led me to a place further down the enclosed street.

The gray ball of light flared brighter when we crossed the threshold, illuminating even the furthest corners of the chamber. It floated around, stopping over the elbow of my cradled arm. I walked unsteadily to the nearest bench and allowed my battered body to lay on the cold stone. My eyes closed.

Visions of the gray ball danced before my lowered lids. In my mind's eye, I saw a piece no larger than an aspirin tablet break away and fly toward me. It pushed past my lips and filled my mouth with the sweet taste of sun-warmed honey. I swallowed, unable to believe I felt no fear.

I became aware of Tolquen's presence in the room, and of the gray light hovering over my exposed chest. I buttoned my shirt, surprised that the action caused me no pain. Raising my arm, I looked at the flesh in suspicion. My arm was healed.

I sat up with a jolt. The skin of my chest, battered and bleeding when I lay on the bench, was whole. Except for the undeniable fact that my shirt and pants were sticky with vomit and blood, I could've believed the injuries were part of a dream. Even the dizziness brought on by lack of blood had passed. I felt rested and famished.

"What the hell is going on?" I asked, my voice strained.

"I told you the shell was given to you as protection," Tolquen said from across the room. "It also has the power to heal, just as mine did."

"Shit, I thought it only did that when the person was to become an Incubus," I said.

"Now you know."

"Know what?"

The curtain parted and Dokulu entered. My attention focused on the food he held. I almost knocked him over when I grabbed the fruit. Speaking became impossible and I didn't even try. When the food was gone I sat back with a sigh of contentment, cradling a cup of water between my hands.

"Better now?" Dokulu asked, smiling. He leaned against the wall nearest the door.

"Much, thank you. I couldn't eat another bite." I smiled back at him. "You?"

He threw his head back and laughed. "I, too, have eaten my fill."

"Now that we have all dined, I think it is time we got down to business," Tolquen said. "We need to find a way to get Marty out of here while we can."

"I need to get a few things clarified first," I said, holding up my hand. "For starters, you can tell me who went through my luggage at the airport."

"It wasn't me. Believe me, I was as surprised as you when you found that scale," Dokulu said.

"It had to be one of Barghest's people," Tolquen said. "By that time, we had received word from the Macadro to back off, but Barghest issues his own orders."

"Then you're responsible for the writing in the burial shaft," I said, turning to him.

"Only the glyphs you consider Mayan," Tolquen said. "That place is a communal gathering area, and many had a hand in the graffiti."

"Including Mycerro? Did you see him on the plane, Dokulu?"

"I saw him," he admitted.

"Thank god. I thought I was going crazy." I looked at Tolquen. "The underground gathering area is frequented by Barghest's followers, too?"

He nodded.

"How do they get in?" I asked, puzzled. "Emil said the entrance is too small to allow a human to pass."

Tolquen's eyes took on a mischievous glint. "You forget we are not human."

"That reminds me. What about the scales? Does each Incubus have the ability to command a snake?" My eyes widened. "Of course. You sent the snakes through the opening."

Tolquen shifted his weight and stared at the floor. "Not exactly."

"Then where do the serpents come from? One attacked me in Pennsylvania, and I swear there was another, larger animal behind it. Of course. It was the bull."

"Very likely," Dokulu agreed.

"Then each of you has the power to command these creatures?"

They exchanged nervous glances but refused to comment. I thought I knew the answer, so I changed the subject.

"Dokulu, the first night I met you, you sat down with me and ate regular food. How'd you do it?"

"We can choke down the stuff when the need arises. It's one of the things we must force ourselves to do to escape detection. We must get rid of the impurities at the first opportunity."

"So after you left me that night, you went out and..."

"Exactly."

"And after the first attack, when Tolquen carried you to the truck, I saw your chest move."

"If we concentrate hard enough we can give the illusion of breathing, but no air is taken in."

"But what about the attack itself? How was it possible for one Incubus to take you down? He must've been very strong."

Dokulu looked abashed. He stared at the floor without offering an explanation.

"He was not attacked," Tolquen said. "He allowed the other to take him. I would not wish to be close to him when the Macadro hears of his little transgression."

"Transgression?"

"It is customary, when two of us meet after a long parting, for the elder to offer his heart to the younger as a greeting. The younger of the pair always eats first. In that way, the elder regains his strength, plus a portion of the strength of the newer Incubus, when he returns the favor. Dokulu could not resist the opportunity to eat and be eaten."

"An interesting way of ensuring the oldest of your race remains the strongest. Isn't it ever done the other way around?"

"It has been," Tolquen said. "There have been times when one of us grows tired of being. Such instances are rare. The older will insist that the fledgling eat first, then will refuse any reciprocal offering, allowing the new Incubus to keep his strength. If he wishes to cease, he will demand three takings, but I have never, before this night, seen such a thing happen. And I know of no one who asked for the ending."

"The third taking," I said, leaning forward. "What was that all about?"

"You already know when we eat of a mortal we gain everything in one taking," Dokulu said. "But with us it's different. If I were to eat once of Tolquen, I'd gain a measure of his strength and his life span without depleting him of either. However, if I were then to take his heart a second time without first allowing the heart to fully reform, I would gain all the power and endurance he's accumulated over his life."

"What would happen to him then?"

Dokulu shrugged. "If I stopped then, he'd still exist as an Incubus, but it'd be as if he were new. He'd be almost powerless, and would have to begin again to accumulate strength and longevity. He'd be scorned among our kind."

"And if you didn't stop after the second taking?"

"If I were to consume him a third time, again before he had the chance to grow a complete heart, I'd attain his life and he would cease to exist. Like the ones outside."

"But what if he did manage to form a new heart before the third taking?"

"Then the process would need to begin again," Tolquen said. "It must be done three times in rapid succession, or the being will continue to exist. He would be less than nothing to another Incubus, if the taker stopped after draining his power. We would never take twice unless we intended to finish the task."

"Or to punish someone," Dokulu said.

"You're trying to tell me you'd prefer to die outright than to exist in a weakened state?"

Dokulu nodded. "You must understand that, to us, our power and our strength are everything. I can't imagine what it would be like to wander the earth for eternity, scorned by others of my kind. I'd be a complete outcast. Such an unfortunate creature wouldn't have the fortitude to reclaim that which was taken from him. He'd have to spend an eternity trying to regain it, but all the while the others would still be more powerful than he." Dokulu shivered in distaste.

"Then why take the chance? Each time you offer to someone, you run the risk of such a thing happening."

"But we enjoy being taken," Tolquen said. "It is the most stimulating experience that can happen to us, far better than taking the heart of a mortal."

"If you enjoy it so much, why did the creatures scream?" I said, shuddering at the memory.

"The screams were of outrage," Dokulu said. "To us, giving is the most personal thing we can do. But like most intimate acts, the giving has its dangers. Why do you think we only offer to those younger? We must sleep after the taking to allow our hearts to rejuvenate. The younger the entity, the longer it takes for the body to complete the process. I always make sure the younger is asleep before I allow myself to drift off, and I awaken before he does."

"You can control that?"

"Not at first," Dokulu said. "But the older we get, the easier it is. I can function for several hours before I must sleep."

"The problem can be eliminated by refusing to allow the other to eat in return," Tolquen said. "That way, you keep what they have given you without putting yourself in danger. Remember that."

I glanced up to see both men staring at me. "Why should I remember that? I'm not an Incubus, nor do I have any intention of becoming one."

Tolquen and Dokulu exchanged another uneasy glance. "Just remember it," Tolquen said. He stood and sniffed the air. "It is almost dawn. I think it would be a good idea if you could get some rest. Dokulu and I will scout out the area."

I stood and stretched. The thought of getting a few hours of rest was appealing. With my arm healed and my stomach filled, it was becoming difficult to keep my eyes open. "Sounds like a plan."

"Good. I will get something to put on the floor so the stone will not be quite so uncomfortable."

He was off and running, and in a short time I was snug in a soft bed of assorted vegetation, covered with woven blankets. Tolquen and Dokulu left me shortly afterward.

Just as I was about to drift off, I heard the sounds of scraping footsteps on the hard-packed earth of the outer corridor. I sat up and strained my ears, but the noise didn't come again. There was no change in the hovering gray sphere. I concluded I'd imagined the sound and lay back down to spend what remained of the night.

Chapter 19

I AWOKE SOMETIME later and, using the dim light cast by the hovering gray ball, looked at my watch. The crystal had shattered and the watch had stopped. Muttering an impatient curse, I took it off and tossed it aside.

The slow, aimless movements of the glowing sphere claimed my attention. It flared brighter and swooped around the room. I watched the light for several minutes while it moved around, highlighting the paintings on the walls. At last my mind registered something that had bothered me for days.

There were no bugs.

On all my previous visits to Mexico, bugs had bothered me. Out here in the jungle, some grew as large as my hand. So far, I hadn't seen a single bug in the underground city. I couldn't remember seeing a bug in the cave we excavated, either.

Throwing the blanket aside, I stood and walked closer to the tapestry doorway. A bucket of water, together with my bags, stood just inside the room. I splashed some water on my face and started a systematic search of the chamber. As I expected, there were no spiders, roaches or mosquitoes, and nothing to indicate a bug had ever lived within the walls of the underground city. Could the presence of the Incubi be responsible for this phenomena? I'd have to ask Tolquen.

I pushed the mystery out of my mind and opened the largest duffel bag to extract the envelope containing my pictures. Picking up the first photograph, I tilted it toward the meager light from the sphere and tried to make out details. It was no use. The chamber was too dark.

I glanced at the sphere. Perhaps I could get it to burn brighter.

As if in answer to my half-formed thought, the gray ball swooped through the air toward my corner of the room. I cringed and put up my hands. The sphere paused above my head and intensified, bathing the photographs in soft light. I waited several seconds to see what it would do, but it made no threatening moves. Trying to ignore it, I settled into my makeshift bed and flipped through the stack.

An old black-and-white picture of my parents fell from the pile. Taken just before my mother's disappearance, it was the only image I had of her. I looked at the features, so similar to my own, and wondered yet again what my life would have been like if she had helped raise me. Although we hadn't heard from her in over 20 years, my father and I had never given up the hope that she would one day return to us. Now that my father was gone, I was the only one to keep that frail hope alive. Unwanted tears stung my eyes, and I set the dog-eared print to the side.

I took out the pictures of the Olmec heads. The one I sought was on top of the pile. It was disconcerting to look on the carved face of someone I knew. I looked at the photo for some time. I placed Tolquen's picture to the side and flipped through the stack until I came to the image of Dokulu.

His head was a much better likeness, indicating the artist was more familiar with his subject's features. I looked at Dokulu's carved face and couldn't resist a smile. The ancient artist had captured his easy-going personality with a few well-chosen blows of the chisel. I could almost see the twinkle in his eyes as he gazed for all eternity at the hills surrounding Tamoanchan.

I scooped up the pictures, ready to shove them back into the envelope, when a shadow in the background of one caught my eye.

"More light," I said without thinking. The gray sphere obeyed, moving closer to my bowed head. I almost didn't notice, transfixed as I was by the image in the photograph.

The brighter light allowed me to pick out the shadowy figure of a man, leaning against the trunk of a rubber tree. Shadows obscured the face, but the form of the body was familiar. The man was Tolquen.

I reached for my index and noted I had taken the picture fifteen years before. My hands shook with suppressed excitement. I spread the pictures out on the floor and studied each one. Selecting nine, I arranged them on the ground and stretched out beside them for a better look.

There was no doubt about it. Each of the nine photographs showed a person in the background, watching me. I leaned forward until my nose touched the paper, but could not make out the faces. Stifling a curse of frustration, I stood and ran back to the duffel bag. I found my magnifying glass and returned to the pile of blankets.

Each of the nine photographs showed one of the Incubi in the background. Tolquen appeared in four of the pictures, all of them taken within one hundred kilometers of the lost city. I set those aside and looked at the remaining five.

Dokulu was easy to recognize. His height and relaxed stance allowed me to pick him out even when his facial features were obscured. I found him in four of the remaining pictures.

The last one took a while, but in the end there was no mistake. I had taken that picture at La Venta museum, during a birthday outing with Emil. The dazzling white hair reflected the sunlight, giving an illusion of a halo encircling the well-formed head. It was Quentin, the man from the airport. His smiling face looked right at me.

I WAITED UNTIL Tolquen came to wake me up. Drawing the tapestry aside, he came into the room and surveyed my angry scowl.

"Good morning." His tone was tentative, as though he sensed my mood.

"How long have you been following me?"

He took the pictures from my outstretched hand and glanced at them. "You just discovered that? We never made any attempt to hide our presence from you."

He handed the pictures back to me and I studied them again. He was correct. In every case, the Incubi were in plain view. I never noticed them before.

"But why follow me? I was only fifteen years old when I snapped this picture." I held up the photograph. "I didn't know then that I wanted to be an anthropologist."

He shook his head. "I am afraid your questions will have to wait. There is a more urgent matter requiring your attention."

"What's wrong?"

"What is right?" He tossed my backpack across the room and indicated with a gesture the pair of pails near the door. "You have five minutes to wash and dress and do anything else you need to do. I will be back." With that he left.

His mood rekindled my anxiety. Jumping up, I shrugged into the first article of clothing I found. Tolquen returned while I was tying my shoes.

"Where's Dokulu?" I asked. "Is there any food left?"

Tolquen shook his head in frustration. After several minutes of rummaging around in his bag, he produced a couple of brown bananas and a withered mango.

"Not exactly first-class accommodations," I said, studying the unappetizing offerings. "Can't I pick something fresh?"

"There is no time. Eat these and I promise you will get something more substantial along the way."

"Along the way to where?"

"Do you never stop asking questions?"

My eyes narrowed in suspicion. "Not when I don't know what's happening. The least you could do is explain why you feel the need to order me around like a trained animal."

"We do not have time for talking," Tolquen said. "We have to get you out of here."

"For the tenth time, why?"

Tolquen sighed. "The camp of archaeologists is aware that Emil Larson is missing. They know he did not spend the night in his tent, and they also know you have not been around for more than twenty-four hours. They naturally put two and two together and came to the conclusion Emil went looking for you and never came back. And then someone came up with the bright idea of calling Norman Mathews. He told them to call in the *federales*. They are combing the area, and Mathews is on his way here right now. He could arrive at any minute."

"In that case, the best thing for me to do is go back to the dig," I said.

Tolquen crossed his arms over his chest and looked at me, his head tilted to one side. "What are you going to tell them when they ask about Emil? That he was eaten by a band of renegade heart-eaters? They would lock you up before you could finish the tale."

"There's no way I can tell the truth of what happened last night, but I have to let them know I'm alive and he's dead."

Tolquen caught me by the shoulders and gave me an impatient shake. "If you tell anyone Emil is dead, they will want to hear how it happened. Then they will want you to produce the body. Do you think Mathews will believe you?"

I thought for a moment and sighed. "You win. It'd be foolish for me to return to camp."

Tolquen smiled in relief and let go of my shoulders. "Good. Let us get your stuff and go."

I followed him through the city. He led me in a different direction from the entrance I knew. The gray sphere preceded us, lighting the path.

"Where're we going?" I asked, struggling to keep up.

"You are going with Dokulu. He will take you into the jungle and get you lost. Then he will guide you toward the coast. After that, I do not know yet. It is obvious you cannot get on a plane or use any transportation that would require you to produce identification. The authorities would pick you up in a minute. We will have to find another way."

"Aren't you coming, too?"

Tolquen shook his head. "I have not left this valley for thousands of years. The time has not yet come. I shall remain here and try to find a way to get you out of Mexico."

"You just said I can't get out legally. Do you know any other way?"

"I might." Tolquen's grim countenance and gruff speech reminded me that the man beside me, for all his kindness and willingness to help, was a killer.

I swallowed hard. "What happens to the bugs?"

He smiled. "You noticed that, did you? I was an Incubus for many years before I figured out they do not come around us. I think our scent scares them away."

"As far as I can tell, you don't have an odor."

"Humans do not have a very good sense of smell. The bugs sense our many incarnations. They have reason to stay away."

"What incarnations?"

"You will find out soon enough."

We came to the end of the tunnel and Tolquen paused beside the portal. "Now would be a good time for you to get that beacon of yours back in its shell."

I looked at the gray sphere, then back at Tolquen. "And just how do you propose we go about that? I'm certainly not going to touch it."

Tolquen rolled his eyes. "All you have to do is tell it."

I turned to the ball hovering three feet from my head and took a deep breath. "Come," I said.

The ball swooped toward my neck. The entity disappeared inside its protective casing, then the whole medallion shuddered seductively and nestled against my bare skin. I welcomed the warmth it emitted for a brief second and traced the etchings on the surface with my hand. The star took its place over the image of the bull. Slowly, the odd light faded away.

"All right," Tolquen said, shattering the spell of intimacy the warmth of the shell produced. "Are you ready to make a run for it?"

I took a deep breath and nodded.

He opened the concealing curtain and stepped through the exit, holding the vines away until I emerged into the light of day. We ran, hands tightly clasped, into the nearest stand of trees. Under the thickest grove stood the solid form of a waiting truck. I didn't see Dokulu at first. Then I spotted him. He stood in a thick patch of shade, his face lifted to the wind.

I ran to the truck and threw my bags into the back.

Tolquen embraced me, lowering his face into my hair. "Take care, and trust us. If you need me, I will come."

"I need you now," I said. "Won't you come with me?"

He shook his head and stepped back. "Not yet. You must go. Dokulu, it is time."

Dokulu shook his head. "It's too late."

"What do you mean?" I said in a weak voice. The shell lay quiet against my chest. "I don't feel anyone out there."

"Nevertheless, they're here," Dokulu said. "They're strong, too." He turned to Tolquen and their eyes locked. "Don't you feel them?"

Tolquen nodded slowly, his eyes locked with Dokulu's.

My muscles shook with fear. "How many?"

"Too many for us to handle alone," Dokulu said in a grim voice. "The other?"

"He is not ready. He restss," Tolquen whispered. His voice took on a higher tone and he hissed softly.

I licked dry lips. "What other?"

The bushes rustled and moved. I cried out and grabbed Dokulu's arm, then released it when my fingers closed over his cold, slippery skin. Scales formed under his shirt, and his neck grew long and thin.

"Oh, my god," I said, unable to tear my gaze from the transformation. "Hail Mary, full of grace..."

Something jumped from the bushes. I drew breath to scream, then felt Tolquen's hand close over my mouth. His long, graceful fingers had melded into a flat, cold flipper with scales that scratched my skin. I swallowed another scream and fought the dizziness that rolled over me in sickening waves.

...the Lord is with thee....

"What the hell is she still doing here?" the newcomer asked in irritation.

I recognized R.J. Hargrove and sobbed in relief. He seemed to appear in answer to my prayer. Tolquen released me. I couldn't make myself look at him.

"R.J. Thank god. Get me out of here, fast."

"We let her resst," Dokulu said. "It wass a misstake."

"Is there someplace to hide her?" R.J. said. "We're surrounded. I barely made it through."

"You?" I said in a weak, choked voice. "Is everyone in Mexico an Incubus?"

R.J. turned to me and smiled. "I hope not. That'd make hunting very difficult."

I placed both hands on the hood of the truck to keep from falling. "Moldy Chinese snake, huh?"

R.J. shrugged. "I had to tell you something. You weren't ready for the truth."

"What makes you think I'm ready now?"

"It'sss too late to worry now," Dokulu said.

I glanced at him and shoved my hand in my mouth to keep my heart from spewing from my chest. His clothes hung from his body in limp folds. His head had elongated and grown thinner. His facial features had melted away, except for the black hair crowning his head.

His transformation into a plumed serpent was almost complete.

"I told you Barghest wasssn't that ssstupid," Tolquen said. "Thisss time he will not sssend fledgelingsss."

"I think you're right," R.J. said, worried. "Come on, Marty. We have to get you out of here."

"Don't take the lady away just yet," said a voice from beyond the clearing. "She'll miss the party we've planned in her honor."

My shell gave a agitated twitch when the owner of the voice stepped out of the trees. "You're very perceptive, Tolquen. The last group was a test of your defenses. This time, Barghest has sent only the strongest."

Chapter 20

FOUR INCUBI MOVED to surround the speaker. They stood beside him for a minute, staring at me with glowing eyes. As if on cue, their heads elongated and their bodies grew thin. In a few seconds, four piles of discarded clothing formed a perfect circle around their leader. Four long, plumed serpents tested the air with forked tongues.

The arrival of the new contingent caused my fear to evaporate. It was strange, but there it was. Instead of the terror that had held me immobilized, I felt fortifying anger invigorate my limbs. I felt the support of Tolquen and the others, and knew they were prepared to die on my behalf. Their unflinching courage shamed me into showing a little backbone.

"I promise you, they are strong indeed," the leader said, laughing. "It looks as though the odds are in our favor. Give us what we want and I will call them off."

"What is it you want, Ahuizotl?" R.J. asked.

The name made me start in renewed fear. "Ahuizotl?" I said in an undertone to R.J. "The Aztec leader who sacrificed twenty thousand of his own people just to dedicate one temple?"

"He's the one," R.J. confirmed in a low voice.

"Nice guy."

He nodded. "The nicest."

I stared at the demon before me, surprised to see a short, rather stocky man who reminded me of Danny Devito. I relaxed and suppressed the urge to laugh. Even I found it impossible to be afraid of a butterball.

"We want the girl, of course," Ahuizotl said. "The exchange of one insignificant human for three of the oldest seems laughable, but Barghest is not unreasonable. Give us the girl and we will go."

"If she's so insignificant, why do you want her?" R.J. said. "Go tell Barghest we've decided to keep her around for a while."

"The decision is not yours to make. Once she has all the information she needs, the Murdoch will wish to come with us," Ahuizotl said, his voice confident.

I smiled and shook my head. Beside me, Tolquen and Dokulu waited, their transformations to snake form complete. I could tell them apart by the hair on their reptilian heads, which was exactly the same as their human incarnations.

I reached out a wary hand to touch Dokulu. Since I knew what to expect, the alien feel of his skin didn't shock me. I even rumpled his hair. He brushed against my waist, then raised his head three feet into the air. His mouth opened and he let out a deafening roar. The sound filled the thicket and bounced off the trees. A minute later, an answering roar reached us from the mountains behind us. I saw Ahuizotl's face set in a grim scowl.

"We're not alone either," I said, eyes narrowed. I did some rapid thinking. Less than twenty yards separated the two factions. However, the call that answered Dokulu's reptilian howl had been too far away to reach us any time soon. I had to stall for more time. "Tell me, what information do you have that would make me want to go with you? Tolquen and Dokulu have already seen to my education."

"Really," Ahuizotl said. He waved a hand and two of the four snakes took off in different directions, slithering low to the ground. They disappeared into the underbrush. The smile returned to Ahuizotl's face. "Then you know they have been watching you, following you."

"What do you take me for, a fool? I know that."

"I'm glad to hear it." Despite his calm words, he looked disconcerted. "I guess they told you they enjoy murdering innocents so that they might live."

"It seems to me that's a distinction you could claim for yourself."

The vines to my left rustled and swayed. I tried not to jump in response. Tolquen slithered off in that direction. A glimpse of R.J. showed that his body had grown long and cylindrical. Scales formed on his arms and face and a long, forked tongue darted from his mouth with rhythmic frequency.

He dropped to the ground, leaving his clothing behind. He crawled to my feet and wound himself around my legs. The slow, gentle contractions of his long body felt caressing. I closed my eyes for a minute and gulped air. When I was calmer, I turned my attention back to Ahuizotl.

"I see they have educated you well," he said in a tense voice. "Still, I cannot imagine they told you everything."

"Like what," I said in a deep voice.

R.J.'s sleek scales rubbed my chest. His head nuzzled my breast. His forked tongue darted out to graze my skin with feather-light strokes. I felt the muscles of my groin tighten with pleasure.

"Did you know their Macadro contacted your parents before you were born?"

My passionate response died. My body stiffened in outrage. "I don't believe you."

Another bush rustled from the opposite side of the thicket. Dokulu wound his way to the area and disappeared into the vines. That left R.J. and me on our side, and Ahuizotl and two more serpents on the other. The odds were indeed poor. I pushed the thought away and concentrated on the ridiculous little person across from me.

"It's true," Ahuizotl said. "Your parents knew of our existence long before you were born. Your father made a pact with the Macadro. They met frequently over the years to exchange news of you."

"You're making this up," I said in a shaky voice. "You know my parents aren't around to confirm or deny your story. Why should I believe you?"

"What reason do I have to lie?" He spread his hands and his smile was gentle.

I swallowed against the knot in my throat and shook my head. "My father was a scholar. If he knew about your race he would've published the information."

Ahuizotl laughed and moved a step closer. "Would he? All parents want the best for their children. What could be better than seeing your only daughter established as a queen, to be loved and revered by her subjects? He wanted that for you."

I took a step back to keep the distance. "No. You're a liar, Ahuizotl. I will not be your queen."

"You have no choice." He moved closer. "We have awaited you for thousands of years. We know you are the one."

"The one what?" I said, backing further away.

"The first female of our kind," Ahuizotl said. "You will be the mother of a new race of companions for us. Both sides welcome you. We wish you no harm."

I had to stop the retreat when my back met the bole of a huge banyan tree. I looked around, searching frantically for an escape route. There was nowhere to go.

As if sensing my rising panic, R.J. slid from my body and took a defensive position in front of me. He coiled into a tight ball and raised his head several feet into the air. I heard him hiss while he swayed from side to side.

"Then what do you want?"

"I see Tolquen has failed in his duties as teacher," Ahuizotl said, laughing. "We want what the others want—an advantage. The Macadro wishes to be the one to initiate you in the ways of your people. Can you blame Barghest for having the same wish? It has long been whispered that the one who makes the first woman will return stronger than ever. He will be invincible among us, and humans will worship at his feet. He will be a god in this modern world, and his followers will return to the splendors we knew of old."

So that was the ancient Prophecy Tolquen alluded to. No wonder the Macadro didn't want me to know. "I refuse the honor," I said, raising my head in defiance. "You can't force me to become one of you."

"We can help you to change your mind."

"I don't think so."

He crossed his arms over his chest and smiled. It was a signal. The vines burst into rustling action. The two remaining snakes moved in for the kill.

R.J.'s sleek, coiled muscles tensed to strike.

Ahuizotl held up his hand. The attacking snakes let out howls of frustrated rage, but ceased their forward progress. "Is there nothing I can say that would change your mind?"

I shook my head. "Nothing."

"Perhaps your mother could help to persuade you."

My head snapped up and I stared at him with narrowed eyes. "My mother disappeared twenty years ago. She must be dead by now."

Ahuizotl threw his head back and laughed. "Tolquen did not tell you anything, did he? Your mother lives."

"I don't believe you."

"Nevertheless, it is true. She resides among us. Come with me and you shall be reunited."

"No. I know there are no female Incubi. You're lying."

"Am I? It's true you must be the first of your kind, but females have lived among us since the dawn of our making."

My stomach heaved. "The Mamacunas."

"So you do know. That is right."

"No. You're filthy, vile. How could you do this?"

"It is beyond our power to force such a life on anyone," Ahuizotl said earnestly. He looked so serious that I believed him.

"They never told me."

"Your father knew. He visited her often."

I put my hands over my ears to shut out the sound of his voice.

"No. She'd never leave me of her own free will. She loved me. You forced her."

He shook his head. "Come with me now. Speak with her. She is anxious to see you again."

He held out his hand. I stared at it, fighting nausea. I remembered my mother's gentle face and soothing voice. Something snapped inside me. I sprang forward, intent on throttling the bastard. Ahuizotl laughed and held out his hands, as if welcoming me into the fold. Before I could take two steps the shell, quiet until then, decided to awaken.

A big brown blob hurled out of the pink opening, exploding into the air with such force that it threw me back against the tree. The shapeless goo quivered on the ground between Ahuizotl and me. He covered his heart with his hand and retreated a pace.

In another second, the goo solidified into the massive shape of a snorting bull. The creature pawed at the ground, blowing air through its nostrils. Then it raised its head to look at Ahuizotl.

I cowered, sobbing, against the tree. The bull lowered his head to expose its horns—fourteen inches of perfect bone. It charged without warning, running straight at Ahuizotl's chest. I screamed and covered my face with my hands.

All around the thicket, the servants of Ahuizotl attacked in response to the threat to their leader. Deafening roars of anger and hatred filled the air. The vegetation rustled and long, slithering shapes moved into position. A pair of venomous jaws loomed over Tolquen's coiled body. Before I could shout a warning, the serpent struck. Tolquen's jaws found a place on the body of his opponent and latched onto its chest. Both bodies rolled through the dust, worrying and shaking and trying to gain an advantage over the other.

The serpents flanking Ahuizotl moved in on the charging bull. They attacked from both sides, coiling around the great beast's legs in an effort to bring him down to the ground. I saw their jaws sink into his hide, but the stinging bites bothered him about as much as a circling gnat. The great body shook, heaving the snakes into the brush at the bull's feet.

One of the serpents screamed in human voice. The bull didn't even flinch. It caught the writhing body under its front paw and bent its head. Its teeth ripped the flesh of the snake with one gentle nip, exposing the human heart.

The burning light in the serpent's eyes changed from yellow to red. It sank its teeth into the thick hide of the bull's chest. Then incredibly, horribly, the snake tried to change its shape.

Thick, hoofed legs formed near the tail and turned from green to brown. Its belly thickened and sprouted a mat of coarse hair. A genital sac grew between the legs and then enlarged until it split into three separate mounds. Above the area of the waist, the thing retained its snake shape.

I vomited into the nearest bush. The thicket and its nightmare horrors faded before my dazed eyes. I slapped my cheek to keep from passing out. I knew I had to stay awake and aware.

The bull took the heart of the snake-bull into its mouth and bit through the connecting flesh. It swallowed the pounding organ and turned to the next victim. The second snake fell almost as easily.

I got to my knees and looked around the thicket. R.J. had disappeared. Thrashing bushes and frustrated roars allowed me to find Tolquen and Dokulu, but I couldn't make myself draw closer to them. I had no idea how they fared.

Using the tree as support, I got unsteadily to my feet. A snake, battered and wounded, slithered from the bushes to my right. I couldn't tell who it was. It inched its way toward the half-snake-half-bull creature and ate its fledgling heart. Its wounds healed at once. It slithered back into the concealing vines.

Ahuizotl faced the bull in the center of the clearing. The beast lowered its head and pawed the ground, then moved forward with blinding speed. Before it could find its target, two Incubi in similar shape sprang from the trees. Ahuizotl cheered them on, then jumped onto the hood of the truck to evade their murderous horns. They ducked their heads in response to Ahuizotl's instructions, and made ready to charge my lone defender, horns lowered.

The bulls came on, mowing down saplings and bushes in their path. Their eyes glowed red in anticipation of the kill. The creature from the shell stomped its foot and snorted in derision.

I watched him charge, head lowered. His horns sank into the first bull's flesh with a sickening, flabby thud. His head rooted around until it found the heart, and he swallowed it down.

Before he could turn, the second bull attacked. I saw its horns make contact, then I screamed. The shell at my breast gave another violent heave and disgorged the snake, fully formed.

It paused long enough to roar its displeasure before entering the fray. It made straight for the second bull and went unerringly for its heart. Ahuizotl's creature bellowed and turned its head to bite.

I tore my gaze from the animals to search the clearing. I noticed that Ahuizotl had disappeared. I glanced around, wondering where he was. My body stiffened and I strained my senses, using everything I had to locate him before he could spring. The leaves of the banyan tree over my head crackled in the slight breeze, giving me the clue.

I bent my knees and jumped away. Ahuizotl dropped to the ground in front of me, blocking my path. His eyes glowed green. I knew, from previous experience, that meant he was madder than hell and tired of the game.

I turned to run, but he moved to grab me. His arms encircled me in a grip that forced the air from my straining lungs. Blackness swirled around me. The arms tightened. Ahuizotl laughed in my ear and brought my wooden body tight against his chest.

"I see no reason to wait," he said in a voice shaking with lust. "I could take you myself. Then I would be strongest and the others would pay homage to me."

He turned me to face him and ripped my shirt from my chest. I tried to cover myself, but he had imprisoned my arms. His grip was too strong to break. He lowered his head.

I closed my eyes and sobbed. I braced myself to feel his ripping teeth. It was several seconds before I realized I felt nothing. His arms released me and his body moved away.

I opened one eye, anxious to know what was happening.

Quentin, his long blond hair tousled, struggled with Ahuizotl on the ground before me. While I watched, he threw the shorter Incubus out of the clearing, then surged to his feet to launch the pursuit.

"Get the hell out of here, Marty," he shouted on his way past.

Bending down, I grabbed Tolquen's shirt from the pile and slipped it over my shoulders. I hesitated, loathe to leave the creatures from the shell. There could be more of the Incubi in the surrounding jungle, waiting for a chance at me.

"Didn't you hear me? I said run!"

One of the snakes shot out of the bushes and made a lunge for me. Quick as lightning, another appeared from nowhere to intercept it. I saw the knot of kinky black hair atop the second snake's head, and knew it was R.J. They locked together, their tubular bodies melding into one. Slavering fangs reflected the sunlight, and hoarse grunts of strain filled the air.

I turned and fled without another backward glance.

Chapter 21

I RAN BLINDLY, crashing through the undergrowth, making no attempt to disguise my passage. From the clearing behind me, the sounds of the struggle increased. Furious cries split the air, echoing off the mountains and giving the illusion of many reptilian voices raised in answer. I covered my ears and ran on.

I had no idea in which direction I ran. When I encountered the first stone buildings of the Toltec city, I stopped and sought cover in dense foliage. I cowered there, listening for following footsteps. I closed my eyes and tried to control my breathing. When I was calmer, I raised my head to take a look around.

An officer of the Mexican Police force, drawn by the sounds of my foolish flight, appeared. He clutched a rifle in his arms. Another joined him, and they separated to search the nearby buildings. I suppressed a sob of fear and tried to think.

I had to get away from the occupied areas. Using the blocks of a ruined structure as cover, I moved as silently as I could in the direction of the surrounding jungle. I inched along, pausing every few seconds to hold my breath and listen. Judging by their fading footsteps, the two officers moved in the opposite direction. I breathed a sigh of relief.

I waited until I could no longer hear them moving through the ruins, then gathered my resources for a mad dash. Heedless of clinging branches and dislodged stones, I fled. Behind me, I heard someone scramble over the blocks in pursuit. I bit back a sob and poured on the speed, expecting at any moment to be brought down by a flying bullet. He didn't fire. This development puzzled me, but not enough to make me want to pause and look around.

I reached the trees and hurled past them, seeking thicker growth and dimmer light. My pursuer followed me into the jungle. I heard him enter a few seconds behind me.

Despair filled my body, weighing my limbs and constricting my chest. Whoever he was, he could run faster than I. His tramping footsteps told me he would soon win the race. He gained with each passing second.

The knowledge gave me a sudden burst of last-ditch energy. Arms and legs pumping beyond their normal ability, I shot through that grove like the hounds of hell were in pursuit. But still he gained on me.

I was almost to the end of the grove—and my strength— when someone popped out of the bushes ahead. A figure walked directly into my path, giving me no time to stop. It happened so fast. One second the path ahead was clear. The next, blocked. I had been herded into a trap, and could see no means of escape.

I didn't even slow. I lowered my head, grit my teeth, and kept running.

At the last possible second, the person stepped out of the way. I laughed in delight, positive I would win. I was so giddy with relief that I didn't notice the hands that reached for me, or the leg that shot out to trip me. Before I knew what was happening, I lay face down in the dirt.

All the fight went out of me. I sobbed and swallowed mud. I didn't even have the strength to lift my head and look at my attackers.

The one who pursued me through the woods ran up to join his compatriot. It was several seconds before I realized he was panting— out of breath.

"Did you knock her out?" he said, fighting to draw air between words.

"I don't think so."

The second voice reached my ears, sounding better than the sweetest music. I rolled over and looked at the pair who stood over me. Both were covered in sweat due to the sticky, humid jungle air. This sign encouraged me. I had yet to see one of the Incubi perspire. The woman wore her favorite Marvin T-shirt and rumpled slacks. Her gray hair stood out from her head like a tattered halo. I had never seen anyone who looked better.

"Shelley? And Mark Andrews. Am I glad to see you guys."

"Hush," Mark said, putting out a hand to help me to my feet. "Do you want the cops to hear? I think they're far enough away, but I don't want to draw them back."

"Good point," I said, lowering my voice to a whisper. The others did likewise.

I almost took Mark's hand. Then I remembered R.J. I rolled out of his reach, coming to my feet in one smooth movement. I held out my hands, ready to run. "Why were you following me?"

"I thought you could use some help," Mark said.

He looked normal enough in his working uniform of scruffy jeans and blue shirt. But I needed more proof that he was indeed human. I studied his face.

"Why didn't you call my name? Tell me who you were?"

"You want me to alert the *federales* you're here? I thought you were trying to avoid capture."

I looked from him to Shelley. Both their chests rose and fell in even rhythms, but I already knew the Incubi could give the illusion of breathing when it suited their purpose to do so.

"Are you all right?" Shelley asked. Her lined face wore an expression of concern. She took a step in my direction.

I backed away. "Don't come any closer."

A sudden idea occurred to me and I grasped the shell in my hand. I lifted it, careful to keep the engraved side toward my chest. I didn't want them to see the smooth surface where the animal carvings should've been.

Shelley exchanged a bewildered look with Mark. "What's the matter? Tell us. We're here to help."

"You can help me by keeping your distance until you tell me which side you're on." I brandished the shell, watching their faces for the least sign of fear. "I mean it, Shelley. I don't want to have to kill you."

"You're going to kill her with a seashell?" Andrews asked, his tone incredulous. "Must be one hell of a shell."

"Maybe. You tell me."

Neither showed the fear I saw in the other Incubi. I started to wonder if they might be normal after all. To test the theory, I moved closer with the shell. It didn't make a single threatening move.

They exchanged worried glances. Shelley licked her lips. "What're you talking about?" she asked.

I backed away, still holding the shell. "Why are you here with him? Why are you following me?"

"We're not following. We're trying to help. From the look of it, you could use it, too," Shelley said, hands on hips. "I leave you alone for two days and you have the police of two continents looking for you. Then you brandish a seashell and tell me it's a lethal weapon. What's happened to you?"

"Two continents? What are you talking about?" I let the shell fall into position between my breasts.

"We got a phone call from Sheriff Wilson in Pennsylvania shortly after you disappeared yesterday," Mark said. "You're wanted for murder."

"Me? That's ridiculous."

Shelley peeled mud from my face and regarded me, her heavy-lidded eyes troubled. "That's what I said, but they found a dead body inside your house. Someone ripped her heart out, then stashed the remains in the cellar."

I opened my mouth to protest, then shut it again. There had been no body when the Sheriff searched my house, but that wouldn't help establish my innocence. The Incubi had all the time they needed to frame me. I couldn't escape the trap they set. I sank down on the nearest rock and covered my face with my hands. "Oh, god. What the hell am I going to do now?"

Mark shifted his weight, uncomfortable with this display of emotion. Shelley dropped to her knees beside me.

"Then you know something about this?"

"Yes, but I didn't do it, I swear." I looked at her, wondering if she'd think me crazy. Then I shrugged and took a deep breath. "Remember our conversation the other night? You told me all I had to do was find him."

"I remember."

"Well, it's not a him, its a they, and they found me before I left Philadelphia. They're following me."

"Oh shit," Shelley said, stunned. "How many?"

"I don't know for sure, but lots. Too many. And they're strong."

"What are you talking about?" Mark asked.

"Her heart-eaters," Shelley said with an impatient flap of her ink-stained hand. "They're following her."

Mark paled. "You mean they exist?"

"They do, but they're not like I thought," I said.

"What are they like?" Shelley asked.

I groped for words. "In a lot of ways, they're just like us. In others, they're horrible. They're immortal, too. I never expected that. I always thought they were regular people who ingested drugs and ate hearts on religious holy days. I never dreamed they were anything else."

"How do you know they are?" Mark asked, dropping down beside Shelley. He put a hand to his mouth and bit off a chunk of fingernail. Blood oozed from the tip of his finger and he wiped the drop on his pants.

"Don't do that," I whispered. "The scent will draw them."

His eyes widened and he stopped chewing on his nails. "The scent of what?"

"Your blood." I scanned the injury and felt relief when it didn't close before my eyes. I hugged my knees to my chest and managed a shaky laugh. "I've been with them since I disappeared from camp yesterday morning. I watched them kill Emil last night. There wasn't anything I could do to stop it. They wanted me and he got in the way."

"What?"

"Emil Larson's dead?" Mark repeated.

I nodded. "He came to look for me and walked into a trap. It's my fault."

Mark sat beside me and patted my back. "You can't blame yourself."

"I can and do." The memory of Emil's death brought on a return of fear. I had to get Mark and Shelley away from the valley before they could share Emil's fate.

But I had to admit it was wonderful to be with someone who didn't glow. I was loathe to make them leave, and was ashamed of myself for feeling that way.

"What're you two doing out here? And why were you following me? I thought you were more of the Incubi."

"What are Incubi?"

"That's what the heart-eaters call themselves. I just barely got away from another of their welcoming committees in the old city."

"You've been there?"

"Yes. It's Tamoanchan. I received a tour from Tolquen."

"Who's Tolquen?" Mark asked.

I told an abbreviated version of the story. When I finished, there was stunned silence. Mark lifted the shell and stared at it, enthralled.

"Wow. It really is loaded, then. You said your guide, Rich, is one of these things?"

"Yes. But he's a good Incubus. There's some power struggle going on, over me. Both sides want me. They think I'm supposed to be their first female member and usher them into a new golden age of prosperity. They want to be worshipped again."

Mark whistled and shook his head. "It's weird to hear you talk about ancient gods as living, walking people."

"Imagine how it feels to meet and talk to them," I said. "That's really weird."

"I'll bet. There's no hope of trying to explain this to the authorities. They'd never believe it."

Shelley nodded. "We'll have to think of another way."

"I can't ask you two to get involved. It's too dangerous. If you'll forget you saw me, that'll be help enough. I'm running from everyone, and there's no one I can turn to."

"All the more reason you need our help," Shelley said, getting to her feet.

"I don't suppose I can talk either of you out of this? If they know you're helping me, they'll come after you, too."

Shelley shook her head and smiled. Mark hesitated for a second, then made a similar gesture. I smiled my gratitude and wiped the last of the mud from my face.

"Thank you, both of you. Do either of you have any ideas about how we're going to get out of here? Between the Incubi and the *federales*, we seem to be surrounded."

"We have a van stashed in the woods, over the next rise," Mark said, gesturing deeper into the jungle. "We could be there in less than ten minutes."

"That's a start, but where do you propose we go?"

"Let's take one step at a time," Shelley said. "Getting to the van is step one."

"You two stay put a minute," Mark said. "I'll scout ahead a bit to make sure no one's around."

"You have to look for plumed serpents and bulls," I said. When I heard the words I realized how insane they sounded.

But Mark was an ally in a thousand. He didn't even blink. "Gotcha."

I looked at him, noting his flushed cheeks and the sparkle in his eye. "You're enjoying this."

"Of course. I always wanted to be a secret agent. This is the closest I'm likely to get."

"Then you believe me, about the Incubi?"

"No," he said with complete honesty. "But I'm willing to give you the benefit of the doubt."

"I believe you, kid," Shelley said, flashing a scowl at Mark. "I know you better than he does."

"Thanks. Unfortunately, I have a feeling he's going to have all the proof he needs, sooner than he thinks."

"Wonderful. I can't wait." He left us to make sure the path was clear.

I turned to Shelley. "You didn't tell me how you came to be in the jungles of Mexico at just the right time."

"I overheard a phone call from that sheriff to Norman Mathews."

"Tell the truth. You listened in."

"Of course I did. I always listen when it involves you. Where do you think I get my information?"

"What did the sheriff say?"

"He was pretty mad."

"Was this after he found the body in my house?"

Shelley shook her head. Her graying hair, never willing to submit to a style under the best of circumstances, frizzed in the humid air. She brushed it back with her hand and emitted an impatient curse. "Before. He got an anonymous phone call. Someone called the station to report they saw you struggling with a big sack."

"And the sheriff believed that? He's the one who told me to leave. How did he get into my house?"

"He got a search warrant, then called back and insisted Norman meet him there to act as your representative."

"You're joking. I'll bet Norman loved that. So he was on the scene when they discovered the body. Interesting."

Shelley gave up on the hair. Pulling a rubber band from the enormous purse she had slung over her shoulder, she pulled her mane into a severe ponytail and knotted it at her nape. "Yeah, but I don't think he enjoyed it. He looked awful when he got back to the office. He called his secretary and told her to get him on the next plane to Mexico. So I had her get me a ticket, too. Then a call came through from the dig, explaining that you and Emil were missing."

"How'd he take that news?"

"Not well. He was concerned. He called the sheriff, though, and told him you were missing."

"Great. Add another nail to my coffin."

"That's basically right," Shelley said, nodding. "Of course, the sheriff was convinced you were trying to flee. He issued an APB for you and Emil."

"Why Emil?"

"Beats me. Maybe he thought Emil assisted you to escape. Whatever the reason, you're both wanted in the States. When Norman heard that, he told the people down here to call in the authorities."

"I heard that. What am I supposed to do now? I'm running out of places to hide."

"We look a lot alike," Shelley said. "You could use my passport."

"We don't look that much alike. Besides, I can't get you involved in this. What would you do for a passport? You'd be stuck here, maybe for years."

"I'm already involved."

"But not criminally. Let's keep it that way as long as we can."

"If you say so." Shelley glanced up. "There's Mark. He's signaling for us to follow. Are you ready?"

"I guess. Let's go."

We ran toward Mark, keeping low to the ground and as close to the bushes as possible. No one shouted, and no one moved to intercept us. We topped the rise and I saw the van ahead. I stopped next to the trunk of a large tree.

"Come on," Shelley urged. "We're almost there."

"Why didn't you try to hide it?" I said, suddenly uneasy. "It's like a beacon, telling everyone we're here."

"I checked it out," Mark said. "No one found it."

I stayed where I was, waiting. My stomach felt knotted and unsettled. I glanced around, trying to identify the source of the unease.

"There's an Incubus close by," I said in a soft voice.

Mark and Shelley moved closer to my side. I felt their bodies tense as they surveyed the surrounding terrain.

"How close?"

I shook my head. "Not too close, but not far enough. What are we going to do?"

"I vote we run for the van," Mark said. "If there's one around, we stand a better chance of outrunning it in the vehicle."

"Good point," Shelley said in agreement.

I drew a deep breath and let it out slowly. Mark's argument made sense. "Okay. I'm right behind you."

I followed them across the rocky ground, my inner fear growing with each step I took. As if sensing my mood, the shell around my neck grew heavier, weighing me down. I got ten yards from the van before I stopped, unable to take another step.

"I can't," I said, panting. "Something's wrong."

"Are you sure you're not imagining it," Mark said in irritation. "Everything seems fine to me."

I shook my head and backed away from the van. "No. There's an Incubus in there, and it's not a friendly one. We have to get out of here. Now."

I turned to run back the way I had come. I heard the van's cargo door open. Shelley screamed. I stopped dead.

"Leave them alone," I said.

"I'll be happy to," the Incubus said. "As soon as you come back here."

"Run, Mar—"

I heard the sound of flesh connecting with something more solid. Mark's shout died on a grunt of pain. I closed my eyes and clenched my hands into fists. I'm ashamed to say it, but for one fraction of a second, I considered taking Mark's advice. More than anything, I wanted to run. But I knew I didn't have the stamina to evade the Incubi for years to come, just as I knew they would never give up the hunt. For good or ill, my destiny was so firmly locked with theirs that any freedom I might enjoy would be a momentary illusion. They would always be there, waiting for me to lower my defenses. Besides, I couldn't leave my friends to a fate I refused to face. I turned to face my adversary.

He held Shelley close to his elongated body. His eyes glowed green and scales still covered the skin of his arms. Mark lay in the dust at his feet, staring up in mute terror. While we watched, the Incubus completed his transformation to human shape and stood, smiling at us through lowered lashes.

I didn't feel the least bit surprised.

"Hello, Norman," I said in an even voice. "I wondered when you'd show up."

Chapter 22

"I GUESS THAT meddling Tolquen told you about me."

His lips formed and filled in, and the scales faded from view. He did not, however, let go of Shelley.

I faced him and I hoped I displayed more guts than I felt. My knees were shaking and my dry tongue seemed welded to the roof of my mouth. "Tolquen had nothing to do with it, other than to tell me the Incubi can't have sex. I always wondered why you insisted on waiting till after the wedding."

"There was never a question of a ceremony," Norman admitted. "I needed to know what you were working on, and pretending interest in you was the only way to get close enough to find out. You should have accepted the obscurity we offered. We might have allowed you to live in peace."

"You expect me to believe you would've left me alone?" I asked, scoffing. "What about the people you killed in Pennsylvania?"

Norman shrugged. "Someone acted without orders. They've paid the price."

"What about the body in my house?"

"Your sheriff is a suspicious man," Norman admitted. "We had to make sure he never found out the truth. You provided the perfect scapegoat, my dear. He suspected you from the beginning. I just helped him along."

While we talked, Mark backed away. When he was out of reach of Norman's lightening-quick grasp, he got to his feet and hurried to my side.

"How do we bring him down?" he asked.

Norman laughed. "If she could, she'd have done it by now. Unfortunately, she left her protectors behind. I'm not sorry to say they were destroyed."

My muscles flinched uncontrollably. Emotion clogged my throat. For a moment I couldn't speak. First Emil, now the snake and bull from the shell. And I was responsible for their deaths. I thought they were invincible. Finding they were not almost defeated me. I waited, struggling for control. I had to convince Norman to let Shelley and Mark go. To do that, I had to pretend nonchalance and await my chance.

When I thought I could trust my voice, I asked, "You were there?"

"Not in the battle. I stuck to the plan. Barghest wants you alive. I have the honor of escorting you to meet him. We can use this van."

I licked my lips, stalling for time. "I'll go with you. Let these two go."

He laughed and tightened his grip on Shelley. Her face contorted in pain. She bit her lip to keep from crying out. "I think not. They know what I am. If you cooperate I might let them live long enough to meet Barghest. If not, they'll die here. It makes no difference to me."

Mark stepped forward. I grabbed his arm to haul him back.

"Let go," he insisted, trying to pull away. "We're as good as dead anyway. While he's busy with us, you can escape and find the good Incubi."

Norman looked up, feigning a smile of regret. "Didn't I tell you? I must've forgotten. Tolquen and his spawn were destroyed by Ahuizotl. The Macadro lives, for now. However, I think you'll find Barghest more sympathetic to your feelings."

Grief contracted my heart, robbing me of the will to fight. Norman's news forced me to accept the inevitable meeting with Barghest, but I'd never accept the consequences. I squared my shoulders, more determined than ever to deny him the union he sought.

Norman, using the ability if the Incubi to read my thoughts, laughed. "How noble you are, Marty. Prepared to sacrifice your worthless life rather than join the immortals. Admirable, but foolish. Get into the van."

I hesitated, then moved to obey. As long as Norman held onto Shelley, I had no choice but to do what he asked. I still had the shell, and the star inside. Unfortunately, I sensed its diminished strength. The absence of the snake and the bull depleted its power, and I didn't know if enough remained to mount a serious attack. Something told me Barghest wouldn't approach me alone.

The shell stayed quiet, marshaling its strength, biding its time. I wondered if the star waited for the meeting with Barghest to make its presence known. I'd have to wait and see and trust it to protect me.

I was about to step into the front passenger seat when Norman stopped me. "In the back. You ride with me. Andrews will drive, and Peterson can sit in the front with him."

I flashed him a look of contempt and did as ordered.

Mark took his seat and reached for the ignition. I held my breath, hoping the van wouldn't start. No such luck. It roared into life and Mark put it in gear. He followed Norman's directions to the letter, negotiating treacherous mountain passes until we neared the border with Guatemala.

"Is that where Barghest lives?" I asked, gesturing toward the fence that separated the two countries. "How do you expect to get past the border patrol? You forget we left our passports behind."

Norman grinned but didn't answer. Instead, he reached out to rip the shell from its chain around my neck. It happened so fast I didn't have time to stop him. He opened his window and tossed the shell outside.

"You don't need it anymore," Norman said, amused by the panic I could not hide. "It's empty, worthless. Barghest will give you true wealth beyond your imaginings. Wearing cheap trinkets from his rival will only enrage him and make it more difficult for you."

He leaned closer and draped his arm across the back of my chair. "I see the mention of Barghest frightens you. I could spare you, you know."

I cleared my throat. "What do you mean?"

He lifted a wisp of hair that had escaped my ponytail. "I'd be gentler. And quick. I promise you'd feel no pain."

"You'd allow me to die?"

He chuckled and bent to nuzzle my neck. I tensed, praying he wouldn't sense my hatred.

"Not die. We couldn't kill you, none of us. That would defeat the purpose."

"What purpose? What is the prophecy all about?"

"Ah. Tolquen withheld that information, and wisely. The outcome wasn't certain."

"And it is now?"

I saw Shelley lean back in her chair, listening. I leaned closer to Norman, hoping my demeanor would keep him talking. It was possible he would let something slip that we could use against him.

"Of course. Barghest knows I'd never let you escape."

"But you would betray him by making me the first female?" I said, tolerating his touch to hide my surprise. Ahuizotl had said much the same thing. It seemed Barghest had placed his trust in demons who were selfish and untrustworthy to a fault. But how could I use that to my advantage? "You can do that?"

"I can."

"Wouldn't that make you a traitor? Why would you risk it?"

"The risk would be more than worth it," Norman assured me. "According to the Prophecy, the Incubus who converts the chosen female will return stronger than all the others, even the Macadro. He will rule our kind. The human population will be at his mercy."

"What do you mean, return?"

Norman frowned. "That part of the Prophecy is likely gibberish. Nevertheless, both the elders believe making the first female will give them dominion over the other."

"Is that what the prophecy is all about?"

He frowned. "That's part of it. It depends on which side succeeds. Even we don't know what the outcome will be. The rantings of the old witch who began it all are vague, but we know there'll be a struggle over you."

I swallowed hard. For once, having my suspicions confirmed gave me no gratification. "What are the possible outcomes?"

"On one hand, a new golden age."

"That's what Tolquen said, but what does it mean? Prosperity for who?"

"For us. It means we'll be worshipped and adored, of course. It's our right."

"And the alternative?"

Norman shrugged. "Barghest believes that if the Macadro wins we'll cease to exist."

"How?"

"Ah, that's the question," he admitted. "That's the weak point in his theory, and the main reason I think he's wrong. We can't be destroyed by any but a stronger Incubus, and no fledgling could accomplish that. Personally, I think his fears are ridiculous, but the Macadro shares them." He laughed and put a hand on my shoulder. His sharp yellow teeth were uncomfortably close to my chest, his unwavering gaze fastened on my left breast. "What do you expect from a couple of prehistoric Neanderthals?"

"We're about to cross the border," Mark said from the front seat.

Norman didn't look up. "Get in the right-hand lane, behind the red car."

We inched our way forward. I bit my lip and tried to think. Norman sat between me and the door, blocking escape that way. I looked out the window and craned my neck to get a peek at the guards. They stopped each vehicle to inspect passports. As I watched, the guard in our lane forced two cars to turn away, denying entry into the country. I wondered how Norman proposed to get around that.

The guard turned another car away and we moved into second place in line. I tensed, watching the border patrol go over the passports of the occupants in the vehicle ahead. He scrutinized them for several minutes before ordering a search of the car.

Mark turned to Norman. "Do you want me to get out of line? I still have enough room to turn around."

"Certainly not. The other car proceeded through. Pull forward."

Mark shrugged and did as Norman told him. He moved the van to the gate and rolled down his window. The guard asked for passports in a bored voice. I looked at the passenger door, debating. I was about to risk making a run for it when Norman's arm fell across my shoulders like a lead weight, holding me in place. He leaned forward to speak to the guard.

"You don't need our passports," he said in a calm, reasonable voice.

The border guard's head snapped up and he looked at us with suspicion. His eyes locked with Norman's. I blinked and turned away, defeated.

The eyes of the guard glowed yellow in response to Norman's amused scrutiny. They watched each other for a long time. Finally, the guard's gaze shifted to me. He smiled and motioned us through the gate.

Mark tore his wide-eyed gaze from the guard and obeyed. I saw his knuckles turn white when he gripped the wheel. Beside him, Shelley sobbed and covered her face with her hands.

Another Incubus, waiting on the Guatemalan side, allowed us to pass. The wheels of the van barely stopped turning beside the guard's station. Once through, Norman directed Mark to follow a narrow dirt road into the jungle. In less than an hour the road faded away and we traversed a rutted path into the mountains. The van's shocks were no match for the pitted, tangled animal track. I dipped and swayed around until a stomach-clenching dip forced me into Norman's waiting arms.

I struggled and pushed but couldn't break free. Thankfully, we didn't have far to go. When I knew I'd get sick from Norman's close proximity, he barked an order to halt. He released me. I slumped against the cushions of the seat, gasping for air.

The view out the window chilled me. We stopped on a narrow ledge, the end of the path. On the left, the ledge ended about six inches from the outer rim of the van's tires. It was a sheer drop to the valley below. I looked at Shelley.

Her condition concerned me. She stared out the window with

glazed eyes, ignoring Mark's hand on her arm. Norman grinned in delight. Moving so swiftly his limbs were a blur, he got out of the van, wrenched Shelley's door open, and pulled her out onto the ledge. Anger filled me. I followed him out and beat on his back with both fists.

"Leave her alone. Can't you see she's terrified?"

Norman faced me, grinning. "I don't have time for cowards. If you can get her to move she'll live a while longer. If not, she dies here."

He moved away. I dropped to the ground beside Shelley. I put my arms around her and tried to comfort her. After a few minutes, her trembling eased and she was able to nod her head in response to my concerned comments.

"I'm all right," she said at last. "Forgive me, Marty"

"For what?"

"I never believed you. I thought I did, and I said I did, but I didn't. Until now."

"Same here," Mark said. He bent over us and placed a reassuring hand on my back. "I'm a believer."

"That doesn't help us any, but it sure is good to hear," I said, forcing my lips to smile.

"What are we going to do?" Shelley asked in a stronger voice.

"I have an idea," Mark said, dropping his voice to the merest thread of a whisper. "If we could get behind him, we could push him over the cliff and escape in the van. These Incubi can't fly, can they?"

"No," I said, shaking my head. "But they can change shape."

Mark paled. "Into what?"

"A snake or a bull, as far as I know. If they can convert to anything else, I haven't seen it."

Shelley, who still stared straight ahead, stiffened. "We're too late," she whispered.

I followed her gaze. While we talked, Norman worked. He opened the cargo door of the van and extracted the supplies Shelley and Mark had brought along. Then he moved to the center of the van, placed his hands under the carriage, and lifted.

"Oh my God," Mark said in a weak voice.

The van rolled onto its side, then tipped over the ledge. We heard it break apart long before the ruptured gas tank exploded at the foot of the mountain.

Norman looked at us and laughed. "There will be no escape that way, I assure you. And before you get any more bright ideas, let me warn you I can do the same to each of you any time I wish. Shall we go?"

His harsh laughter filled the ledge. The air throbbed with it. It bounced off the rocky walls and echoed throughout the still mountain pass.

I couldn't imagine a more secluded location anywhere on the face of the earth. And no one knew we were there.

Chapter 23

"BRING THE WATER and the flashlights," Norman ordered. "You won't need the food."

The harsh sunlight glinted off his thinning hair and showed lines and wrinkles I had never noticed before. He seemed to tower over us, his tall frame gaining stature as a result of the unbelievable strength he had displayed.

I blinked and studied him again. He appeared human in a clean, starched shirt opened at the throat, and pressed trousers. I wondered which of the ancient gods he had been. Something nasty and despicable, I had no doubt.

We each hefted a jug of water and a light. Norman led the way down the ledge, back the way we'd come. After about twenty yards, he turned away from the path and indicated a narrow pass between the cliffs. He made us precede him through the opening.

The hard dirt showed signs of recent use, not all of it human. I saw hoof prints and long, tubular indentations indicating the passage of other animals. From the absence of droppings or mats of fur, I deduced the tracks were made by Incubi in their various incarnations. The thought made my muscles tighten to the breaking point.

I knew we'd finally found an ancient ceremonial center, but my curiosity died a natural death. I had no desire to see it, or the ceremonies conducted within.

Norman walked at the back of the line to keep an eye on us. Even if I had a plan that might work, I had no hope of communicating it to my fellow captives. The path was so narrow we had to walk in single file between the cliffs, making secret conversation impossible. No cooling breezes could penetrate the walls of stone. It wasn't long before my clothes were plastered to my sweat-soaked skin. My heavy denim jeans felt like lead weights. In addition, the thin mountain air robbed me of strength. It was all I could do to pull my body up the steep grade. I was out of breath before I had walked twenty feet, and from the sounds of their wheezing breaths, Mark and Shelley were in no better shape than I.

We hadn't gone far when the path came to a sudden end at the face of another cliff. We found ourselves surrounded by towering rocks. The path broadened at the end to allow us to huddle together. Mark ran a hand over the walls, feeling for unseen footholds. He glanced at me and made a wry face. The rock was as smooth as it appeared.

At last, Norman appeared. He walked past us to the barrier and pushed against the rock. It moved inward without a sound. He grabbed the flashlight from Shelley's limp grasp and switched on the power. Inside the cliff, a broad tunnel led into darkness. Cool air reached out to dry the sweat covering my body.

"Where are we?" Mark asked.

"You anthropologists and students of Mayan lore know it as *Bolontiku*," Norman said.

I exchanged looks with Mark and Shelley. "The Land of the Nine Gods? We thought *Bolontiku* was a euphemism for hell in the Mayan religion."

"I know," Norman laughed. He ushered us into the passage and pushed the huge boulder back into position. Once the door was closed, all sound and light vanished. Norman turned on a flashlight and allowed the beam to illumine the walls. They were close, but dry. "As you can see, it's a real place."

Norman moved away from the door. Mark took his place there. His face grew red and his breathing labored as he tried to move the stone. I turned to Norman and asked questions, hoping to divert his attention from Mark's efforts.

"And *Oxlahuntiku*? Is that a real place, too?"

"The Land of the Thirteen Gods," Norman said sarcastically. "That's the name they gave the Macadro's lair. It exists."

"Interesting that the Maya considered Barghest's hiding place hell and the Macadro's heaven," Shelley said. "Doesn't that tell you anything, Norman?"

"It tells me humans are fools. Just as Mark is a fool. You don't need to hide what you're doing. Go ahead and give the rock a good push. All three of you at once. I'll wait."

Norman turned the beam to light the door, then leaned against the wall of the tunnel. Shelley and I went to help Mark.

Though we pushed and pulled until we were once again drenched in sweat, we couldn't make the rock shift a fraction of an inch. I gave up when I felt a muscle pull in my shoulder.

Norman laughed. "Our strength is no match for you. Accept it."

"What do you want, Norman," Mark said, panting. "Why show us this?"

"You haven't seen anything yet," Norman said. "Come with me. I'll show you wonders you've only dreamt of."

"I think I'll pass."

"You have no choice. We've wasted enough time. Come."

Norman got behind us and pushed us along. I turned on my flashlight in an attempt to banish the gloom. Even with its aid, the going was rough. The passage descended at a steep angle for some time, then ended at a flight of crude stone steps. With Norman driving us on, we had no choice but to go down the uneven stairs.

The steps seemed to go into the very heart of the mountain. I tried to count them, but lost track at 217. Unlike the caves of the hidden city, this tunnel was unadorned. Indeed, the chiseled walls were rough and unfinished, indicating the ancient carvers hurried through their work. I could understand why. The place reeked of death and despair. With each step we took, the odor grew stronger until it surrounded us like a thick blanket of smoke. Shelley wretched and gagged and clung to the wall for support. By the time we reached the end of the steps my legs felt like thin strands of melting rubber and my heart slammed against my ribs. I knew if I could hear it beating, it must be driving Norman mad.

I glanced in his direction. He smiled and licked his lips. I looked away.

We moved through another long passage that ended in another flight of steps. When we reached the bottom, Norman allowed us a few minutes to rest before resuming the trek. I opened my water jug and took a large mouthful, then spat the vile liquid into the dust. I saw Shelley raise her jug. Before she could take a sip, I knocked it out of her hands. It flew against the wall, spilling crimson liquid all over the chamber.

"Very funny, Norman," I said, making no attempt to hide my anger. "You're repulsive."

Mark, his eyes wide, checked the last jug. It, too, contained blood. "Why?"

"Their blood is addictive," I said, wiping my tongue on my shirt. "One drink and you'll crave it forever."

"I guess Tolquen told you more than I thought," Norman said, smiling. "It was worth a try."

"You're an asshole," Shelley said in contempt.

"Ooh," Norman said, feigning fear. "The big bad scientist called me a naughty word. Come along. There's so much more to see."

When we reached the next set of stairs I groaned aloud.

"I won't go," Shelley said, stopping short.

"I won't go, either," Mark agreed.

I went to stand beside them. "Now what are you going to do? You can't kill me. Even if you could, I'd prefer to die here. How many of your friends are waiting for us down there?"

"Use your head," Norman snapped. "You can feel our presence. How many Incubi do you sense?"

I flashed him a wary glance, then closed my eyes. I stood for a long time, trying to get a feel for the place.

Finally, Mark placed a hand on my arm. "Well? What do you think?"

I shook my head. "I can't feel any more Incubi. But that might not mean anything."

"I'm telling you I'm the only one here," Norman said. "Now move."

Shelley stayed where she was. "No."

Norman rolled his eyes and came forward. He lifted her with one hand and threw her across his shoulder. He grabbed me with his free hand. Then he turned to Mark.

"Follow or not, as you wish. I won't come back for you. If you're still here when I leave this place I'll stop to have a little snack. If you want to stay alive you'll keep as close to these two as you can."

Left with no choice, Mark followed Norman down the stairs. The farther we went, the worse the odor became. The rotting smell mingled with the damp, fetid aroma of fungi and slime. The surrounding walls were covered with sick growth. Here and there, a small stream of greenish water trickled from the ceiling, feeding the dank pools that formed on the slippery rock. It was all I could do to keep my balance. With Norman dragging me along, I stumbled and slid down the treacherous stairs.

We emerged in another dark tunnel, but the light of the flash revealed carvings and paintings decorating the walls. It was a relief to have something other then our captor to look at. When Norman set me free, I turned on my light and took a look around.

Mark whistled. "These can't be Mayan."

Shelley joined us in front of the crude mural. "They look like the paintings at Lascaux."

"I think you're right," Mark said. "The technique is the same, and so are the animals."

"Except the snake with the glowing eyes," I said, pointing. "And look at this. This scene is definitely Mayan."

Next to the snake, a mural depicted a plumed serpent watching a man tied to a ceremonial altar. A priest waited over the prisoner, a flint hatchet resembling Tolquen's *u-kab-ku* held in his hand, ready to open the victim's chest.

"Look familiar?" I said, turning to Mark.

He nodded. "The gold disc found in the *cenote* at Chichen Itza has a similar scene carved on it."

"It's also found on the Temple of the Warriors," Shelley said.

"It's more than that," I said. "This scene is about the Incubi. Look at the man on the throne. Blond hair, blue eyes. It's Quentin, the one they call the Macadro."

"Enough of this," Norman said, grabbing my wrist. He seemed to gain immense satisfaction from the pain of others, especially me. "You're wasting time."

He walked down the corridor, ushering Shelley and me before him. The corridor went on for at least a hundred yards, then stopped. The light showed another boulder blocking the path.

Norman moved it aside and, turning to me, grabbed the flashlight out of my hand. He took Mark and Shelley's, too. Then he pushed us into the room beyond.

We didn't see the steps until it was too late. Luckily, there were only half a dozen or so. One by one we tumbled down, landing in a pile of brittle bones at the bottom.

We didn't need the light to show us the kind of bones they were. The pitiful remains of thousands of human beings filled the pit, and not all of them were clean of flesh. We found the source of the stench. Shelley sobbed and Mark cursed. I stifled a scream and tried to stand. My feet sank into the pile, snapping bones like they were dry twigs.

Norman tossed three of the flashlights out into the passage. He turned the last light to shine in our faces. I heard him laugh.

"What is the matter with you all? Didn't you become anthropologists to study bones? I wouldn't struggle if I were you," he said, shaking his head. "We've occupied this place for a long time. The pile is quite deep."

"Help us out of here, Mathews," Mark shouted. "You've had your fun. I'll admit I'm scared half to death."

"This is nothing compared to what you're going to feel when Barghest arrives."

"You're a bastard," Mark said. "I'll bet you're looking forward to watching us sweat. I'm not going to give you the satisfaction."

"You misunderstand me," Norman said in a suave voice that

turned me cold. "As much as I'd like to, I'm afraid I can't stay. I have my orders and I must carry them out."

He turned to go. Shelley screamed and tried to follow. Her struggles only succeeded in burying her body deeper in the pile. Every time she moved, clouds of powdered flesh rose up to choke us. I reached out a hand and tried to calm her. She flinched from my touch.

"Please, Norman, don't leave us here," Shelley pleaded.

Norman stopped at the doorway and turned around. "You bore me. Mortals never knew how to die with dignity. Your crying and sobbing all over the place gets tiresome very quickly. That's one reason I'm glad I don't have to hang around."

Shelley sniffled and quieted. Norman's observations were as good as a slap across the face. I felt calmer immediately.

"At least leave the light," I said.

Norman grinned. "I think not." He paused, then switched off the flash and set it beside the door. "On second thought, it wouldn't do to piss off Barghest's mate. I'll leave it here."

The cave returned to darkness. I saw Norman's eyes glow through the gloom. With their light, I could just make out his movements.

"Goodbye, for the present. The next time we meet, dear Marty, you'll have a different attitude toward me."

"I doubt that."

"I don't."

He walked through the doorway and pulled the stone into place behind him. The last thing I saw before darkness closed in was the faint yellow glow of amusement in his shining eyes.

The stone closed with an audible click, sealing us in with the bones.

Chapter 24

I ADMIT IT. For a minute, I panicked. The absence of light was so profound it settled over me like a living, breathing entity. It grew and pressed closer, stealing my ability to reason. Within seconds, I lost all sense of direction, all memory of light.

The bones of thousands of decomposed bodies pressed against me, giving the impression of many fleshless hands reaching out to steal my blood-soaked flesh. My screams blended with Shelley's, echoing off the cavern walls, bouncing against my eardrums like drumsticks hitting a steel drum. Something rose out of the darkness to slap me. It was several seconds before I registered the fact that the hand still bore a coating of warm, pliable skin. When the second slap came, I almost welcomed the stinging feel of it.

"Shut up, both of you," Mark said, loud enough to be heard over Shelley's wild sobs. The walls of the cave caught and repeated his voice, driving the living timbre of it through my hysteria. "This isn't doing any good."

The words gave me something on which to focus. My paroxysm melted away, leaving me ashamed of my behavior. I got control of my rampaging imagination and nodded. Realizing he couldn't see my action, I spoke. "You're right. I'm sorry."

"Don't apologize. See what you can do about Shelley."

Her screams quieted to a series of demoralizing moans and sniffles that were, somehow, worse. Straining every muscle in my body, I followed the sound of her voice. Leaning toward her, I placed a hand on her shoulder. She flinched in terror, trying to pull away. She sank deeper into the pile of bones. If she continued to fight she'd soon be buried in the things. I shuddered.

"Take it easy, Shelley," I said, using the tone I reserved for disruptive students. "Stop blubbering and help us find a way out of this."

Her hand closed over mine. When she finally spoke her voice sounded stronger, more assured. "Marty. Thank God. It's so dark. I can't see a thing."

"Cave darkness," Mark agreed. "It's enough to drive a person mad. I suggest we all keep talking until we can make it to the flashlight. The sound will help keep us oriented."

"Good idea," I said.

"Agreed," Shelley responded. "Who's closest to the steps?"

"I think I am," Mark said. "It's so damned dark I lost all sense of direction, though. Anyone know for certain what you were facing when the lights went out?"

"I think...No, I can't be sure," Shelley said. "Marty?"

"I'm not sure, either. We need a light. Anyone have matches, or a lighter?"

Mark's laugh was grim. "I gave up smoking three months ago. For my health. Right now, I'd trade thirty years of life for one stinking cigarette and a match to light it with."

"Wait a minute," Shelley said. "I might have a match."

"You?"

"She collects them," I said while Shelley tried to get her free hand into her purse. "She collects everything. If you need anything, just ask for it."

There was a little pause, during which I heard her rummage through the enormous bag. "Sorry," she said at last, disappointed. "Nothing."

"Don't worry about it," Mark reassured her. "We'll have to do this the hard way. Give me your hand, Marty."

I stretched toward the sound of his voice, fingers extended. His warm, human grasp banished the last of my fear. I clung to him with my left hand and to Shelley with my right.

"Good," Mark said. "Now I'll move around a little—try to find the steps."

"Hurry," I said. It was becoming harder to keep my grip on Shelley. I felt her sink another inch. Before too much longer, her face would slip below the surface of the bones.

I felt him push forward, toward the place we agreed the steps were likely to be. It was a mistake. The movement caused the bones to shift, burying me deeper in the pile. By the time Mark moved a foot my shoulders were covered.

"You'll have to hurry," I gasped. "I'm sinking."

The weight of the skeletons pressed against my chest, making it difficult to breathe. Although I hated to lose the contact of flesh on flesh, I had to pull back.

"Marty? Do you have her, Shelley?"

"Yes. I think she's stable now. She stopped sinking."

Mark swore. "It's like trying to swim in Jello. Every time one of us moves it shakes the whole pit."

"You have to try it," I said, pushing bones away from my mouth. "We'll die if we stay here."

"I'll give it another shot. Try to hang on, kid."

He didn't wait for a response. Bones snapped as he pushed his way through. I closed my eyes to keep the dust out, but there was nothing I could do to keep from breathing it in. The musty stench rising from the churned pile made me gag and wretch.

Mark's grunts of exertion masked another sound, coming from my right. I wasn't aware of anything wrong until Shelley's hand tightened on mine, crushing it. I let out a cry of pain and tried to pull away. She held me fast, moaning deep in her throat.

"What is it? What's the matter?" Mark sounded both startled and exasperated.

Then I heard him suck air through clenched teeth. "What the hell is that," he whispered.

"What?" I asked, craning my neck. "What do you see?" Then, all at once, I remembered why we were here. Terror overwhelmed me. For a second I think my heart stopped beating. "Barghest," I said. "He's come."

I looked around, careless of the bones surrounding me. I'd rather die from suffocation than submit to Barghest's master plan.

Dislodging the pelvic bone lodged against my back, I turned my body, squinting through the gloom to find the source of Mark's anxiety. I wanted to see the fiend before I died.

A second later I saw it—a tiny shaft of light no larger than the slit between closed mini-blinds. Something was trying to squeeze through the opening. I didn't wait to see what it was.

"Move," I ordered, then winced when the shout bounced off the stone, magnified ten-fold. I pushed Shelley away with all my strength. "Go in the opposite direction. Go."

I didn't wait to determine whether or not they followed my advice. Arms and legs pumping, I swam through the sea of bones in Mark's direction. One brief glance behind me and I knew I wouldn't make it.

The thing succeeded in squeezing through. I saw light, but not the kind I wanted to see. The yellow ball hung in the air for a second, then started across the huge expanse of cave, making unerringly for me.

Shelley screamed and doubled her pace. On my other side, Mark followed her example. The dust they created rose up in billowing clouds, reflecting the yellow light generated by the thing. Soon it was so thick I could see nothing but the glowing ball descending upon me at a breathless pace.

I stopped fighting. It was finally over. I knew it. There was no defense against the Incubi when they chose this incarnation, and I was tired. I turned my body to face it, sinking deeper into the snapping bones. By the time it reached me, only my eyes protruded from the grave.

It didn't slow at all. It swooped down, growing stronger, then stopped just above my head. The light intensified, revealing the steps. Mark made it first and called to me.

"Run, Marty. You're only a yard away. Hurry."

I couldn't take my eyes from the ball. An idea came to me, but I was afraid to believe it was true.

As if reading my thoughts, the ball dipped lower, grazing the top of my head. I closed my eyes and smiled in relief.

"I don't know if I can get my hands up," I whispered.

It was easier than I thought. My arms slid from the pile like greased poles through sand. I hesitated, then extended them.

I'd never touched it, but I knew I had to. I expected it to burn my skin. Instead, it felt cool and solid to the touch. I wrapped my fingers around the sphere and let it rise, pulling me out. When my feet cleared the bones, the sphere stopped rising and made its way to the stone landing by the stairs. Then it lowered me until I stood beside Mark.

He had the flashlight in his hand, but he didn't use it. He didn't need to. Yellow light filled the cave, allowing us to discern Shelley's form. She seemed paralyzed with fright, unable to extract herself from the shifting pile.

I looked at my sphere and gestured toward Shelley. The ball dipped in answer, then lifted her from the pile. She soon stood with us on the landing.

"I'll be damned," she said in awe. "What is it?"

"My star," I said with pride. "One of my protectors. It was still in the shell when Norman pitched it from the van. I guess it followed us."

"I'll be damned," Mark echoed. "You mean it's friendly?"

"Obviously. Now we need to convince it to stay and deal with Barghest."

"Can it?" Shelley asked, her eyes widening.

"Oh, yes. I saw it kill at least eight Incubi without a hitch. Barghest won't be a problem."

"Killer shell, indeed," Mark said. "I swear, Marty, I'll never doubt another thing you say."

Just when I had almost recovered my waning courage, the sphere moved away, soaring toward the opening at the far end of the cave.

"Where's it going," Shelley said. "Make it come back."

I tried everything I knew. The sphere didn't even hesitate. It flew toward the opening and squeezed out with an audible pop. The darkness descended over us once again.

Mark switched on the flashlight, letting its light play around the landing. We all spotted the bright orange container at the same time. "Norman left one of the jugs," Mark said.

I grabbed it and pulled out the stopper. "It's filled with blood." I pitched the jug away.

Left with nothing else to do, we sat on the landing and watched the small fissure the shell had made in the cave. A tiny beam of sunlight dribbled through. It wasn't enough to light the cave, but it was something to look at. I hoped the sphere would return. The minutes dragged by. Finally, I turned away. My euphoria over the sphere's arrival died, leaving me more deflated.

My muscles chose that moment to give out. I sank to the cold stone and hugged my knees to my chest.

Shelley put an arm around my shoulders. "Maybe it went for help."

I shook my head. "Norman said the others were dead, and Quentin badly wounded. There's no one else on our side."

"Then it's outside, waiting for Barghest," Mark said. "Maybe it plans to deal with him before he can get to us."

"That's the answer," Shelley said.

"I hope you're right."

Mark got to his feet. "Of course I am. Come on. Let's see if we can get this door open."

"You don't know what these Incubi can do," I said, following the others. "Barghest is almost as strong as Quentin, and Quentin is hurt. It would take an army of spheres."

"And that's what we have," Mark said, studying the immense rock blocking the passage. "You said it can split into dozens of killing machines. We'll be fine. You can take that to the bank. Now come on and give me a hand."

Ten minutes later we heard the unmistakable sound of metal grinding against rock. Someone was on the other side of the door.

Moving as one body, the three of us backed away until there was nowhere to go. My gaze locked on the rock, watching it shudder, then start to swing. I felt evil. Rushing forward, I threw my weight against the rock. It was a futile attempt, but I had to do something.

"Help me," I pleaded. "Please."

Shelley hastened to obey, with Mark right behind her. Bracing my boots against the uneven landing, I leaned into the door with everything I had. Mark turned to place his back against the rock, then froze in disbelief. He pointed.

Shelley looked in the direction he indicated. "Shit," she said. "I hate snakes."

"What did you say?" I glanced over my shoulder and nearly collapsed.

One after another, snakes, as big around as my thighs, dropped through the hole across the cave. Collecting my wits, I grabbed the flashlight and trained it in that direction.

The first snake through had a luxuriant crop of shocking white hair on the top of its head. I recognized the second as the snake from my shell. The three that followed had black plumes—one curly, one straight and one kinky. The last snake was bald. The sphere dropped neatly through the opening and hovered above the reptiles, waiting for them to complete their transformations.

I threw the flashlight on top of the bones and placed my hands on my hips. "What the hell took you so long?"

Quentin, in naked human splendor, rose from the bones and cocked his head to one side. "Just like a woman. Always complaining."

"Humph. I see Norman exaggerated the extent of your injuries. Hello, Tolquen, Dokulu, R.J. Welcome to our humble cell."

The last snake completed his transformation and stepped forward. "How's it going, Peanut?"

"Doctor Larson," Mark said, his voice weak with surprise. "We thought you were dead."

Emil smiled. My heart flipped in my chest. "No longer," he said.

"You might change that sentence to say, 'For the moment,'" someone said behind me.

I whirled to face Norman, my euphoria dying. The rock had been pushed away. Several Incubi crowded the opening. Even so, I had no trouble picking Barghest from the pack. Tall and stately, he looked more like the leader of an ancient race than Quentin ever could. His eyes glittered under deep, bushy brows, and the angles of his chin were deadly sharp. High cheekbones threw his thick, full lips into shadow. Muscle atop muscle rippled at his slightest movement.

He pushed past his mob of followers to reach for me. I shrank back, my foot inches from the sea of bones.

"Don't touch me."

I saw anger in his eyes. He raised his foot to take another step; the step that would secure me in his animal grasp.

Literally caught between the devil and the deep blue sea, there weren't many options. Stealing myself against the feel of thousands of human bones pulling me into their grave, I took one last breath and prepared to join them in blessed oblivion.

"She's serious," Norman said. He rushed to Barghest's side and grabbed the big man's arm. "You must bring the female forward."

Barghest, his eyes glowing green, didn't seem to hear the impassioned plea. His gaze never left my face. I felt him reach out with his mind, attempting to establish a lock with mine. A finger of malice, tangible and electric, rose up to touch me. I stood transfixed, waiting for him to speak. His thoughts swept toward me with the inevitability of the relentless surf, and with ten times the power. Unlike the struggle with Mycerro on the plane, I had no hope of holding his malignant will at bay.

I felt the cloud approach my mind and marshaled what remained of my defenses. I couldn't pull my gaze from his. With every beat of my heart I expected to feel him establish an entry and succeed in his goal to dominate my mind.

Then, the minute I felt his premature triumph, the link severed with a rent I could feel through every cell in my body. The sensation robbed me of breath. I fell to my knees, gasping, and tried to ignore the pain.

Behind me, the Macadro laughed. "Come, Barghest. Did you think I'd allow you to corrupt her with that old ruse? She must make her choice. Take your parlor tricks and leave this place. The contest is over. You've lost."

Barghest appeared unconcerned. He bowed his head toward Quentin, but his smile indicated he wasn't ready to concede defeat. "Perhaps. But there is one who could yet persuade the Murdoch to join with me."

He raised his hand. Norman, after a gloating glance at me, stepped aside. One after the other, the followers of Barghest made way. A small, slim woman, clad in a flowing white robe, stepped out of the passage and glided into the cave. A gleaming gold belt cinched her tiny waist, and a steel dagger, its hilt encrusted with fiery jewels, dangled at her side. Her flowing auburn hair fell over her shoulders to rest on her firm breasts. The goddess came to my side and placed her hand on my cheek.

"Hello, my darling Martine," she said in a lilting, musical voice. "We are reunited at last. Stay with me. We can be together for eternity."

I forgot Mark and Shelley. Everything and everyone shriveled into insignificance when I looked into her brown eyes and saw the love I felt mirrored there. I placed my hand over hers and nuzzled my face against her palm. When I spoke, my voice broke with tender emotion.

"Mother," I was all needed to say.

Chapter 25

SILENCE DESCENDED for several minutes. Then the cave exploded in angry sound. Almost everyone moved at once. The uproar created a useful diversion.

Mark rushed forward and, with an impressive shove, knocked my mother from my side. He took her place before me. "Wake up, Marty," he shouted. "Can't you see what she is?"

Behind me, Emil and Tolquen raised their voices in admonition for Barghest's tactics, while the demon laughed again in triumph. Somewhere in the distance, I was aware of Shelley's soft sobs. My mother's arrival had shifted the tide of the battle. No one seemed to doubt the outcome, with the possible exception of Quentin. He alone watched the proceedings in waiting silence.

I remained on my knees, my gaze still locked with my mother's. She smiled, confident I would bend to her will. I considered my options. In the end, there was nothing else I could do.

I lowered my head and rose to my feet, careful to keep my arms crossed over my chest. The occupants of the cave grew silent. Mark made one last attempt to reason with me, but the look I flashed him made the plea die on his lips. With his shoulders slumped in dejection, he stepped back. I saw the hatred in his eyes before he turned away.

Mark's last action broke the spell. My mind cleared, allowing me to think. I recalled the cold feel of my mother's hand on my cheek, felt again the awful desolation I'd experienced when she abandoned me to join Barghest's camp. I had blamed myself for her defection. All those years of thinking I was unworthy came flooding back.

I stood up straight and looked at Shelley. She had filled the gap, loving me without question despite what I had done or would do. She had risked her career to come to my rescue. There was no way I could subject her to the same fate my mother embraced.

I turned to Barghest, the path I had to take finally clear in my mind. "I refuse the honor," I said again, this time with conviction.

His smile vanished. Cold anger glowed in his eyes. Beside him, my mother howled in outrage and let loose a string of epithets so foul I cringed from the sound. Whatever resided in the body that had been hers, there was nothing left of the gentle soul I had once loved.

Twenty-one years with Barghest had made her a creature of the darkest side of the human psyche.

For once, I had made the right choice.

Barghest's band of Incubi moved in to surround me. Before they could reach me, I pulled forth the dagger I had pinched from my mother's belt and held it against my chest. I looked at Mark and knew he understood. He slipped behind me, dragging Shelley with him.

"She's going to kill herself," Norman gasped. "Grab her."

I flashed him a defiant look and pressed the dagger into my flesh. "If one of you miserable has-beens comes near me I swear I'll do it."

Barghest rolled his eyes and looked past me. "Mortals can be so dramatic."

"Yes," Quentin said, amusement coloring his voice. "Don't you just love it?"

"No. I don't."

Barghest reached out, his short, muscular fingers brushing my arm. At the same time I leapt backward.

I never made contact with the bones. I was caught in mid-air and held. It took several seconds to realize there were real arms around me, a warm body next to mine. I opened my eyes and wound my arms around Dokulu's neck.

"What are you waiting for," I urged. "Let's get the hell out of here."

He laughed and shifted my body. "Hold on. I have to get your friends, too."

"Oh yeah. Well? Don't just stand there."

The sphere moved in to run interference. Swooping low, it flew close to Barghest's chest. He was taken aback long enough for Dokulu to grab Mark and Shelley and tuck one under each arm. Then we were off.

He slithered across that pit of bones without disturbing a single particle of dust. I didn't look down to see how he accomplished it. When we arrived on the other side Emil reached out to help me back to solid ground.

I barely had time to turn around. Someone reached out to drape another shell around my neck, then pushed me toward the opening.

"Get out of here," R.J. ordered.

"I can't fit through that."

Tolquen looked from my hips to the slit in the rock and grinned. "No, you cannot. Allow me."

Placing his hands on my shoulders, he pushed me back a pace.

Then, balling his hands into tight fists, he punched at the rock surrounding the narrow opening. In seconds it was wide enough for Mark's broad shoulders. Dokulu lifted Shelley and pushed her through.

Quentin and Mark were engaged in earnest conversation, heads bent together. I opened my mouth but the words remained unuttered. Mark turned away and pushed past me. Dokulu lifted him out of the cave.

"You're next, Peanut," Emil said. "Move."

"Wait a minute. I want to know what happened at the glade. Where have you been hiding all this time? Were you at Tamoanchan with Tolquen?"

Quentin elbowed Emil out of the way. "Your questions will have to wait, my dear." He gestured into the cave. "There isn't time."

He was right. Barghest and his followers, with Norman in the lead, came closer. I couldn't help searching for the figure of my mother. She was there, in the front of the line. Her beautiful face had twisted with the power of her hatred. She resembled an animal more than a human being.

She advanced, her venomous gaze locked on my face. Quentin's Incubi formed a line of defense. They shielded me until I could make my exit.

Barghest's eyes glowed green, indicating he was madder than hell. I held out my hands to Quentin and forced my gaze to his normal blue eyes.

"Take care."

Instead of lifting me out, he pulled me into his arms. Warm lips brushed mine. "No matter what happens, run. Keep running. Don't stop until you're well away from the mountain."

After that remarkable exhibition he almost threw me through the hole. I landed on the prickly remains of a dead bush; its fragile twigs snapped under my weight. The wind was knocked out of me. Nevertheless, I scrambled back to the hole and peered into the cave.

I bit back a scream at the sight of the raging battle. R.J. and Norman, their bodies twisted together, rolled through the bones. Below the neck each retained human form, but their heads were sleek and reptilian. Each tried to sink their massive jaws into the other's chest. Both were covered in blood.

I couldn't see Tolquen or Dokulu. From the sound of it, they were engaged in their own mortal struggle somewhere farther inside. Emil stood beside Quentin, who sat on top of the bones as if he didn't have a care in the world. His eyes were closed and a faint smile curved his lips.

"Don't just sit there," I screamed. "Help them."

At the sound of my voice Emil looked up. A look of pure fury crossed his features. "Run, you idiot. Go."

My mother took advantage of Emil's distraction. She lunged toward him, her hook-like fingers seeking the skin above his heart. Emil brushed her away and followed her reeling body into the pit. A second later, her shattered scream reached my ears. The pagan, savage sound of it froze the marrow in my bones.

Emil returned to Quentin's side. Fresh blood covered his chin and chest. I couldn't feel remorse. My mother had died when I was ten.

Before I knew what was happening I was no longer looking into the cave. Mark grabbed me around the waist and took off, half-running and half-rolling down the hill.

Behind us, the sounds of the battle increased. Reptilian howls rent the sunny air. Under the rock, a bull's impatient snort signaled his intent to charge. I needed to know what was happening, but Mark ignored repeated requests to release me. He kept on running, dragging me along.

We were almost 200 yards from the opening when I felt the first rumble. It started in the soles of my feet and traveled up my legs, shaking my entire body. I threw myself to the ground.

"Come on," Mark urged, pulling my hands. "We're not far enough yet."

I struggled to draw breath. "Far enough for what?"

Shelley, who had proceeded down the slope, came back to add her weight to Mark's. Together they pulled me another 50 feet.

The hillside rumbled again. The tremor was so violent it knocked them off their feet. They landed beside me, and together we turned our heads to look back up the mountain.

"It's an earthquake," I gasped. "Emil. Tolquen. We have to get them out."

I crawled. Mark clasped my ankle and pulled me back.

"It isn't an earthquake," he said, panting. "I hope we're far enough away." His eyes narrowed to squint through rising dust.

The hill heaved under by stomach. I just had time to cover my head with my arms before a rain of pebbles and stones fell upon us.

When the shower ceased I looked at Mark. "What's going on? What did Quentin tell you?"

He didn't answer. The quakes came continuously, gaining strength. My body shook until I thought my bones had turned to jelly.

Around us, uprooted trees thundered to the ground and giant cracks split the earth. I jumped to the side when the ground opened under my feet.

Mark scanned the area. Then, grabbing my wrist, he pulled me to my feet. "Come on."

I followed, with Shelley right beside me. We ran another 30 yards, then threw our bodies behind a large outcropping of rock.

We made it just in time. The hill gave one last violent shudder. It lasted so long I thought my teeth would shatter. Then a deafening rumble, beginning in the bowels of the earth, split the air. Too late, I realized the import of Quentin's thoughtful trance.

I barely had time to sob. The hillside collapsed upon itself, sending a mountain of dust and boulders shooting into the air. What goes up must come down, and these did with a vengeance. Our rock barricade splintered and chipped, but somehow remained intact. The last standing tree crumpled like a piece of tin foil. Its roots rose from the ground and the trunk split with a loud crack. Branches and leaves rained over us, burying our bodies. The fall of debris seemed to go on for hours.

When things at last quieted, I rose to my knees, then got shakily to my feet. I started uphill, dreading what I would find.

The mountain was unrecognizable. A crater, like the creamy side of an ice cream cone with a bite taken out, marred the once majestic view. The edge of the crater was no more than 30 paces from our rock shield.

I was too numb to think. Eyes wide with horror, I turned my face to Mark.

He was filthy. Shelley was even dirtier. They were caked with dust and blood from small cuts. I knew I looked the same.

"So endeth the Incubi," Shelley quoted, her voice soft but even. "It was a terrible way to go, but I can't say I'm sorry."

"That's a rotten thing to say. They saved your sorry butt, and mine too."

Mark didn't look at me. "He told me to get you away from the hill as fast as I could. He was worried about you, Marty."

He sounded preoccupied, lifeless. He stared at the destruction for a long while, then turned his eyes to look at my face.

"He knew when we reached the rocks. He knew when we were safe. When you were safe."

I couldn't think of a thing to say. Shelley asked the question my mind couldn't form.

"How did he know, Mark?"

"For a second, I saw it all. All of history, through his eyes. We were linked," Mark said in a sing-song voice that made me shudder and look away. "He asked me if you were safe. I told him yes."

Shelley moved to place her arm around his shoulders. She opened her mouth to speak, then closed it without uttering a word.

In the distance, sirens squealed. Within minutes they drew closer to the mountain. Mark blinked, then went on in a rush of words.

"They want us to say the earthquake caught them exploring a hidden burial chamber. That way, if the government decides to investigate, our story will fit with the uncovered facts." He looked at Shelley. "He wants us to tell them we saw Emil alive and well before the cave-in. He wants us to clear Marty."

Shelley nodded, her face grim.

Dazed and confused, I latched onto the only thing he said that made sense. "You were linked? You read his thoughts?"

The emergency vehicles arrived and proceeded up the hill. We didn't have much time and there was something I had to know.

"Yes," Mark said. "I read his thoughts."

"Can you feel him now?"

He closed his eyes and shook his head. "When the hill went up, the link snapped. There's nothing."

HOURS LATER IT was all settled. The last of the rescue teams scoured the hillside, looking through the debris for survivors of the tragedy.

I was wrapped in blankets, sipping tepid water from a smelly canteen. I couldn't seem to stop shivering.

Shelley sat beside me. Neither of us had spoken a word since the emergency vehicles arrived. We let Mark do all the talking. He convinced the officials we managed to get out of the cave just seconds before the quake. The other members of the team, including the missing Emil Larson, weren't as fortunate.

Mark explained Emil's earlier disappearance as archaeological fervor. After hearing rumors of a secret cache of Mayan remains high in the Guatemalan mountains, Emil sent a message through Rich Cerves for me to join him here, without telling the others. Mark and Shelley didn't know of the great discovery until much later, when they followed Rich on one of his trips to bring supplies to the makeshift camp.

It was a terrible story, but the officials bought it. The

governments of most South American countries were used to the strange behavior of scientists, and knew they guarded their finds with jealous secrecy. Shelley and I confirmed the story with nods and grunts. Thank heaven for the Latins. They took Mark's concoction for fact and left us alone.

That left only the body in Pennsylvania to deal with, but Mark had an explanation for that, too. He blamed the body on Norman. I thought it was a nice touch.

One by one the trucks pulled away. Mark made arrangements for us to go to the nearest town for rest and recuperation. After that we could return to Mexico at our leisure.

When there was no more explaining to do, Mark joined us at the rocks. He looked tired and strained but he managed a delighted grin.

"It's over, Marty," he whispered. "You're cleared of any charges and free to go. With Norman out of the way, I wouldn't be surprised if the university asked you to join the dig officially. Shelley and I will pull for you."

I tried to smile. "I'll think about it, Mark. I appreciate everything you did. Both of you."

Shelley flapped her hand. "Forget it, kid. You'd do the same for me."

I nodded. "Yes, I would."

"You still don't have the proof you need, about your theory and all," Mark said in sympathy. "None of us will ever be able to speak of what happened here."

"I know, and it doesn't matter," I said. "I know I was right."

Mark nodded.

I threw off my blanket and let the late afternoon sun warm my back. It really was over.

We walked toward the truck. My body felt like a telephone pole—stiff and covered with an unspeakable coating. The others didn't move too quickly, either.

I was in the truck before I saw it, a delicate blossom clinging to the one thriving tree on the entire hillside. Following an impulse, I climbed out of the truck, my pain and bruises forgotten. Plucking the bloom from the tree, I started up the hill.

Mark and Shelley watched but didn't follow. They sensed my need for solitude, I suppose.

I counted steps until I arrived at the approximate area where the fissure had been. Then I placed the red flower amid the debris.

"For all of you," I whispered. Strangely, I would miss them—all of them.

I didn't look back. Shelley made a place for me on the seat beside her.

"Are you all right?"

I laughed. "Never better. Really."

The driver revved the engine and turned the truck down the mountain, away from the hidden crypt.

The red rays of the setting sun caught and reflected the star on my new shell. Turning it, I saw etchings. The bull and the snake. Faint, but there.

I turned the shell so the carvings rested against my skin. It was cold and lifeless. Just an ornament, after all.

No, a souvenir; a remembrance.

I leaned my head against the seat and closed my eyes. I was asleep before we reached the base of the mountain.

~*~

Charlotte Dobson

Charlotte Dobson has won seven awards for fiction, including three for her suspense novel, *Crystal Waterfall*. She also writes an occasional article for the Novel Writer's Workshop Cyber-Journal. *Incubus* is her first venture into the horror genre.

When she isn't writing, Charolotte enjoys geneology, astronomy and travel.

A native of Virginia Beach, she has lived in Rhode Island, Florida, and Tennessee in addition to almost every major city in Pennsylvania. She currently lives in Connecticut with her husband and their three cats.

Visit Charlotte's web page at:
http://hometown.aol.com/chardob/charlottedobson.htm

CPSIA information can be obtained at www.ICGtesting.com
Printed in the USA
BVOW08s2140050114

341009BV00001B/2/A

9 780759 901315